DADDY'S ANGEL

LAYLAH ROBERTS

Laylah Roberts

Daddy's Angel

© 2020, Laylah Roberts

Laylah.roberts@gmail.com

laylahroberts.com

Cover Design by: Allycat's Creations

Editing: Celeste Jones

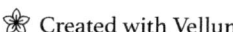 Created with Vellum

BOOKS BY LAYLAH ROBERTS

Doms of Decadence

Just for You, Sir

Forever Yours, Sir

For the Love of Sir

Sinfully Yours, Sir

Make me, Sir

A Taste of Sir

To Save Sir

Sir's Redemption

Reveal Me, Sir

Montana Daddies

Daddy Bear

Daddy's Little Darling

Daddy's Naughty Darling Novella

Daddy's Sweet Girl

Daddy's Lost Love

A Montana Daddies Christmas

Daring Daddy

Warrior Daddy

Daddy's Angel

Haven, Texas Series

Lila's Loves

Laken's Surrender

1

The panic was like a lead weight on her chest.

An attack loomed. Her hands shook, her stomach rolled over nauseously.

Can't breathe. Can't breathe.

Larry paced back and forth, oblivious to the fact she was falling apart. That was Larry.

All about himself. The prick.

She instantly felt bad for thinking that. But Larry wasn't her favorite person in the world right now. Actually, he never was.

I don't want to do it.

The words hovered on the tip of her tongue.

I won't do it!

She could just imagine herself telling him that. It would never happen because she was a wimp who couldn't stand up to her own agent.

People are depending on you, Arianna. You need to be stronger than this. You cannot disappoint them.

So she sat there, barely listening as Larry harped on about the charity concert looming on the horizon. About how she needed to get into the recording studio. Appearances, meetings, promotion.

Enough!

She forced his voice to become background noise. Because if she listened to him, she knew she'd lose complete control.

Breathe in. One. Two. Three. Four. Breathe out. One. Two. Three. Four.

Tears stung her eyes. She blinked them back. Her hands continued to shake, and she twisted them together.

You can do this. Just breathe, Arianna. Just breathe.

"Arianna are you listening to me?" he finally snapped.

Crap. Damn. She raised her gaze to meet his. She knew a lot of people considered her agent a handsome man.

She didn't see it.

He was too slick. His suit was tailored perfect. His hair was never out of place. His face was unlined and he was tanned year-round.

It was unnatural. She'd known him for four years and never once had she seen a bit of spinach between his teeth or his fly down or a hair poking out of his nose. Not that she actually wanted to see that, of course.

But any of those things might have made him more relatable. Friendly. Approachable.

Larry was none of those things. Larry was a shark.

Which is why her parents had hired him. Yep, she hadn't even hired her own agent. They'd gotten rid of her last agent, Gordy, because he hadn't been making her enough money.

What did she need with more money? She didn't want the flashy cars and exorbitant mansions. But her family did. Larry did. And they all relied on her to perform.

She hated it. She detested what her life had become. And now this. . .

I can't breathe. Can't breathe.

Go to your happy place. Stars. Mountains. Quiet. Trees.
Now breathe.

"Arianna. Are you listening?"

"I can't do it. These threats. . ."

"Look, darling," he said condescendingly. She hated when he talked to her like that. Like she was an idiot. As though he thought he was charming, and she'd fall to the floor and kiss his feet.

Never gonna happen, Larry.

"You need to calm down. I know these threats seem scary. But it comes with the territory. You've gotten threats in the past and nothing ever came from them."

But how had this person gotten her home address? All correspondence went to a private box and was collected by Larry's assistant. How had they managed to slip these threatening letters under her damn door?

"Arianna! Have you been taking your pills?"

She glared at him. Asshole. "My medication is none of your business, Larry."

She hadn't been taking those pills for months. She didn't like the way they made her feel. Like she wasn't herself. She wasn't even entirely sure she needed them. Her parents had forced her to go to that creepy Doctor Jones. She was certain he was medicating her unnecessarily. She had her panic attacks under control.

Well, as long as someone wasn't sending her threatening letters. But that would make most people panic, right?

"It is if you're not taking care of yourself. I care about you, Arianna."

Urgh. Total sleaze. And he didn't care about her. He cared about money. He wanted her docile. When she took those pills, she didn't get nervous when she performed. But she also couldn't feel the music, couldn't create. Oh, she could still sing. But it was other people's lyrics.

She wanted to sing her own music. But Larry always vetoed that.

"Larry, these threats are real. Shouldn't we go to the police?"

He narrowed his gaze. "The police! For a few letters? They'd laugh at us. We don't need to call in the cops for another hoax. You cannot let a couple of threats stop you from doing this concert!"

He was probably right. She was being weak. She was scared.

He leaned his fists on the desk between them, looming over her. She hated when he did that.

"Do I need to speak to your parents about this? They could fly in. Be moral support."

She flinched. Christ, twenty-six years old and still worried about what her parents thought. What they might do.

Stop embarrassing us, Arianna.

Just talk, Arianna. Stop crying, you're not a baby.

Why can't you be normal?

Christ. She shook off those memories. "No."

"Good. Look, if you're that worried, let me hire you a bodyguard."

"No."

His gaze narrowed and she tensed.

"Then buck up, Arianna. You don't have time to fall apart. That sort of selfish indulgence is for artists who are already set for life. This concert might be for charity, but it will bring in a lot of publicity for your last album. You need to start working and stop looking for excuses to get out of your obligations. You're doing the concert!"

He stormed out and the door slammed shut behind him.

Such an asshole. God, she hated him. She took in one short breath then another.

She'd fire him, but despite his failure as a decent human being he was a good agent. And if she fired him, her family would get upset with her, they'd come to visit. She needed to do everything she could to avoid that. She just couldn't cope with that much confrontation right now.

Or ever.

Larry wasn't going to give up. And this charity event coming up had been booked a year in advance. She'd be letting people down if she didn't attend.

She rubbed her hand over her face then opened up her laptop. She'd sent copies of the notes to the only person she thought might actually listen to her. Caleb was her favorite person in the entire world. Sometimes it felt like he was the only person who actually saw her. Arianna the person. Not Arianna, the world-famous singer. Not Arianna, the cash cow. Not Arianna, the snob.

She grimaced at that last thought. She knew that's what many people thought of her.

If only they knew. Truth was, she didn't always know how to relate to people. She'd spent her childhood with tutors and therapists.

The only time she felt normal was when she lost herself in the music.

It had been her saving grace, but it was also her nightmare. Because with her music came fame and money. Which all sounded good. But when you just wanted to live a quiet life, when your family used you to fund their lifestyle, when you were constantly guilted into doing things you didn't want to do.

It also became her hell.

She opened up her email, relief filling her as she saw he'd replied. Caleb and his two closest friends, Wolfe and Aleki, were working overseas as bodyguards for some rich, foreign princes

She opened the email.

Squirt,

You were totally right to send these to me. I've contacted a friend who runs a security company in Montana. He's going to send some bodyguards. Now, before you argue that it's just a couple of notes, you

and I both know that you don't overreact. Which means you think it's something more. So either you take the bodyguards or Aleki, Wolfe and I are coming home to take care of you ourselves? Got me?

You need a permanent bodyguard anyway. I can't believe fucking Larry hasn't taken care of that already. As famous and beautiful as you are, you're bound to attract weirdos. Just look at the way you have the three of us twisted around your little finger. I'll get onto finding someone permanent.

Until his guys get there, you stay inside and safe. I'm not kidding, Arianna. You disobey me in this, and I will put you over my knee like I did when you were eight and you climbed that tree when I told you not to. Don't think I won't.

Love you, Squirt. Stay safe. Do what these guys say. They're the best of the best. Unlike that dick, Larry.

Caleb

PS my friend Kent is a Daddy Dom and so are most of the guys working for him. Just thought I'd give you a heads up. Hint. Hint.

SHE ROLLED her eyes at that last bit. She knew Caleb, Aleki and Wolfe were all Daddy Doms. They'd all been in the SEALs together and had formed a tight bond. Caleb often told her she was a Little. She knew why he'd think that. But there was no way she could ever indulge that side of herself.

If she only had herself to worry about, then she'd leave all this. Take off, find somewhere peaceful where she could live without other people's expectations.

But she had to think of her family. As her mother liked to tell her, she owed them after years of being a constant disappointment.

She reread the email, grinning at his reminder of the time he'd spanked her. She hadn't talked to him for a month afterwards. It wasn't like she'd been in danger or anything. She was the best damn tree climber around.

Caleb had lived next-door to her growing up. He was seven years older, so mostly she'd just been a pain in his ass.

But she knew he loved her. He'd never cared that she was weird or different.

Still, there was no way she was going to enter into any kind of relationship with these bodyguards. But maybe hiring someone permanently wasn't the worst idea. It could help keep the panic at bay.

She took a deep breath, let it out slowly then typed back a simple message.

Thank you. Hi to Wolfe and Aleki. Love you all.

Ari xx

2

"Got a job for you both." Kent strode into the meeting room, looking slightly harried.

Bain raised an eyebrow at Dominic who just grinned. They weren't used to seeing the chief looking so frazzled.

"I saw that look," Kent stated. He sat in a chair at the round table with a huge sigh. "Do you know how fucking difficult Clint is being? He doesn't want a traditional stag night; he wants a combined night with Charlie and the girls. Only Charlie doesn't want that. She's told me in no uncertain terms to make certain he isn't around during. . .well, whatever it is the women are getting up to. Abby is taking charge of that. Although I need to find out if they're planning on leaving the ranch as they'll need security."

"Chief, ease up, man. You're acting like you're the wedding planner." Dominic smirked. "You're just the best man."

Kent glared at them both. "Just the best man? I'm in charge of making sure Clint has a suit, that he remembers the ring, that he gets to the wedding on time, that he doesn't just kidnap Charlie and elope."

Bain grunted. That's the way he'd do it. He'd gone through the whole huge white wedding thing once. Waste of fucking time and money.

But it had been what Jillian wanted. And at the time, he'd been so in love with her, he'd have given her anything. Nearly did. Just about bankrupted himself keeping her happy.

Never again.

"Be a good thing if he did."

Dominic gave him an assessing look while Kent just sighed. "And miss out on seeing Charlie walking down the aisle? On the happiness shining from her face? Watching my brother fall to his knees in fucking joy? Getting to dance with my girl for half the night afterwards? I'd rather put up with this stress. But if Clint moans one more time about his monkey suit. . .I'm going to have to hogtie and gag the bastard."

Dominic grinned. "You said something about a job, Chief?"

"Right, onto the work I actually get paid for," Kent grumbled.

They all knew it was an act. The Jensens were a tight family. The fact that they'd opened their ranch up to accept people like them, men who wanted relationships where they were in charge, where women were protected and cherished, and that they treated everyone here like family. . .it spoke to their huge hearts.

Kent might bitch about his brother, but he'd be there in a second if Clint needed him. Moving here, accepting this job had been a lifeline for Bain after separating from Jillian. It had turned into the best decision he'd ever made.

"Ever heard of Arianna Silvers?" Kent asked, opening a folder and pulling out a photo. Yep, sometimes they still did things old-school around here. Bain liked that.

He looked down at the pretty singer. The photo was one of those publicity shots. A gorgeous woman with wavy, dark-red hair and pretty green eyes stared out at him. She had way too much make-up on, and her clothes probably cost more than he made in a month.

The least favorite part of his job was having to guard rich, stuck-up celebrities. They didn't get these jobs that often, thank Christ, because usually these sorts of people had their own permanent bodyguards.

"Have to be dead not to have heard her music," Dominic commented.

Both men looked at him.

"Not that it's my cup of tea." His cheeks reddened. Not his thing, huh?

"She in trouble?" Bain asked.

Kent frowned slightly. "Could be. She's had a couple of threats sent to her."

"Happens when you're in the limelight," Bain said cynically.

Kent shot him a look. "Well, these threats have scared her. She has a charity concert coming up and she's worried."

"Wouldn't she be better with a permanent bodyguard or hiring a security company? Where does she live?" Dominic asked.

"She has an apartment in New York where she mostly lives. These are copies of the threats she's received. The first one came approximately six weeks ago."

He turned around a piece of paper.

I SEE YOU, my little songbird. You sing so pretty for me. Don't worry, I'm coming to rescue you from the cage they put you. Then we can be together forever.

"Fuck," Bain said with a frown. "No signature? Nothing on the envelope? Where was it mailed from? Cops find anything?"

Kent cleared his throat. "That's the thing. These weren't sent. They were hand-delivered to her apartment. An apartment with security. And none of these have been passed onto the police."

"What?" Dominic asked. "Why not?"

"I'm not sure. I haven't spoken directly to Arianna." Kent frowned.

"She got her assistant to call you, huh?" Bain asked. "She's so afraid and yet she couldn't call you herself?"

Kent stared at him for a moment. "No, actually. An old Navy friend of mine contacted me about this job. Caleb Pierce."

"Caleb Pierce?" Dominic repeated.

"Know him?" Kent asked.

"Heard of him. Isn't he overseas guarding some rich prince?"

"He is," Kent confirmed. "He's a good man. I owe him a favor, he's never called it in. Until now."

"He involved with her?" Bain tapped his finger against the photo of Arianna.

"Not like that. Apparently, they grew up together. He said she's a close friend. She sent him the letters and he contacted me. Asked me to send some people out until he can arrange something more permanent."

"Does she even want us there?" Dominic asked, glancing over at Bain. This could be a tricky fucking job if she didn't.

"Apparently she agreed to you both coming. She's expecting you. She, or perhaps her assistant, sent me some details. She's bought you both first-class tickets on a flight out to New York and her driver will collect you. Everything you need has been emailed to you, along with copies of the other two threatening letters. This could all fizzle out, like so many of these things. But she's scared. Caleb is worried and I owe him. See if you can get her to send those letters to a lab so we can have them tested. Guessing she has her reasons for not wanting the cops involved."

Probably more worried about her reputation and career than her life.

This was going to be so much fun.

"Fucking hate these jobs," Bain muttered to Dominic as they collected their bags at the airport. They each had duffels with personal items along with hard, locked cases containing firearms. Standard for jobs like this.

Hopefully, like most of the others, this one would turn out to be a dud and finished quickly.

Dominic grinned at him. He was currently sporting a salt-and-pepper beard. His bright blue eyes twinkled with merriment. "Which is why Kent doesn't usually send you on these jobs."

"My fucking luck that Macca wasn't available." He'd just arrived home with his new girlfriend, Gigi. She was Australian, she'd moved halfway across the world to be with Macca.

He was fucking lucky to find someone special like that. Someone who was willing to uproot her life. Bain had never had that. His ex had been selfish. More interested in material things than him.

But that meant Macca wasn't available for this job and unfortunately for him, neither were any of the others.

So he got babysitting duty. At least Dominic was with him. He'd let the other man do the talking. Actually, Kent had ordered him to let Dominic do all the talking. They were all aware that Bain didn't have much of a filter. Catering to some rich brat's every whim just wasn't something he was good at.

Give him an enemy to take down, a good fight, he was there.

But getting his charge a double-shot mocha almond latte from a café halfway across town wasn't something he was ever going to jump to do.

And yes, the last time he'd been on babysitting duty for some small-screen actress whose fame had been waning, that's exactly what she'd demanded.

He'd told her he wasn't some glorified errand boy and she could make her own damn coffee.

Yeah, letting Dominic do the talking wasn't a bad idea.

"At least she sent a driver," Dominic told him as they approached an older man holding a sign with JSI written on it. "That's more than most do."

Bain just grunted. He hated having someone else drive. He might have a few teensy-tiny control issues. They followed the older man, who'd introduced himself as Joe, out to a dark town car and climbed in the back. Bain tapped his fingers against his leg. Probably just as well he wasn't driving. Manhattan traffic would do his head in.

"Nice ride, Joe," Dominic said, making small talk with the driver as they weaved their way through traffic. "So you worked for Ms. Silvers for long?"

"Me and the wife, we've worked for Miss Ari for close to six years now. Just after she went big with her first album. The wife does all the cooking and cleaning. Well, not that there's much of that to do seeing as Miss Ari just lives on her own. We probably should have retired by now, but we can't leave Miss Ari on her own."

That surprised Bain. Hard to believe a famous singer like Arianna Silvers would be on her own for long.

They pulled into an underground parking lot. Bain climbed out of the car and looked around as Joe shuffled to the back to pull out the bags. He quickly grabbed both of his bags, before the older, stooped man toppled over under the weight.

"Come, come. This way." Joe waved his hand and shuffled forward at a painfully slow pace.

Bain looked over at Dominic who just grinned. When Joe said he should have retired already, it seemed that probably should have been around ten years ago.

"Are there cameras down here?" Bain asked.

Joe had to use a card at the entrance to the garage to get in, but it wouldn't take much for someone to get hold of one of those. At the elevator, the old man swiped his card again.

"Oh, I don't know," Joe answered. "Rob, he's the head of security for the building, he'd probably know."

Bain spotted one above the entrance to the elevator, but none in the actual basement garage itself.

"Are we going to the lobby?" Dominic asked, as the lift rose.

"Oh no, that's the good thing about this place. You can go straight up to the penthouse where Miss Ari lives."

Bain sighed. He could feel a headache forming.

"So all someone needs is that card and they can not only get in the garage, but go straight up to the penthouse apartment?" Bain demanded. "Without checking in at all?"

"Well. Yes. But only me and Miss Ari have these cards," he boasted proudly. "Oh, and the wife of course. And Larry, her agent. Can't remember if her parents have one. Don't think so since Miss Ari wouldn't want them showing up whenever they liked."

Christ. Hopefully the client had a better memory than her driver. The elevator opened into a small foyer.

"Tell me that the same card doesn't access the penthouse?" Bain asked Joe.

"Course not," Joe replied.

Joe entered a six-digit pin code into a panel next to the door. Then there was a click and the door opened. Bain looked around, spotting a camera discreetly mounted in the corner of the foyer. There was only the one, though.

"Gonna have to talk to her about improving her security. More cameras. New keycards for the elevator. Have to check if there's some sort of alarm when people reach the foyer."

Dominic just nodded with a frown.

They followed Joe inside, where he was soon greeted by a short, round woman with white hair and a wide smile.

"This is the wife. Estelle."

"Hello, so nice to meet you," she said warmly. "Can I take your bags for you?"

Dominic shook his head. "We'll carry them, ma'am. If you could just show us where we're sleeping, we'll go introduce ourselves to Ms. Silvers."

"Of course. But call me Estelle, please." She turned and unlike Joe, thankfully moved at a faster pace. "Joe, don't you touch that apple cobbler, it's for Miss Ari. Girl hasn't been eating at all lately," she confided in them. "Apple cobbler is her favorite, I'm hoping it will stimulate her appetite."

She led them down a passage. "Now, Joe and I are here every day except the weekends, so if you need anything let one of us know. Miss Ari thought you'd be happy in these two rooms." She opened a door and they followed her in. His eyebrows rose. The room was huge, with a large window that showcased the Manhattan skyline. "Each room has a private bathroom. And the rooms connect through that door." She nodded at a door to the side.

"Where is Ms. Silvers bedroom?" he asked abruptly.

The woman gave him a puzzled look then the smile dropped slightly from her face. "It's at the end of the passage. Joe will have told her that you're here, if you'd like me to take you to her. I'll give you a short tour."

"Thanks. Just give us a minute."

The woman nodded and left the room. Dominic moved into the room next door as Bain quickly set up his gun, putting it in a side holster and grabbing his jacket to hide it. Dominic knocked and then returned. They both moved out into the passage where Estelle waited.

She took them on a tour of the penthouse. Which was fucking huge. What did one person need with six bedrooms, eight bathrooms, a jacuzzi, an infinity pool as well as a large study?

Rich people. He'd never fucking understand them.

Okay. Perhaps he had a slight chip on his shoulder when it came to people with money.

Estelle finally led them towards their client's study. She knocked and waited as someone with a soft voice called out.

"Miss Ari, the two gentlemen from JSI are here."

The woman, who was standing in front of the huge windows that looked out towards a large park, turned to look at them.

He felt like someone had sucker-punched him. He actually froze for a moment. The photos he'd seen of her hadn't prepared him for her beauty. Wavy, red, thick hair. She was short but had curves in all the right places. A small waist, wider hips and fucking gorgeous breasts.

Fake? He guessed they probably were, but she hadn't gone overboard with them. Moss green eyes studied them both. She wore ripped jeans that probably cost more than he made in a week and a tight, blue-green T-shirt. She had to be one of the most beautiful women he'd ever seen, hands-down. And there was just something about her that drew him in, that made him want to get close to her, to touch her, to see her smile.

She opened her mouth just as there was a shout from the foyer.

Bain immediately gestured to Dominic. He walked towards Arianna, standing in front of her, while Bain moved out into the corridor. Grabbing hold of his gun, he held it lightly at his side.

"Arianna!" A short, thin man dressed in a suit stormed down the passage. He froze as he spotted Bain.

"Holy fuck, you're enormous!"

"Who are you?" Bain demanded.

"I'm Larry," the other man sneered. "Arianna's agent. And I'm guessing you're the bodyguard she hired without consulting me? Well, you're fired. Get your stuff and get out."

Bain quickly glanced over at Dominic and watched as their

client stepped out from behind his friend. He narrowed his gaze at her. Didn't she know that she was supposed to hide behind the bodyguard? Dominic gently pushed her back behind him.

"Get out of the way, you overgrown ass. Jesus, you need to ease up on the 'roids."

"Larry!" Arianna snapped, sounding appalled.

Bain just glared down at the asshole in an expensive suit. Larry sneered and moved past him into the room. Bain took a look down the corridor and went to check that the front door was secured. Larry seemed the type to only care about himself.

When he moved back to the study, he could hear yelling. What the fuck? He strode into the room, to find Larry pacing up and down. Dominic stood next to Arianna, by the dark wood desk. The room surprised him. There were built-in bookshelves on two walls, filled with paperbacks. A fireplace was featured on the far wall with a couple of comfortable looking chairs resting in front of it. The whole room was cozy and welcoming.

Larry's thin, weasel-like face scrunched up like he was consti- pated as he flung his hands around as he yelled.

Jesus. Did he have to scream every word?

"You had no right to hire them without consulting me, Arianna! I'm your agent. I should have vetted them first! Fuck, we could have at least got one who has guarded a celebrity before. What about that guy who guarded that actress, Jenna Stone? I think he's free."

"He's free because she was murdered," Dominic stated. He frowned at Larry. Took a lot to rile Dominic. He was one of the most easy-going guys Bain knew. That's why Kent usually sent him on these jobs.

Larry ignored him. "Or at least one who isn't a hundred." Larry looked Dominic up and down with a sneer. A hundred? Dominic had just hit fifty. This guy was a complete prick. He turned to Bain. "Or one who looks like he shoots up with steroids daily. Mind you, the fact that he's black isn't a bad move."

Arianna made a small gasping noise and Bain turned to see her gaping at Larry, looking ill. As though she felt his eyes on her, she turned her gaze to his. She almost immediately dropped her eyes from his. Something stirred in his gut. Had she dropped them due to shame? Or something else? He didn't give a fuck what this asshole said about his size or his skin color.

Bain had long since stopped caring about what others thought of him.

He crossed his arms over his chest, aware that the arms of his jacket strained across his biceps. He heard another strangled noise coming from the little singer and looking over at her, saw the way she stared at his body.

Liked the way he looked, did she?

Sorry, sweetheart, you can use my body as protection but nothing else.

Even if sleeping with a client wasn't against JSI terms of employment, he wouldn't do it. Not with someone like her. Larry continued on with his tirade. Occasionally she would open her mouth, but then he'd go off on another spiel.

Did the ass ever shut up?

He watched her wince as Larry grew particularly loud. Then she appeared to pale as he said something about calling her parents. Although why that would bother her, he didn't know. According to his info on her, she was twenty-six. Old enough to make her own decisions. Without her parents or this dickhead's permission.

Still, irritation filled him at her obvious discomfit.

"A bodyguard could be a good move if we spin it right. Not this one, obviously." He pointed at Dominic. "But I guess the other one will do until we can find someone with more of a following."

A following? Did bodyguards have followings?

Larry turned to him. "Are you on Instagram? Are you known? Is there anything I can use to get some media attention for Arianna?"

Bain just glared at him. He wasn't even going to dignify those fucking questions with an answer. What the fuck? An Instagram following? Was he fucking insane? He was a security operative.

"Come on? What's your problem? Don't you talk? Doesn't he talk? Arianna, how am I meant to work with him when he doesn't fucking talk? It's bad enough dealing with your shit."

Her shit? What did that mean? That she was a problem to deal with?

Arianna's eyes widened at those words and she actually took a few steps towards Bain, standing between him and Larry. Bain glanced over at Dominic; whose eyes had widened in surprise.

Surely, she wasn't. . .was she trying to protect him? From Larry the dickhead? Did she not understand how the whole bodyguard thing worked?

Dominic watched Arianna with interest, but Bain couldn't see her face from this angle. He moved forward so he was standing just a few feet back and to her right. Just in case Larry made some dickhead move on her.

"Larry," she said in a low, warning voice.

"Look, darling," Larry wheedled. "I didn't mean it like that. Arianna, you know I love working with you. It's so refreshing. I think you're so courageous the way you deal with all your problems."

Problems? What the fuck? What was up with this guy? First, he yelled at her now he was trying to sweet-talk her, except his tone was condescending as fuck. And if the tension in Arianna's body was any indication, she thought so as well.

"It's just, you can't make decisions like this on your own. We've talked about this. Anything to do with your career has to go through me. I'm your agent. I get paid to handle this shit, so you don't have to worry your pretty head about it."

Could the guy be more of an ass?

Then he ran his hand down her arm. Yep, seemed he could.

Arianna shook off his hand immediately, moving backward. Bain quickly reacted, stepping forward to place a hand on her back and steady her. She stiffened and stepped hastily away from him.

Right. He got it. She didn't want the help touching her.

Larry waved a hand around. "Obviously this isn't going to work, babe. Just give me a couple of days, I'll find you a bodyguard that's far more suitable to your situation than these two. I just wished you'd told me you were feeling so unsafe. You know I'd do anything for you."

Jesus, could this guy lay it on any thicker.

"I did tell you," she said in a low voice. "You brushed me off. How did you even know they were here?"

"I have no idea what you're talking about. Obviously, you dreamed that. The two of you can run along now. I have this all figured out." Larry gave them both a dismissive look. Bain couldn't work out what Larry's issue was. Was it the fact that they weren't famous enough for him? Or that he hadn't chosen them himself and therefore didn't get to control them?

A bit of both he was guessing.

"Well, Larry, we can't do that, I'm afraid," Dominic told him, watching the other man with that grin still on his face. Bain bet he was the only one who could see the irritation in his eyes. "Arianna hired us. We only go where she tells us to. And I don't think she wants us to leave."

Larry sighed. "You've met her for two minutes and you think you know her? Look, I get that you're after your two seconds of fame, no doubt being seen with Arianna will bring all sorts of jobs coming your way. But it's my job to look after Arianna's interests. She listens to my advice. Don't you, darling?"

Larry grabbed her arm again. Bain stepped up beside her, scowling down at him. He didn't like how handsy the agent was with her.

"Let her go. Now."

Larry glared up at him, but he did remove his hand from her arm and step back. "You are being ridiculous! I'm no danger to her. Arianna and I have been together for years."

Together? He made it sound like they were a thing. But Bain had seen her reaction to the other man. There was nothing romantic about their relationship. In fact, Larry seemed to enjoy bullying Arianna one minute then being a condescending ass the next. Why the hell did she put up with this guy?

His surge of protectiveness caught him by surprise. It was just because she was the client. That's all.

"They're staying, Larry. Caleb hired them so I know they're the best. He's going to find me a permanent bodyguard."

Larry moved his gaze from her to Bain then his lips curled up. "Fine, keep your bodyguards. I guess I can do something with them, but it's a missed opportunity, Arianna. You get a guard with more of a following and it's only going to help with sales of your next single. It flops and I'm gone. Not going to grab hold of a sinking ship, babe."

Fucking asshole.

He could feel the slight woman standing beside him tremble, but she never made a noise, and she slipped slightly in front of him. What did she think she was doing?

"But don't worry," Larry said with an oily smile, as though he'd sensed he'd gone too far and was now working clean-up. "I can make anything work. I'll have the media lapping all of this up. I can probably spin this. Yes, why didn't I think of that before?"

"Think of what?" Dominic asked.

This guy was getting on his last nerve.

He clapped his hands together gleefully. "Singer's courage in the face of her stalker. That's some great publicity right there."

"No," Bain told him.

"No? What does that mean, no?" Larry blinked.

"It means that we can't allow you to make these threats public," Dominic said smoothly.

"Excuse me? Do I tell you how to do your job? This is gold, I just can't believe I didn't think about working this angle before. I can get behind this, definitely."

"Protecting Ms. Silvers is *our* job," Dominic interjected before Bain could do something stupid, like plant his fist in the weasel's face.

Damn, that would be satisfying.

First thing first, though. He needed to get the client out of the line of fire. He stepped to her side and moved so he was standing halfway in front of her.

"Our job is to protect Arianna, and making these threats public could just serve to anger her stalker or it could give them what they want. Feed into the delusion. It could increase the risk to her," Dominic said reasonably.

Bain didn't know how he managed to stay so patient.

"What the fuck do you know about stalkers?" Larry gave Dominic a derisive look. "I'll do what I have to in order to keep Arianna's career alive and the money coming in. You do your job, I'll do mine."

Larry scowled at Bain. "Will you get out of the way? I need to talk to Arianna. We have work things to discuss."

Bain crossed his arms over his chest. Like fuck he was leaving her with this dickhead.

But then a small hand touched his forearm. He glanced down into wide, moss-green eyes set in a calm face. He had to hand it to her, she knew how to hide her emotions. If he hadn't felt her trembling, he'd have thought she was completely unaffected by this douche.

He felt certain she was about to ask him to remove Larry. And that would definitely be his pleasure.

"Could the two of you please give us a minute?" she said to Bain then turned to Dominic.

She wanted him to leave? What the fuck? He glanced over at Dominic, who was frowning. Two frowns in the space of an hour from Dominic. That didn't bode well for his state of mind.

"Ms. Silvers?" Dominic asked. "You want us to go?"

She nodded. "Yes, please."

Larry gave them a superior look as Bain stared down at her.

"We can get rid of him for you."

"I'm her agent," Larry sneered. "She needs me. Not like the two of you. Bodyguards are a dime a dozen."

"Larry," Arianna said warningly.

"Have they even signed NDAs, Arianna?" Larry walked over to where a decanter sat, half-filled with what looked to be bourbon. Despite the fact it was only two in the afternoon, he poured himself a generous glass and took a sip. "They shouldn't even be here without signing those, you know that, Arianna."

What a condescending fucking ass.

"Ms. Silvers?"

She looked from him to Larry then sighed. "Please leave us. I will speak to you soon."

She obviously didn't give a shit about what he and Dominic thought or advised, she'd rather listen to this guy bullshit and bully her.

He knew his reaction wasn't entirely reasonable. He barely knew her. She was the client. She obviously knew Larry well. He just didn't like being dismissed by her.

Turning, he strode from the room, aware of Dominic behind him. The other man closed the door quietly.

"Bain, man—" Dominic started to say.

"Fucking bullshit. How are we meant to guard her when she won't let us? Did you see the way he talked to her? And she didn't say a word back."

"Bain. Calm down. So he's a douche? He's not the client."

Thank God for that. But it seemed they needed to have a chat with the client. She needed to learn that they protected her. Not the other way around.

3

They were summoned back to her office an hour later. Okay, maybe he was being a bit grouchier than usual. But that douche just put him on edge.

When they walked in, Arianna was standing at the windows, looking out. She turned and gave them both a small smile.

"Please, have a seat." She gestured at the sofa and two armchairs across the other side of the room. "I'm sorry about Larry."

"That's all right, Ms. Silvers." Dominic sat on the sofa, but Bain remained standing.

"Call me Arianna. We're going to be living together, right?" She went bright red after saying those words. "I mean. . .uhh. . .umm. . ."

She studiously ignored his gaze as she sat and nervously picked at a thread in her jeans. That was a surprise. He thought she'd be more polished. He'd done a bit of research on her. She came from a wealthy family, youngest of three children, her family was well-immersed in society. There hadn't been much information about her brother, but her sister was on her third marriage, this time to some famous model.

He'd expected someone snobby and cold.

"Thank you for sending a driver," Dominic said, smoothing things over.

"Oh, no problem. Joe and Estelle have worked for me for years. Estelle does most of the cooking and cleaning. If you have any favorite meals or don't like anything, you can let her know."

That was amazingly good of her. And again, unexpected.

"Thank you," Dominic said gently. "Arianna, we need to have a talk about your security and protocols. Have you ever had a bodyguard?"

"Uh, no. I mean, I've had temporary security for concerts and things. But no, never. I, umm, oh, Larry insists on you signing NDAs. I'm so sorry. He said he'll send them over with a courier." She gave Dominic an apologetic look then glanced up at Bain.

"You. . .would you like to sit?"

"No," he said abruptly.

Dominic sent him a warning look. Then turned back to her. "Don't worry about Bain. He prefers to stand. He thinks it makes him look more intimidating."

"He doesn't need any help to look intimidating," she said. Then her cheeks went red again as though she realized she'd said that out loud. "Sorry."

"You shouldn't have stepped between me and that jerk," Bain told her abruptly. He ignored Dominic's exasperated groan.

"W-what?" She managed to actually meet his gaze for a few seconds before looking away. "What do you mean?"

"Our job is to protect you. We stand between you and danger. Not the other way around. Don't do it again."

"I. . .I. . .Larry wasn't a threat to me."

He just raised his eyebrows. "He was acting erratically. He touched you."

"He's always like that," she murmured. "He doesn't like me making decisions without him."

Bain glanced at Dominic who gave him a puzzled look. Didn't Larry work for her?

"Look," Dominic said, leaning forward with a gentle smile. "It might take a bit of time for us to figure each other out. Why don't you get us a list of any upcoming events you have? Do you have any plans to leave the apartment today?"

"Oh no. I hardly go anywhere," she murmured. "I'll be home most of the time. It's just when I have to go to the recording studio or rehearsals for the upcoming concert."

"We'll need information about the venue and security," Bain told her.

"S-sure, I'll get Larry's assistant on that. Just let me get my notebook." She moved to her desk and opened a drawer, pulling out a notebook that had glittery sequins on the front. That surprised him.

She sat and started writing a list. She needed a bright and sparkly pen to match her notebook.

Okay, man. Getting off course. She isn't a Little.

"We'll need to go through protocols with you," he told her.

"Okay."

"Also need to talk to head of security of this building."

She wrinkled her nose. "His name is Rob Andrews."

"Something we need to know about him?" Dominic asked.

"I just. . .I don't want to be mean, but I don't think he's terribly competent. After that first letter was delivered, I asked to see the camera footage. I thought we might need it for the police. He said the camera in my foyer was broken. When I tried to ask for it the second time, he said he would check it. When I followed up, he said there was nothing on it. He wouldn't give it to me. Said he'd only release it to the police. Which I can't understand since I'm the only one living on this level."

"And this third time?" he asked. This guy sounded fishy as hell.

"I couldn't get hold of him for a few days, apparently he was ill. He said when he was able to look that it had automatically been erased."

"Why didn't you call the police?" Dominic asked.

She looked away from them both. "Larry said they wouldn't do anything about a couple of threatening letters. That I'd look like an idiot, especially as nothing was showing on the cameras. Maybe he's right. . .maybe I'm worried about nothing."

"This person got to your apartment and slid a letter under your door," Dominic told her. "That is a threat to take seriously. You did the right thing."

She nodded.

"And don't worry, we'll deal with Rob," Bain told her quietly.

THIS JOB WAS QUIET.

Other than the confrontation with Larry, and butting heads with Rob, the head of security, these past few days had been peaceful.

Almost boring.

Rob had refused to let them change the security for the penthouse access. Because no one had contacted the cops, he hadn't bothered to keep any of the footage.

The guy was an incompetent dickhead. They had Corbin looking into his background, but so far he'd found nothing. Still, Bain had a bad feeling about him.

But they had put in another camera in the small foyer to cover any blindspots, and an alarm system which notified them whenever anyone entered.

The strangest thing? They'd barely seen the client. She spent all her time in her bedroom, even getting her meals taken there.

The few times he had seen her, she was barely able to make eye contact, basically racing back into her room. She was friendlier towards Dominic, obviously preferring to talk to him. Which suited Bain just fine.

"Hey, man. You set for tomorrow?" Dominic joined him in the living room. Arianna never used the room, so they'd taken it over.

"Yeah. You get that information from Larry?"

"Finally," Dominic muttered with a frown. "That guy's a prick. He stalled on purpose just to be difficult, even though we're protecting his client."

Larry was a class-A prick for sure. He did his best to block or undermine them. Tomorrow, a series of interviews had been booked for the lead up to the concert. At least Arianna had agreed to limit it to three interviews, and they were being held here at the apartment.

"You sure you want to stay with Arianna?" Dominic asked. "You can take the door and I'll remain with her."

"No. I got it."

Dominic just gave him a look.

"It's my job, I'll do it."

"Just. . .don't be too hard on her, okay? If you gave her a chance, you'd find out she's actually really sweet."

"Sweet? She ignores me. She runs each time she sees me coming. She spends all her time in her room, making Estelle serve her food there instead of coming out and eating with the staff. I wouldn't exactly call her sweet."

Dominic sighed and leaned forward in his chair. "I think she's a bit intimidated by you."

"What?" He was a big guy. And he could be a bit abrupt. But he was here to protect her. Why would she be intimidated by him? She got up onstage in front of thousands of people regularly and she was scared of him?

"All I'm saying is give her a chance. You might find you quite like her. And you got to admit, you judged her before you even met her."

Had he done that?

Yeah. He totally had.

"Fine. I'll give her a chance."

"I think she doesn't have many people to talk to. She's a bit shy. Well, maybe shy isn't the word. Socially awkward? Hmm, maybe the two of you have more in common than you think."

"Shut up," he snarled at the other man stood and walked away, chuckling to himself.

Something in common with the ice princess? Yeah, he so didn't think so.

BAIN WALKED over at the knock on Arianna's office door. For the last two hours, a crew of make-up and hair stylists had been in here, primping Arianna in preparation for these interviews.

He didn't know how she could stand it. But he supposed women liked that sort of shit, didn't they? Seemed like a waste of time to him.

Now everyone had cleared out. Including Larry, who had gone off to greet the first interviewer. When Bain opened the door, he was surprised to see Estelle standing there.

"Hello, dear," she said sweetly. She held a small tray with two glasses of water with lemon in them.

"Here, let me take those for you." He reached for the tray, but Estelle shook her head.

"I'm fine, dear. I need to talk to Miss Ari."

Arianna turned, gifting the woman a small smile. Come to think of it, it was the first time he'd seen her smile all day. Maybe she didn't like all this primping and attention? But why do it? He shook that thought off. Wasn't his problem to try and work her out. He just had to guard her body.

The older woman approached Arianna. She looked perfect. Not a hair out of place. Almost like a freaking doll. Estelle set the water down on the small table that sat between the chairs that had been set up for the interviews. Arianna picked up a glass and he noticed that her hand shook. Estelle put her wrinkled hand over Arianna's hand. Steadying her? Comforting her? In that moment, Estelle almost appeared to be the stronger one.

He frowned, watching as Estelle slid something out of her pocket, handing it to Arianna. What the fuck? Were those pills?

"What the hell are those? Are those drugs?" He stormed over.

Not your business. Not your problem.

But if she was taking something illegal, he sure as shit wasn't going to just stand by and watch without saying something.

Estelle turned, standing between him and Arianna. Guarding her? From him? He was the fucking bodyguard. And if Estelle was enabling her drug habit then he needed to get her away from Arianna.

"What the fuck did you just give her?" he demanded, tempted to grab hold of the older woman and drag her away.

"None of your business, dear," Estelle said, but that sweet note in her voice was gone.

"Don't you take those," Bain snapped at Arianna.

She stared up at him with wide, frightened eyes. That didn't sit right with him. Was Dominic right? Was she intimidated by him?

"What are you taking?" he demanded.

"That's none of your business." Estelle glared at him.

A small hand crept up and slipped into the older woman's hand.

"It's okay, Estelle," she whispered. "I've got it from here."

The other woman glanced down at the younger one. "You sure?"

Arianna smiled up at her. And he felt his heart skip a beat. She was gorgeous. And it wasn't due to her make-up, hair or clothes. Her beauty shone.

"I'm sure. Thank you so much for bringing me the water. Why don't you and Joe go hide before Larry starts demanding things."

"All right. It's time for my shows, anyway. Just relax, dear. It will all be over soon."

As soon as Estelle left, Bain gave Arianna a stern look. "You can't take those pills."

She sighed. "They're herbal. Something to help me relax."

All right. So at least they weren't what he thought.

"Relax?"

"I get nervous during these interviews."

That shocked him. "You don't like doing this sort of stuff?"

She snorted. "No. I've never been great in social situations. People often confuse me. I worry about saying the wrong thing. I. . .just. . .maybe these have no effect and it's a mind over matter sort of thing. . ." she trailed off, looking embarrassed. "I know I should be strong enough not to need them."

Those words were like a punch to the gut. She thought he was judging her.

And aren't you?

"Doesn't matter if they are. Make you feel better, then take'em," he told her gruffly.

She studied him for a moment then half-turned away to swallow them. As though she was ashamed? Why the fuck would she be ashamed? Huh, he was beginning to see Dominic might have been right. He had pre-judged her. And maybe, just maybe, he'd fucked up.

"Don't tell Larry," she pleaded, turning back. "I would have taken them earlier but he's always around."

Was that frustration in her voice?

"What's it got to do with him?" And why the fuck did she think he'd tell Larry anything?

She licked her lips nervously. "He didn't tell you?"

He folded his arms over his chest. He was aware they had a limited time before Larry was back with the first interviewer.

"Tell me what?"

She gave him a cautious look. "I thought he'd said something. I, uh, I have a prescription for anti-anxiety pills I'm meant to take. He wouldn't be happy if he knew I had replaced it with herbal pills. I just don't like the way those other pills make me feel. Like I'm numb."

He frowned. He knew little about all of this. And he sure as shit wasn't going to tell her what to do when it came to her health. Wasn't his job. There was one question he had to know the answer to, though.

"Why do this if you don't enjoy it, Ms. Silvers?"

"Please call me Arianna," she said.

He'd insisted on calling her Ms. Silvers in an attempt to keep space between them. And at the same time, he'd been complaining that she kept running away from him.

You're an idiot.

"Fine," he said impatiently. "Answer the question."

"I can see why Dominic does most of the talking," she muttered.

He nearly grinned at her words. Her eyes instantly widened, and she looked mortified.

"Sorry," she apologized.

"Don't be. I like the truth. Better than that icy polite thing you do the rest of the time."

"Icy polite thing?"

"Answer?" he asked, growing impatient. Well, more impatient.

"Oh. Um. I do it because I don't have a choice."

He opened his mouth to ask her what the hell that meant, but the door opened, interrupting them.

Probably just as well. None of this was his business. As soon as her friend found her permanent bodyguards, he was out of here.

And he could not wait to get back to the peace and quiet of Sanctuary Ranch.

4

Unable to sleep, he walked into the kitchen. Best thing about this place was Estelle's cooking. Thank God the ice princess had a decent gym, or he'd be at risk of putting on some pounds.

He opened the fridge and pulled out some leftovers to make himself a sandwich. It was two in the morning, but he couldn't sleep.

He'd just made the sandwich and sat at the counter to eat it when he spotted movement from the corner of his eye. Arianna appeared, dressed in what looked to be an old, worn cotton T-shirt and some leggings. Her hair was in disarray. And there was a pair of huge slippers on her feet.

Were those ducks?

"Ms. Silvers? Everything okay?"

She let out a screech and jumped into the air. Her hand went to her chest.

"Holy fucking shit! You frightened me!"

"You didn't see me? How did you not see me?" he demanded.

Was she so oblivious to her surroundings that she missed a six foot five, two-hundred-and-thirty-pound man sitting there?

"Maybe because you're lurking around in the dark," she snapped.

"I'm not lurking," he replied. "I'm sitting here having a midnight snack."

"That's a snack? That would feed me for a whole day."

He sure as hell hoped not. If this was all she ate in a day, she was seriously under eating. No way would she get away with that sort of bullshit if she was under his protection.

But she's not. Not in that way. So chill, man.

"It's a snack. And you better be eating more than this in a day."

Okay, so obviously he wasn't in the mood to chill.

"Are you sure you're allowed to eat after midnight? Isn't that against the rules? If you eat after midnight don't you turn into an ogre. Oh wait, I think it might be too late. . ."

He had to duck his head to hide his smile. Shit. He was in trouble.

Little brat.

This was a side to her he definitely hadn't seen before. He kind of liked it.

"Getting your movies mixed up. Gremlins shouldn't be fed after midnight because they turn into destructive monsters. Ogres are in *Shrek*."

"You've watched *Shrek*." She gave a comical gasp, holding her hand against her chest. "Doesn't that go against the whole tough guy image?"

"Not an image."

"Ah, my apologies. I didn't realize tough guys watched *Shrek*. Mind you, the two of you do bear a resemblance."

"What does a man have to do to eat his sandwich in peace," he moaned.

She tensed. And he had the sudden intuition that he'd said the wrong thing.

"I apologize. I just came to get some water. I. . .I. . .didn't mean to offend. . .I'll just go. . ." She turned to race off. He quickly stood and reached out to grab her arm.

She gasped, turning and he let her go. Fuck. What was he doing? *Way to intimidate her, asshole.*

"Don't run off. You didn't insult me."

"I'm sorry, I. . ." she trailed off, rubbing her hands over her upper arms as though cold.

He should probably say something to ease her obvious nervousness.

"Stop saying sorry," he said gruffly.

"I'm sor—" she immediately bit off the word at his sharp look.

Her eyes wide, her skin so pale he could see some faint freckles spread across her nose. Aww. Jeez. Why did he have to notice that?

It was damn cute.

He sighed. "Sit."

She licked her lips, looking from the stool to him.

"You didn't insult me. Sit."

He grabbed her a bottle of water and screwed off the top. She just stared at the bottle of water worrying at her lower lip.

"Ms. Silvers. . .Arianna, look at me."

She raised her gaze to his.

"Do I intimidate you?"

"Umm. . .yes. . ." she said cautiously.

He grunted. "'Cause I'm so big?"

Her cheeks pinkened. She nodded.

"Can't change that."

"You're also a little. . .abrupt."

"Some people think that's refreshing."

"Some people, huh? Who? Your mama and nana?"

He grinned. "Yep."

She snorted but picked up the bottle of water, drinking some.

"Here, made too much." He slid over his plate with the other half of the sandwich. "Share?"

She looked down at the sandwich then up at him. He felt sure she was going to refuse, but she reached out and grabbed it.

"Thank you." She took a bite. "It's good. Although you need to cut off your crusts."

"Don't like crusts? They put hair on your chest."

"Yeah. Never got that saying. Who on Earth would want hair on their chest?" She started to relax.

He noticed the way she glanced at his chest. Was she wondering if he had hair there?

"One of my nannies used to take me on picnics. She'd make sandwiches like these. But she'd always cut off the crusts."

"I'll try to remember that next time." The nanny took her on picnics? What about her parents? Where were they?

She took another bite and half the toppings slid out and landed on her lap. "Oh no." She sounded so mortified that it caught him by surprise. She kept her gaze down as she attempted to scoop everything up out of her lap and onto the counter.

"Here." He stood and grabbed a cloth, wetting it and handing it to her.

"Thank you," she muttered, still not looking at him. "Such a klutz." She set the rest of the sandwich down on the plate. Her shoulders were hunched. Did she think he would make fun of her?

"Don't waste the rest. Damn good sandwich."

"Oh. . .umm. . .all right." She took another bite, carefully eating it over the plate. He should probably say something to make her feel better, but he wasn't quite sure what the problem was. So she'd dropped some food on herself.

Big deal.

Gradually, she relaxed and started humming to herself.

"Couldn't you sleep?"

"What? Oh no, I was working."

"Yeah? On the song you're humming?"

"Uh-huh. The lyrics are giving me trouble."

"You write your own music? Thought you just sang other people's stuff."

She raised her eyebrows. "How do you know that?"

"Research for the job," he said stiffly. "That's all."

He regretted the words as soon as he saw her shut down. The mask was back, and he fucking hated it. She obviously used it as a shield, and he didn't want her using it with him.

Ever.

What was wrong with him?

"I better get back to work."

"Shouldn't you be going to sleep," he commented, unable to help himself. *Way to go. Now you not only sound like a prick but a grumpy prick.*

If the shoe fits. . .

"Shouldn't you?" she countered. He nearly smiled at the note of heat in her voice. Anything was better than the icy cold.

"Couldn't sleep. These last few years, guess I've gotten used to the quiet."

"Where do you live?" she asked curiously.

"Small cabin in the middle of the woods."

"Really? Huh, just like Shrek."

He had to grin again. "Yep. But fortunately, I don't have an annoying donkey sidekick."

"That's a shame. I've always wanted a donkey sidekick."

"Someone with your money and fame could buy as many donkey sidekicks as you like." He aimed to keep his voice light but was aware of a slightly dark undertone.

"Maybe I just can't find the right one." There was something sad in her tone. "Good sidekicks are hard to find." She stood. "A cabin in the woods sounds nice. Bet you get a nice view of the stars at night. Thanks for sharing your sandwich."

She left and he stared after her. She thought a cabin in the woods sounded nice? She'd hate it. Hell, she'd probably never gone camping in her life. She was a city girl. Rich. Famous.

He needed to remember that.

But as he went back to bed all he could think of was the sadness in her voice.

"Arianna! Arianna, where are you?"

Oh shit.

She looked around her office frantically. Where could she hide? Knowing he had to be close, she dove under her desk.

She groaned. She was acting like a complete idiot. Why was she hiding from Bain?

Maybe because you're attracted to him? Because you keep thinking about him? Because you don't know how to act normal around him?

It could also be because she'd gone and revealed that stuff about her anti-anxiety medication. And if that wasn't bad enough, she'd also likened him to an ogre.

Idiot.

Now, she was back to avoiding him. She had never met someone so completely masculine in her life. He was pretty much the opposite of what she thought she liked in a guy. He was huge. Muscles that went on forever. And tall, at least a foot taller than she was, which put her at a real disadvantage.

And moody. He was always frowning or scowling. Especially when he was telling her off about something.

And yet, she couldn't stop thinking about him. She couldn't be in the same room as him without her body going into hyper alert. It was so annoying.

Especially when she was pretty certain he hated her. He seemed to walk around in a perpetual bad mood, barking out orders.

He was gorgeous. Sexy. And a total crabby pants.

A clearing of a throat had her slowly turning her head. Two legs stood by her desk.

"Uh-oh."

"Uh-oh?" He crouched down, somehow managing to still be intimidating even folded in half. "What are you doing under the desk?"

"Um, I lost a paper clip," she said quickly, congratulating herself on her quick thinking.

He raised an eyebrow skeptically. "Really? A paperclip?"

"Um. . .well. . ."

He sighed. "Why are you hiding?"

"I'm not hiding. There's a paperclip down here."

"Then get out and let's look for it."

"No."

"No?" He gaped at her, looking like he'd never heard that word before. Maybe he hadn't. She guessed not many women said no to him. "What do you mean, no?"

"We both know there's no paperclip," she told him with a sigh. "I'm down here because I was hiding."

"From who? Is someone bothering you?" He stood as though he was going to go search them out. "Who is it?"

"You. It's you." Shit. Why did she say that? Idiot. She needed to go back to guarding her words. It was better for all of them.

"Me? I'm not bothering you."

She bit her lip. "So you weren't looking for me to tell me off?"

"Why would I tell you off?"

"I don't know. You're always doing it. It seems to be your default status."

He scowled. "What are you talking about? I have never told you off."

She held up a hand, ticking things off as he crouched down again. "You told me off for standing between you and Larry. You told me off for telling you to leave me alone with Larry. You told me off for running through the apartment—"

"First of all, I wasn't telling you off, I was informing you about the protocols you need to follow in order to allow me to do my job better."

"How was me running through the house stopping you from doing your job properly?"

"You could have hurt yourself."

"By running?"

"The other day I saw you trip over your own feet and nearly bang your head on the coffee table. I didn't think it was wise to let you run through the house."

She buried her face in her knees, aware of how bright red her face had gone. That hadn't been her finest moment. She hadn't tripped up because she was clumsy. She'd tripped up because he'd stretched, and she'd got a mouth-watering glimpse of his abs and she'd had her eyes on him rather than watching where she was going.

"All right so if you're not here to tell me off, what do you want to talk about?"

"Come out of there."

She sighed then slipped out. To her shock, he held out his hand. He was voluntarily touching her? This was new.

She slid her hand into his slightly rough, warm one. A rush filled her. Jesus. She'd never been so attracted to a man in her life.

Why did it have to be him? Why couldn't it be someone who

actually seemed to like her? He let go of her as soon as she stood, moving back several steps.

Great. That was a boost for her self-esteem. He couldn't even stand to be within a foot of her.

"What did you want to talk to me about?" she asked.

"We need to go over protocols again before we go to the recording studio tomorrow."

She stifled a groan. Awesome. She slumped into her seat and prepared herself. The man sure did love his rules and protocols.

5

That had been terrible.

She pressed her fingernails into the palms of her hands, trying to fight off the impending panic. So it was one bad day, so what? She could salvage it. She knew she shouldn't have gone into the studio today.

She was barely aware of Bain and Dominic. One walked in front of her, the other behind as they moved through the parking lot. She sped up, moving around Bain to get to the car. She just wanted to go home and forget today happened. All the expectations everyone had of her were weighing her down.

"What do you think you're doing? You walk in time with us. Don't fall out of formation."

She turned to snap at Bain. The guy could be such an ass.

Not his fault. No need to take this out on him.

"Sorry," she muttered. She moved back into place.

They're just trying to keep you safe, Ari.

These threats were messing with her head. She couldn't sleep at night and when she did sleep, she often woke with nightmares. Thank God, her room was soundproof so if she was making any noise in her sleep, she wouldn't wake anyone else. When she woke, she couldn't remember what the nightmares had been about. She hated that. It reminded her too much of the nightmares that had plagued her childhood.

All of which meant she was tired and out of sorts. When they got into the car, Dominic moved into the front passenger seat, while Bain got in the back, beside her.

"Seatbelt," he barked.

She slid the seatbelt on. Her head thumped. She needed some quiet. She wished her stalker would make another move. But he hadn't sent another letter since Bain and Dominic arrived.

"What was that just now?" Bain asked.

"What?" She'd stared at him through the sunglasses she'd put on as they were leaving the recording studio.

"Don't do that again. We can't guard you if you don't do as we say, got it?"

Oh, she got it. She understood that he was a jerk. She thought they were starting to get along the other night. But now he was as grumpy as ever.

Well. That made two of them.

"Arianna? You in here?"

He stepped into her office. If she was hiding under her desk again. . .well, he wasn't sure what he would do, but she needed to learn not to hide from him. He was in charge of her safety.

He bent down and looked under her desk. Not there.

"Uh, Bain? What you doing, man?"

"Looking for Arianna." He straightened and looked over at Dominic who raised his eyebrows.

"Under her desk?"

"She's sneaky and she likes to hide."

"Can't imagine why." Dominic grinned.

"Meaning?" he barked.

"Nothing, man. It's just, you're grouchier than usual. And that's saying something."

"She broke protocol today."

Dominic sighed. "She's clearly having a bad day. Why don't you just let it go?"

Let it go? Really?

"I think I saw her go into the kitchen. Just take it easy on her, huh? I think she's more fragile than she appears."

All he was going to do was talk to her. Wasn't like he was going to torture her. Or put her over his knee and spank her.

Which is exactly what he wanted to do.

He stomped towards the kitchen. He knew he was overreacting, but he needed to go over things again with her. He needed to know that she would obey him when it came to her safety.

As he neared the kitchen, the sound of laughter caught him by surprise. The door was partially open and he peered inside. Shock filled him as he took her in. Her hair was up in a messy knot on her head with tendrils hanging down. She wore an oversized T-shirt, some bright pink tights and fuzzy white socks.

She looked. . .adorable.

He froze at that thought. He couldn't find her adorable. She was the client. Nothing more than that.

She spooned up some chocolate frosting and plopped it down on the cupcake in front of her. Then she giggled to herself as she swirled it around. She wiped at her face, leaving a streak of chocolate across her cheek.

Fuck. Adorable was right.

Something shifted inside him. That hard, bitter part of him softened slightly. She looked young and vulnerable.

"Sprinkles, Miss Ari?" Estelle asked, walking up to the counter where Ari sat. Shit. He hadn't even seen her there.

"Of course! Everything is better with sprinkles!" Arianna clapped her hands with a smile and he was lost. Shock held him immobile. He'd never seen her smile like that before. Or look so carefree. She seemed almost childlike.

Don't be an idiot. This doesn't mean anything.

She stuck her tongue out as she concentrated on getting the sprinkles where she wanted. Finally, he forced himself to move away before anyone saw him standing there.

He'd lost all interest in scolding her.

BAIN WALKED into the kitchen later that night wondering if there were any leftover cupcakes. Those things were amazing. He came to a stop when he saw Arianna standing next to the kitchen counter. She was dressed in a nightie with those same duck slippers.

Those utterly ridiculous but adorable slippers. He spotted something hanging from her hand. Was that a stuffed puppy?

"Arianna?" He walked around her when she didn't move. Instinct screamed at him that something was wrong.

He studied her. Her nightgown had a picture of a teddy bear with angel wings and a halo. He could still see the red mark on her face. From the pillow? Had she been sleeping and woken up? For some reason, he found that kind of cute. He ran his gaze over her face. There was something slightly off. She wasn't looking at him. Not properly.

Her gaze was unfocussed. As though she wasn't quite here.

What was going on?

"Arianna? Can you hear me?"

No reply.

Was she sleepwalking? What did you do with someone who sleepwalked? You didn't wake them up, right? She slowly raised her hand and shocked him by sticking her thumb in her mouth. The stuffed dog hung from her hand by its ear. The toy was white with a black patch over one eye. It looked about as worn as her nightie.

Holy. Shit.

He swallowed heavily. Was she a Little? Or was she simply sleepwalking and didn't know what she was doing?

His mind raced. How was he going to get her back to her bed?

"Arianna?" he asked quietly. "Do you want to go back to bed?" He kept his voice low. Soothing. Hoping he didn't startle her. Then again, she hadn't shown any fear when he'd appeared.

She shook her head, her thumb still in her mouth. Did people who sleepwalked remember what they had done when they woke up? He had no idea.

Maybe she was hungry.

"I was going to make a sandwich. Want one?"

Another shake of her head. Okay, then. Maybe she would just make her own way back to bed? He moved to grab some bread and she turned to the freezer. She opened the door and pulled out a tub of caramel ice cream.

His eyebrow rose.

"Ice cream? At this time of night?"

She frowned.

Okay, man, pull back on the scolding tone. Remember, you're trying not to wake her.

Still, eating ice cream at midnight didn't seem very healthy. Was this something she did often? What if she choked while she was getting a midnight snack?

Calm. Easy. You're not in charge of her health.

But he was in charge of her physical safety. Choking could be a concern. She was out of it, and she might well be in Little space if the toy and the thumb sucking were any indication.

Did she regress while sleepwalking? Or was he reading way too much into this?

Either way, she's hardly likely to choke on ice cream, you idiot.

True.

He laid out the bread on a plate, turning to watch her as she stretched up high to grab a bowl. She was so short, she had to stand on tiptoes and even then, she couldn't reach it. He watched as she opened a bottom cupboard next to her legs. What was she. . .oh hell no!

She was going to use the bottom cupboards as a kind of stepping stool. Fuck!

"Arianna let me get it," he said quietly, resisting the urge to grab her.

She turned to him. Her thumb had dropped from her mouth, and she blinked a few times but then she nodded. Thank fuck. What the hell was she thinking? Well, obviously she wasn't. But why was no one in charge of making certain she was safe at night? She could do any number of things in this state. Fuck, she could walk right out the door. He made a mental note to talk to Dominic about that possibility in the morning.

"Here, why don't you sit up at the island." The kitchen had a big island with some stools. He reached for her but then pulled his hand back at the last second. It wouldn't be right to touch her when she was in this state.

Fuck, she was so vulnerable. What if she accidentally wandered outside? What if someone saw her? Hurt her?

He felt ill.

But to his shock, she slid her hand into his. That thumb reentered her mouth.

"Not very good to suck your thumb, angel," he told her, reaching for her hand.

Christ. Fuck, man. You are not her Daddy. She's a client.

He'd suppressed that side of himself for a long time. But it seemed she brought it back out in him. Her eyes went wide as she stared up at him. He sighed. He couldn't think about how fucking inappropriate this was right now. He'd get her a small serving of ice cream then try to get her back into bed.

He led her around to the other side of the counter and pulled out a stool for her. She just stood there.

"Angel, hop up on the stool." He patted the seat of the stool for good measure.

She stared down at his hand then up at him. He groaned. *Shit. Don't wake up just as I'm doing this.* He gently grasped her around the waist and lifted her onto the stool.

She smiled around her thumb and he quickly made his way back around the island. He spooned out a small amount of ice cream into the bowl then grabbed a spoon and placed them in front of her.

She stared down at the bowl of ice cream with a frown, her thumb slipping free of her mouth. Then she picked up the spoon and pointed at the tub then down at her bowl.

Clearly, she wanted more.

She'd made that very clear. And all without saying a word.

"You have enough ice cream," he told her as he finished making his sandwich. "Too much isn't good for you, especially in the middle of the night."

Her lip went out in a pout. Shit. That was fucking cute. He had to harden himself against her. Cute things were his weakness. And she was fucking adorable.

"Eat up, angel. Unless you'd rather have no ice cream."

He nearly rolled his eyes at himself. If she remembered this in the morning, he was fucked. But to his surprise she just hummed and started eating the ice cream. He made himself a sandwich and sat across from her, but he barely tasted it. He was too busy watching her eat. The way she licked that spoon, her very real pleasure in each mouthful.

Fuck. What was wrong with him?

She's the client.

She dropped her spoon with a clatter and wiped her mouth with the back of her hand. He winced. That was going to feel sticky and gross later. He moved to the sink and grabbed a clean cloth, putting it under the tap. When he turned, she was standing right next to him, her toy dangling from her hand again as she stared up at him.

"Fuck, you move like a ghost."

She swayed slightly.

"Tired, angel?"

She nodded and yawned.

"Let's just wipe your face and hands, huh? Get you back to sleep."

She tilted her face up and he washed it gently then he cleaned her free hand, waited until she passed her toy to the other hand before wiping her other hand clean.

Then she slipped her hand into his once more and tugged. He frowned slightly, wondering what she wanted now.

To his shock, she started jiggling around. If he didn't know better...

She tugged at his hand again. This time, a noise of frustration left her mouth. Shit. Was she waking up? He figured he'd best go with her. He wondered how often this happened?

She led him down the passage, past his own bedroom and Dominic's then around a corner to her bedroom.

"Uh, angel, best I stay out here."

She just kept pulling on his hand. Reluctantly, he followed her inside. Surprise filled him as he took in the bedroom. It was enormous. At least the size of his and Dominic's rooms put together. He'd been expecting something sterile and organized.

It was feminine and filled with stuff. There were portable racks of clothes up against one wall. Her bed was king-sized with a velvet, gray headboard. The bedcovers were a pale pink. Down the end was a velvet gray bench that ran the length of the bed. A white, fluffy rug lay under the bed. Not that you could see much of it because of all the clothes that lay on the floor.

Long, gray floor to ceiling curtains rested along one wall. He knew there were huge windows looking out at the park below. He stared at all her clothes. Didn't she have a closet?

A lamp on the bedside table cast shadows of stars around the room and ceiling. A nightlight?

Arianna made a noise of frustration, dancing around as she held onto his hand tightly. She then pointed at a door across the other side of the room.

Shit. She needed the bathroom.

He quickly followed her across the bedroom and she opened the door. Yep, bathroom. Okay, no way was he going in there. He was already breaching so many rules, it wasn't funny.

No more.

"Angel, I'm not going in there with you." What he needed to do was leave. She could handle this part by herself, right?

Except what if she slipped and hit her head? What if she suddenly woke up and got a fright?

She looked at the toilet then back at him.

Shit.

"Angel, go to the toilet. I'll wait out here," he reassured her.

She still just stood there. Crap. How did he get her to move?

He turned her towards the toilet. "Go potty, little one. I'll be right in here."

To his shock that worked, and she moved off to the toilet. He closed the door but kept it open a few inches just in case.

He paced up and down outside the door. What the fuck was he thinking? He should have walked away the moment she turned up. Or gone and woken up Dominic. He should not be alone in her bedroom with her.

The door pushed open and she shuffled out, yawning. Her mouth was so wide, he could see her teeth. No doubt she'd be mortified if she remembered any of this tomorrow. Then he'd be fired and headed back to Montana.

Which should have made him happy, right?

Ari walked towards the bed then turned and looked back at him. He stepped around more clothes, watching as she tried to climb up into the bed. What the hell was she doing with such a high bed? What if she fell from it in the night?

Stop it.

Finally, he couldn't take it any longer. He grabbed her around the waist and settled her in bed. Then moving on instinct, he tucked the covers around her.

Crap. What if she wouldn't stay in bed? He needed to get some sleep himself tonight. He couldn't stay here, watching over her.

She pulled her stuffed dog close and her eyes started to drift closed. Her thumb was back in her mouth. She needed a pacifier.

"Angel, I want you to listen to me. I want you to stay in bed until morning, understand me?"

She didn't say anything, but she did nod her head before her eyes shut and her breath evened out. Fuck. He wished he could fall asleep that quickly.

Then again, she hadn't actually been awake, had she?

Damn, he needed to do some research on sleepwalking. He took a moment to study her. She looked so sweet and young.

She was trouble. Pure and simple.

6

Ari woke up feeling tired and out of sorts.

She blinked back the sleep in her eyes. What she wouldn't give for a full night's sleep, to wake up energized. She grimaced at the dryness in her mouth and grabbed the bottle of water she always placed by her bed. She took a sip. Why did she taste caramel?

Oh. Shit.

She wiped her hand over her face. She guessed she'd sleepwalked last night. That was the fourth time since she'd gotten that first threatening letter. It was always the same. She'd wake up in the morning with the taste of caramel ice cream on her lips, a dry mouth and an icky stomach because she tended to overindulge.

Although this morning, her stomach wasn't too bad.

She sat up and stretched. With a yawn, she got up and pulled on some work-out clothes. Penance for the ice cream. She decided to skip breakfast, not wanting to risk running into either of her bodyguards.

If she was honest, it was just one of them she didn't want to see. She'd spotted him a few times going to and from the gym. She guessed all those muscles were the result of hard work and discipline.

It had certainly taken all of her discipline not to follow around after him, taking in her fill of those muscles on display, gleaming with sweat.

Okay. . .focus, Arianna.

Why did he pull at her like no other man ever had? Why did he feature in her dreams every night?

You're so screwed up.

She was. She was a big mess. And now it seemed she was sleepwalking again. Maybe she should take her medication again. She shook her head. No. She hated those pills. A couple of sleep-walking episodes weren't enough to make her start taking them again. Things were just stressful at the moment and obviously that had triggered her.

She needed to go for a run. Forget everything else. She walked down the passage quickly, hoping no one saw her. If Estelle caught her, she'd insist on making her breakfast and she really couldn't stomach food right now.

She walked into the gym, sighing with relief to see it was empty. She turned the music on and hopped on the treadmill.

Time to lose herself.

BAIN WATCHED as she pushed herself harder. Placing the dumbbells down, he glanced over at the clock. He'd been in here for close to an hour and she hadn't stopped once. She showed no signs of slowing down.

When he'd first walked in, he'd thought she was ignoring him on purpose. He'd been annoyed and had been about to give her a piece of his mind. But then he'd seen the look on her face. Similar to last night.

So he'd kept himself clear of her line of sight as he'd started his work out, using the time to study her. Sweat coated her skin. Her hair had been pulled back into a ponytail and hung down her back. She wore work-out clothes that molded to her body and boy, did she have some gorgeous curves, but he could also see how prominent her shoulder bones were.

Was she eating enough? Getting enough rest?

Fuck. He didn't want to feel this level of concern for her. He was happier when he was thinking of her as cold and rude. He didn't want to get close to her. . .care for her. . .

He sighed. Shit. He also couldn't stand by while she ran herself past the point of exhaustion. He made his way cautiously towards her. He didn't know how long she'd been here before he arrived, but she'd been running for well over an hour now.

Enough.

He just didn't know how to let her know about his presence without scaring her half to death. As he grew closer, she stumbled. She managed to reach out and push the emergency button on the treadmill, right before her legs gave out. She had a hold of the side of the treadmill as he leaped forward and grabbed her.

She screamed as he touched her. Fuck.

"Easy. It's just me. It's Bain."

Her eyes were wide, her breath coming in sharp pants. Her face had gone pale.

"I'm just going to help you, okay?" he said, speaking low and soft as one might to an injured animal. She looked terrified and he hated it.

She managed a nod and he lifted her up in his arms before she could change her mind. He quickly carried her over to a bench, setting her down. Then he grabbed a bottle of water from the small bar fridge, handing it to her.

She looked even worse close up. Wan, with dark smudges under her eyes. Tendrils of hair stuck to her forehead. She just held onto the water, not even looking down at it. Trembles rocked her body. He grabbed hold of her wrist.

"Pulse is way too fast. Pushed yourself too far." He couldn't stop the scolding note in his voice. She just continued to stare at him.

"Drink the water," he bossed, expecting immediate obedience. Nothing. Damn it.

He took the bottle back from her and undid the lid. He held it out, but she didn't take it. Instead, her head dropped back, her eyes fluttering shut.

"Fuck! Don't faint. Hey. Hey. You're okay." He grabbed hold of her, moving her until she was lying on her back on the ground with her feet up on the bench.

Then he jumped to his feet and grabbed a clean hand towel. He poured some water onto the towel and placed it around the back of her neck.

"Still feeling dizzy?"

She nodded then closed her eyes as if that small movement made her feel ill. Probably did, poor thing.

He slid a hand under her shoulders and sat her up slightly. Her feet slid from the bench and he moved her so she was resting against his chest. Then he lifted the bottle of water to her lips.

"Slowly. That's better. Good girl." He took her pulse again. Getting better. He kept holding the bottle up to her lips until it was entirely gone.

She let out a sigh then sat up, moving away from him. He took that as his cue and stood. Then he held a hand out to her. She stared at it for a moment before she slid her far smaller one into his.

"Thank you," she said quietly, unable to meet his gaze.

He should tell her about last night. He should ask her if she needed any help. But he made himself pull back.

"You need to stretch," he bossed. "Eat something. You pushed yourself too far."

"I know. I...I...thanks." She turned and left before he could say anything more.

Damn it. Why did most of their conversations end up with his scolding her and her running from him?

"HEY, ANGEL," Bain said quietly as she walked up and stood beside him at the fridge. "Want some ice cream?"

It had been several nights since she'd last sleepwalked. He'd half-hoped she wouldn't do it again. And half-hoped she would.

Idiot.

She let out a shuddering breath and he narrowed his gaze as he looked her over. Fine trembles rocked her body. Was she cold? The temperature in the apartment was kept too damn warm in his opinion. But then he wasn't a tiny little thing like the woman standing before him.

"Angel, are you all right?"

"S-scared." She stuttered over the word which was a little cute.

"Did you have a nightmare?"

She nodded. Frustration bit at him. He reminded himself to remain calm. She was fragile in this state. He couldn't do anything to upset her.

Then to his shock, she stepped forward and wrapped her arms around his middle.

Uh, what? Holy fuck.

What was going on? Panic filled him before he realized how ridiculous he was being.

She's hugging you, idiot.

Hug her back.

Fuck. Except she was the client. Bad enough he was here like this with her. That he was interacting with her Little without her knowledge. The guilt was fucking eating away at him, but he didn't know how to broach it with her.

Hey, don't know if you know this, but you sleepwalk. And when you do, you seem to regress. Are you a Little? 'Cause maybe I could be your Daddy.

Yeah. That was going to go down fucking well. The other night, he'd tried to keep touching her to an absolute minimum, in no way did he want her to think he was taking advantage of her.

And then she went and hugged him. *Fuck. Fuck. Fuck.*

He should have told her after the first night.

Apparently, it was a common misconception that you shouldn't wake someone who was sleepwalking. You should get them back to bed or try waking them carefully.

But how did he do that without fucking scaring her?

"Arianna, back to bed we go. Well, not we, I mean we need to go back to our separate beds."

Real smooth, idiot.

Shit. Should have stayed far, far away, you asshole.

Calling himself all sorts of nasty names, he gently tried to pry her off him. He should have called for Dominic the moment she stepped into the kitchen. But he felt so fucking protective of her when she was like this that he couldn't even stand the idea of his friend being here.

Before he left, though, he was going to have to bring it up with her. She needed to know what was going on. Maybe get some help for it.

The concert was tomorrow. He'd tell her after, she didn't need more stress right now.

"Angel, you need to let me go. You need to wake up. Go back to bed."

She shook her head and snuggled closer, letting out a content noise. He glanced down to find her sucking her thumb as she leaned on his chest, her eyes were already drifting closed.

Fuck. Fuck.

"Angel, wake up."

She was being stubborn.

"Up."

Oh no. Fuck no. But she held up her arms and looked up at him so trustingly.

Shit. shit. shit.

He closed his eyes. Took a deep breath then lifted her up in his arms, carrying her bridal style.

"Bed."

"Right. Do you need the toilet?"

She shook her head. That was different. No ice cream. No toilet.

"You sure?"

"Uh-huh."

"Okay," he said suspiciously. He had to rein in his Daddy instincts. *She's not your Little. She hasn't consented to being your Little.*

Your job is just to keep her safe.

Fucked if he didn't find himself wishing for more though.

7

She was so freaking nervous.

She shifted around in her seat as Joe drove them to the concert venue. Bain shot her a look. How come he always ended up riding in the back with her? Why couldn't Dominic sit back here? Dominic's gaze was far less penetrating.

Sometimes, it felt like Bain could see straight through her, right to the heart of all her secrets. Christ, wouldn't that be the icing of the cake? She'd already embarrassed herself enough in front of him.

Hiding from him under her desk. Calling him an ogre. Running to the point of collapse. Nearly tripping over her own feet as she ogled him.

"Everything okay?" he asked.

She nodded. They were on their way to the concert and she was so nervous, it was taking all her control not to vomit.

You can do this.

"Fine," she managed to say.

He gave her a skeptical look. She didn't blame him. She was far from fine.

"No questions about anything?" he asked as they approached the venue's secure parking lot for the performers.

"No."

Joe pulled up into a park.

"Good. Wait there until I come around and get you," he ordered.

She sighed. Dominic turned to give her a smile. "I know he can be abrupt and grouchy; our boss doesn't usually send him on these jobs. He's not exactly a people person. But Bain is the best there is. You're safe with him."

She smiled at Dominic. "It's okay. I know I'm not easy."

She winced. She'd been told what a nuisance she was all her life.

Dominic's eyes widened then he barked out a laugh. "I'm sent on most of the more high-profile cases we take, and you are the easiest person I've ever had to work for. Hands down. My last bodyguard job like this, the person I was guarding thought it was my job to go out each morning and get their breakfast. Which was a smoothie consisting of kale, banana, avocado and beets." He shuddered. "And they tried to make me drink it. That stuff went through me quicker than a bobsled flying down a luge."

She let out a surprised giggle as Bain opened the door.

SHE WAS INCREDIBLE.

The music wasn't to his taste. He was more of a rock 'n roll man. But even he could appreciate how beautiful her voice was.

She moved around the stage like she was born to this. Surprisingly, he saw she was right. As soon as she started singing, the nerves disappeared. The crowd was lapping it up. He stood backstage with one eye on the crowd, the other on her. Dominic was on the other side. They had comms set up so they could speak to each other as well as the concert venue's security.

Arianna hadn't received any further threats. Which surprised him. He was still suspicious of the head of security at her building. But the guy had a squeaky-clean background and he had no evidence of his involvement.

At least this venue only held six hundred people on the upper level and a further three hundred downstairs in the bar.

Still, he'd feel much better once her set was over and they could take her home.

He forced himself to concentrate on the crowd. Everyone had been checked at the doors for weapons. There was plenty of security around. It was as safe as they'd been able to make it. So why did he have this impending sense of doom?

They'd gone over her set, how many songs she'd sing, and he knew she was coming up to the last song. She was the last act of the night.

She'd been so freaking nervous before getting on stage. Not that anyone else would have been able to see it. No, she'd hidden it well behind a composed mask. But he'd seen the fine tremble in her hands. The way she'd chewed her lip when she thought no one was looking.

There was a sudden booming noise. What the fuck was that? The sounds of screams reverberated throughout the room as Arianna stopped singing. She looked around in confusion. An alarm started blaring. Fuck! Was the place on fire? Sprinklers erupted, spraying water everywhere. Arianna let out a panicked cry as the crowd surged forward. Security in front of the stage was barely holding them back.

He raced out towards her, grasping hold of her arm and shielding her as people in the crowd started screaming. They surged against security again as he tugged her with him towards the back of the stage. Dominic quickly joined him.

"Apparently there's a fire at the front of the building, it's cutting off two exits," he called out calmly.

They kept her between them as they tried to make their way out the back, but there was confusion and pandemonium. People were screaming, afraid.

Voices crackled in his ear from the comms piece.

"Fuck!" he swore. "They lost control of the crowd. Need to get her out of here."

They finally reached the exit. His instincts were still screaming at him. He had Arianna tucked into his side while Dominic took point. They walked out into the cold air.

"We need to call Joe," Dominic called out. "Fuck!"

The unusual show of anger would have surprised Bain under other circumstances. But it was well justified considering the clusterfuck they walked into. They'd used the back entrance that should have been only available for the bands and their crew, but there was a huge crowd out here. Whether they were from the concert or not, he couldn't tell. But it was only going to take one person to spot Arianna and they were screwed.

He gently pushed her head down. Dominic moved to her other side.

"Keep your head down. They might not notice you."

It was almost as though they'd heard him. He'd thought they might be more distracted by the fire, but it seemed that paled once one of them caught sight of the woman he had pressed against him, her body shaking with trembles of fear.

Fuck. He hated that.

"Arianna! Oh my God, it's Arianna!"

"I love you!"

"Sign my top!"

"Arianna! Arianna!"

Fuck. Shit. They were pressed in. Unable to get through.

Dominic gave him a grim look. Right. Fuck. He saw the other

man speak into his wrist, trying to communicate with security. Likely calling for back-up. But fuck, even if they were free, they wouldn't get through the crowd to help them.

Dominic moved in front of Arianna. Bain attempted to move her between them, but she clung to his arm. He stared down into her terrified face. Her eyes were wide, her face pale. She faltered and he had to grab her, holding her up.

"Arianna, it's gonna be okay." For now, the crowd was fairly well behaved. But things could ramp up at any moment. "I'm here. Nothing will happen. You just need to hold on a bit longer for me. Trust me."

She stared up at him then gave a nod.

Brave girl.

He maneuvered her so she was between him and Dominic. She was so tiny that they had her mostly covered, but if this crowd got violent, they were screwed.

"Get out of the way," Dominic commanded. "Move back and let us pass."

Bain blocked people who tried to push closer. They grabbed at her clothing, trying to touch her. Arianna let out a frightened cry. They'd only managed to move a few feet when the sound of sirens filled the air. The crowd seemed to recognize the sign of authority and drew back slightly, allowing them to push their way through, towards the parking lot. There were people everywhere, rushing back and forth, uncaring of who they hurt in their panic to get away. A horn blared loudly. Fire engines tried to push their way through.

Dominic led them off to the side and around a couple of vehicles.

"Arianna! Hey, there she is!"

Arianna let out another cry, huddling into Dominic's back. Bain slid a comforting hand over her shoulder. "Nearly there."

What the fuck was wrong with people? As the fire engines

moved forward, people started to scatter. Someone slammed against him and he grunted. Arianna turned, looking worried. He tried to give her a reassuring look. She bit her lip, telling him he'd failed.

"Fuck! Joe ain't getting through this!" Dominic told them. "Let's try to head to the second rendezvous point."

It was their back-up plan if things went to shit. Larry had thought them crazy. But Dominic and Bain had insisted. Where was that little shit, Larry? No doubt he'd been one of the first out of there. And probably without even considering Arianna's safety.

They managed to duck around a few more cars, no one paying much attention to them now. Bain used the opportunity to pull off his jacket and slip it over Arianna's shoulders. Partially to help disguise her, but mostly because it was fucking freezing out here and she was dressed in a tiny skirt and crop top that had all these sequins stitched into it.

Moving out onto the street, they turned down an alleyway. Not the safest way to move through the streets of Manhattan at night, but right now, the well-lit street wasn't much safer.

He slipped his gun out of its holster and Dominic did the same, moving in front of them.

Arianna let out a small whimper of distress. She was shaking so bad that her teeth were chattering.

Poor baby.

"It's okay, angel. You're safe," he soothed. "Going to get you home and into your bed soon. All right? Hold on."

Dominic turned to look at him, but he couldn't see the expression on his face in the dark alley.

Arianna let out a small cry, slipping on something. Probably due to those ridiculously high shoes she was wearing. He grabbed hold of her arm, steadying her. "Okay?"

"Y-yes."

He kept hold of her with one hand just in case. They exited the alley and he nearly sighed in relief to find it relatively quiet. They started walking towards the bar where they'd set up the second rendezvous point. He frowned as he noted the way Arianna was limping. He set his gun back in its holster, there was no immediate threat. Dominic did the same.

He slid his arm around her. Fuck, she was still trembling like a leaf.

"Not too much further, angel," he said in a quiet voice. "You can make it. Once we're home, I'll get you a big bowl of ice cream."

He knew he was saying too much, but he'd do anything to get her to calm down. He considered picking her up, but he'd rather have his arms free and him carrying her might garner them more attention. While the street wasn't that busy, there were still some people around.

They reached the bar and moved around to the small parking lot out the back. Dominic had scoped this place out two days ago, so Bain let him take lead. He kept his arm around Arianna, supporting her. He honestly didn't know how much longer she could keep it together. She was exhausted and frightened.

"Fuck. He's not here." Dominic pulled out his phone. He took a few steps away, talking quietly.

Bain kept his gaze roaming the parking lot. He kept them to the shadows.

Arianna burrowed into his chest, clinging onto him.

"You're okay. Everything is going to be all right." He resisted the urge to kiss the top of her head.

"I left my stuff back in the dressing room."

"We'll get it. Right now, main priority is your safety."

Dominic strode over to them, his face serious. "Apparently, Larry got back to the car without us. He lied and told Joe that he'd seen us and that we told him we would make our own way home.

Joe drove him back to his place, which apparently is half an hour away."

"For fuck's sake, they both knew the plan!"

Arianna let out a protesting noise and he ran his hand up and down her back soothingly. "It's okay."

Dominic raised his eyebrows at him, and he shook his head. Later.

"Well, it gets even worse. Apparently, a crowd has gathered outside Arianna's apartment building. Concerned for her safety. It includes plenty of media."

"Fuck! How the fuck did they get there so quickly?"

"It took awhile for us to get out of the building and parking lot then walk here." Dominic frowned. "Estelle is still there since she was waiting for Joe to return after the concert and he's worried about her. I don't think we should take Arianna back there. Not yet, anyway. Not until the crowd has cleared away."

"I have somewhere safe I can take her. You head back to the apartment; help get Joe through to Estelle. I'll look after Arianna."

Dominic glanced down at Arianna, but Bain wasn't even certain she was following everything they were saying.

"You sure you want to take her?"

Bain gave him a look. "Just get us a ride. I got this."

Yeah, maybe he wasn't acting in the most professional manner. But right now, he'd give Arianna whatever she needed if she'd just stop fucking shaking and making those small whimpers.

A town car pulled up fifteen minutes later. Dominic opened the door.

"Hop in, Arianna," Bain said to her quietly as she continued to cling to him.

She took a deep shuddering breath then moved into the car.

Dominic grabbed hold of his arm as he went to slip in after her. "You sure about this?"

No. He wasn't sure about much. Which was a strange situation for him to be in. He always knew what he was doing. But he was going on gut instinct right now.

And his gut told him that he needed to look after Arianna.

8

She couldn't breathe. Oh God. She was going to lose it. Right here in this town car. At least Bain had moved the privacy screen into place. Still, she didn't want him to see her lose it.

Get it together, Arianna.

She attempted to breathe, to calm the nausea bubbling in her stomach. But nothing was getting through. There was heavy weight on her chest.

She could still feel the hands grabbing at her. Only in her head, they pulled her away from Bain, away from safety. They tore at her. Hurt her.

Don't hurt me.

"Arianna? Are you okay? Ari?"

His voice tried to reach through the panic, but it wasn't working. She could still feel it clawing at her, threatening to pull her under.

"Angel? Calm down. You're okay."

Angel. She liked him calling her that. Like she meant something to him. What would this man do to protect someone he cared about?

Everything. Anything and everything he had to.

God, she wanted that.

"Shit. You're having a panic attack."

How did he know that? She was usually so good at hiding them. She dug her fingernails into the palm of her hand. The slight bite of pain helped her push back the panic.

"What are you doing?" he demanded. He forced her hands apart placing his palms on hers. "Do *not* do that again. You hear me?"

His voice was demanding. A pure command meant to be obeyed.

"Don't hurt yourself." He raised her hand to his chest. "Feel my breaths. Follow me. Breathe with me. In. One. Two. Out. One. Two. That's it. Good girl. Doing so well, Ari. So brave. Good girl. Keep breathing. You're safe. In and then out. Well done."

His praise soothed the raw wounds on her soul. The pain from years of being told she didn't measure up to her parents' expectations, to society's views, to Larry's requirements.

She didn't care that he didn't really mean them. In no way could she be considered brave. She hadn't done anything. He was just saying it because he needed to calm her down.

Once the panic started to lift from her chest and she felt like she could breathe more easily, she realized that she was practically sitting on his lap, her hand on his chest. She tried to move away.

He let her go. Disappointment flooded her.

"Going to fucking kill Larry for making Joe take him home. What the hell was Joe thinking? He's your driver."

Oh God. Oh God.

Thinking about it made the panic rage through her once more. She leaned her forehead against her knees with a tired cry. She couldn't do it. She couldn't take any more.

"Just breathe, angel." He ran his hand up and down her back. "Calm down. Good girl. Nearly there. You're doing well."

She felt ill. Shivers rocked her body. She was so cold. And exhausted. She wanted to go home.

Bain pulled her up and drew her close once more. She leaned on him.

It was just for tonight.

Surely that was okay. It wasn't every day that you had to be rushed out of a building that was on fire then were nearly mobbed by a crowd of fans and then driven through Manhattan and out to . . . where were they, exactly?

"Brooklyn," Bain rumbled when she asked. "Friend lives here. We'll stay the night."

She turned her head sharply. What? When had this been decided? Wait. She remembered him and Dominic talking. . .something about a crowd being outside her apartment.

"We'll stay here tonight and go back tomorrow."

She shook her head. Go back? She didn't want to go back. Not tomorrow. Not ever. She was over that apartment. Over this life. All she wanted was to create music. To be free.

His face tightened. "Know my friend's place won't exactly be up to your standards, but it's better than a hotel where you might be recognized. Friends aren't rich, but you'll be safe there."

What? What was he even talking about? She didn't care about where they were staying. The car pulled over to the side of the road.

"Stay," he warned her. He opened the door then she saw the driver open his window. Bain handed him something. Money. Right. She needed to make sure he was reimbursed for that. Although she supposed she'd just get billed for it.

She looked out at a gorgeous brownstone house. This place was probably bigger than her apartment. What was he even talking about?

Sometimes she didn't understand other people.

Bain opened her door and held out his hand without looking at her. She understood he was doing his bodyguard duties. But for a moment there it had felt like there was more between them. Like he might actually care.

You're paying him, Arianna. He's doing his job.

She slipped her hand into his and felt a shiver of awareness cross her skin. Her body wanted to gravitate towards him, to wrap around all those muscles. Maybe it was a safety thing. She was scared and he was so calm and commanding. Capable.

Yeah? So how come you don't feel that way about Dominic?

She shouldn't feel this way about Bain. Most of the time he intimidated her. He was so stern. Blunt. Grouchy.

He guided her up the steps. The door at the top opened and a well-built man dressed in jeans and a rock band T-shirt stood there. His hair was wavy and pushed back off his handsome face.

He stepped aside without saying a word. Bain ushered her inside quickly and the man shut and locked the door behind him, setting the alarm.

Only then did he turn to Bain with a grin. "Hey, man, good to see you." They did one of those manly half-hugs she thought she saw an actual smile grace Bain's face. But she must have imagined it, because when he turned to her, his face was granite again.

"This is Arianna. Arianna, my friend Tom. We went to school together."

Tom stuck out a hand. His smile was sincere and kind. She put her hand in his. The handshake was firm but not overbearingly so. She gave him a small smile.

"Hello, Arianna, nice to meet you. My wife is going to be so upset that she wasn't here to meet you. She's a big fan."

"Nice to meet you too."

"Jen isn't here then?" Bain asked.

"No, she and Mac are away on business."

"Business is good then? Place is nice."

Nice? It was gorgeous. She looked around in delight at the wooden floors and high ceilings. There were photos plastered on most of the walls of Tom with a curvy, short woman with dark hair and a bigger man with a buzz haircut. In most of the photos, the woman stood between the men. But in others she was only with one man. Arianna was surprised to find her kissing the bigger man in one photo. Were the three of them together?

"Come in, you two. Do you want something to drink? Coffee? Hot chocolate? Something stronger?"

"I'm still on duty," Bain said. "But I'll take the hot chocolate."

She blinked up at him. He drank hot chocolate? She'd pegged him as the type who fueled his body on only healthy food.

"Hot chocolate?" Tom let out a surprised laugh. "I didn't think you ate anything sweet, man."

Bain just shrugged.

"And you, Arianna?" Tom asked.

"She'll take a hot chocolate as well," Bain said.

She frowned but didn't object. She'd actually really love a hot chocolate. Despite it being warm in the apartment, she felt freezing.

"Come on into the living room. I have the fire on." They followed him into a gorgeous living room. It wasn't overcrowded with stuff, but it still looked lived in.

"Want me to take your jacket?" Tom asked.

She looked down, noticing that she still had Bain's jacket on and was holding it tight around her. She blushed and handed it over. "Bain kindly leant it to me. Thank you."

Tom gave his friend a look. "Chivalrous of him."

"Very."

Bain just grunted.

"Have a seat," Tom said to her gently. She sat in a corner of the sofa as he went over to a window seat and pulled it up, drawing out a blanket. "Jen keeps this here for movie nights. Even in summer, we have to turn the air up and crawl under a blanket with her." Tom shook his head but his affection for his wife was more than obvious and it made her heart ache.

He went to put the blanket over her, but Bain grabbed it, placing it over her lap instead. Tom sent him a grin.

"Like that is it?"

"Isn't like anything," Bain snarled.

"Uh-huh."

"Make the hot chocolate, will you?" Bain snapped.

She gasped. She didn't know what exactly they were talking about, but Bain was being rude to his friend.

Tom disappeared with another grin.

"That was rude," she scolded.

He just raised an eyebrow and grunted. Then he crouched in front of her. Immediately she leaned towards him. She was feeling out of her element. Unsure. And Bain was her one constant.

Maybe he was going to say something reassuring. She could use that right now. As nice as Tom was, she hated invading his privacy. She was worried about Joe and Estelle and about all the people who'd been at the concert tonight. Was anyone hurt?

She twisted her hands in the blanket.

"Arianna, look at me."

She raised her gaze to his. She was grateful Dominic and Bain had been there tonight. She'd hate to think what would have happened to her if they hadn't been. They'd gotten her out safely. They'd taken care of her.

She couldn't remember the last time someone had done that.

Which was pretty sad. Loneliness flooded her. Sometimes she just wished she had someone who would hug her and tell her everything would be okay.

"Tom has a wife and a boyfriend," Bain said suddenly.

Umm. Okay. That wasn't what she was expecting him to say.

But it was interesting. Wow. She thought that sort of thing only happened in books.

"You won't mention anything about it to them or to others, understand? We're in their house. How they live is their choice. We'll respect that." His tone wasn't mean or harsh, but his words made her flinch back.

Did he really think she would do that? That she would make someone feel bad because they chose to live a different lifestyle than was socially acceptable?

She gave him a sharp nod, directing her gaze over his shoulder. She pulled back in on herself. The indifferent mask she used so often slid over her face.

Don't let him see he hurt you.

Fuck. Fuck.

He'd hurt her. He'd seen it in the way she'd flinched away. And now she'd shut down on him.

You asshole.

He hadn't said anything to be a jerk. He'd just wanted her to know the situation, so she didn't say something. . .

Right, and what makes you think she would?

Ari wasn't who he'd imagined her to be. She wasn't judgmental, snobby or cold. She was sweet and slightly clumsy. Cute. Kind.

Fuck. He stared at her for a long moment, willing her to look at him. But she kept her gaze off in the distance. She looked so tiny bundled up in the blanket. Finally, with a sigh, he stood. Maybe some distance between them was a good thing. He needed to pull back.

She's the client.

"I'll help Tom with the drinks."

He walked into the kitchen to find Tom at the stove, heating up milk and chocolate. Rugger, Jen's huge mastiff looked up from where he was lying by the back door.

"Rugger always gets depressed when Jen is gone," Tom explained as Bain went over to pat the big dog's head. "Silly thing mopes around like his whole world has disintegrated. Thought it best to keep him in here. Didn't know whether your *friend* liked dogs and most people are intimidated by Rugger."

"She's not a friend. She's a client."

Tom poured the chocolate mix into three mugs. "Right, my bad. She okay? She's very pale and quiet. Do you think she's in shock?"

"Had a panic attack in the car." He gripped the counter as Tom pulled out some whipped cream from the fridge. "I didn't realize that's what was happening for a start. She didn't even make any noise. Didn't try to alert me. But she was digging her fingernails into her palms. She stopped breathing."

She'd scared him half to death.

"You obviously got her calmed down. What happened must have been terrifying. I've been watching the news reports. I saw a bit of footage of the three of you, that could have gone downhill fast."

He nodded. Didn't he fucking know it. If that crowd had fully turned on them. . .he felt nauseous at the thought.

He frowned. "She's different than I thought she would be."

"Yeah? Jen's been a big fan of hers for a while. We've been to several of her concerts. She doesn't do a lot of publicity. Makes her seem a bit unapproachable. Jen always reckons that's bullshit. She says she's sad. That you can see it in her eyes. Never saw it. Until just now."

He frowned. "She's rich and famous. Isn't that what most people want?"

Tom gave him a knowing look. "Not all women are Jillian."

"Didn't say they were," he said defensively. Jillian was a sore point.

"No? You've always liked honesty, Bain. You were the one who told me to stop pissing around and make my move on both Mac and Jen. That life was too fucking short to be caught up in what other people thought, right?"

Sounded like him.

"I'm going to give you a bit of honesty. Yes, there are people like Jill out there. There are also good, sweet, kind people like Jen."

He grunted. "I fucking know that." All the women on the ranch were sweethearts. He just wasn't attracted to them. Just as well since they were all taken. A pair of wide, moss-green eyes suddenly filled his mind.

Why the fuck was he attracted to her?

"Yeah? You might know it. But doesn't mean that you don't have biases. Especially with a woman like Arianna, who seems to have it all—"

"She does. I live in her fucking apartment. Probably worth more than I'd make in a lifetime."

Tom sighed. "Just because she has money doesn't make her shallow, it doesn't mean she's happy."

"Didn't come here for a fucking heart-to-heart. I've been hired to protect her because she's got a stalker."

"Yeah? Shit. Poor kid."

She wasn't that much younger than Tom.

"Want whip?" Tom asked.

He shook his head. Tom put a mound of whip on one of the hot chocolates then added sprinkles.

"Didn't know you were the sprinkles type." Bain raised an eyebrow.

Tom rolled his eyes. "Whatever, asshole. This is for Arianna. It's my sprinkle special."

A sudden yell had them both freezing then Bain took off towards the living room. "Ari!"

There was a bark, then to his shock, a loud laugh.

"Shit, Rugger!" Tom swore. "He got out the door."

Bain came to a stop at the sight that greeted him. Rugger was lying half on Arianna, his big tongue licking at her face as she giggled.

"Rugger get off her!" Tom pulled the dog back and Bain felt like he'd been sucker punched as he saw the beaming smile on Arianna's face. Had he ever seen her truly smile?

Tom sighed with frustration. "Rugger, sit. She doesn't want your dog-breath kisses."

Arianna patted Rugger's head and he licked her hand. She giggled again. "Hello, Rugger."

"He's Jen's dog," Tom explained, sitting next to her. Rugger put his big head in Arianna's lap, and she cooed at him as she scratched him behind the ears.

Something surged inside Bain. Was he jealous of a dog? What the fuck was wrong with him? He didn't want to put his head in her lap and have her make soft noises at him. Nope. That was stupid.

"Guess I'll get the drinks," he snapped, turning around and stomping back into the kitchen.

ARIANNA WASN'T sure what she'd done to annoy Bain. She guessed maybe it was the situation. Everything that had happened tonight had probably put him on edge. After handing her the best hot chocolate she'd tasted in her life, with whip and sprinkles, he'd turned on the T.V. to watch the news reports and completely ignored her.

He'd spoken a few times to Tom. But on the most part he'd sat with a glower on his face. Eventually, Tom had offered to show her up to her room. Bain had come up with them, checking her room over while Tom had grabbed her some of his wife's clothes to get dressed into in the morning. She'd had a shower and dressed in the big T-shirt he'd also provided, which he'd told her was brand new.

It still felt a little weird wearing his shirt, but she didn't have much choice and she didn't want to be rude. Like Bain seemed to be expecting her to be.

Tom had made Rugger leave her bedroom, but she couldn't help but crack the bedroom door open, hoping that he might sneak in.

She could use the company. She didn't much feel like being alone tonight.

~

HE COULDN'T SLEEP. He tried to tell himself it was because he was still on-duty. Or that he was still coming down from an adrenaline rush.

But he knew it wasn't either of those reasons. It was because he was a prick.

He sighed. Then he pressed the heels of his hands into his eyes. He knew that Tom was right. He was looking at Arianna and seeing Jill. He was tainting her with his old hang-ups.

It wasn't fucking fair. She was the first woman he'd been this attracted to since Jill. His ex would have loved this life. Wealth. People at her beck and call. Adoring her. Fawning over her.

But while Arianna was rich, with legions of fans, it was obvious that she didn't much like the notoriety. He didn't know why he'd warned her not to speak of Tom's relationship. She'd never once indicated that she was someone to look down on other people. To judge others.

No. That was all on him. He was the one being the judgmental prick.

Time to pull your shit together, man.

He couldn't act on his desire to have her. But he could work on his attitude.

How often had she had people over since he'd been living in her apartment? How often had she gone out? How often had she fucking smiled?

She was sad. And lonely.

Yeah, he needed a big attitude adjustment. He was fucked if he knew what to do, though. Apologize? Be a good start. Work on his professionalism? Also a good idea. He should tell her about her sleepwalking.

He'd called and spoken to Dominic who had managed to find Joe. Apparently, the older man had acted kind of cagey, which worried him. Arianna loved him and Estelle like family, it would hurt her if Joe was up to something. Dominic was working on getting rid of the crowd outside the apartment. He'd also spoken to Larry, the asshole, who was gonna go back to the concert venue early in the morning to get everything Arianna had left.

He'd be having a chat with Larry himself tomorrow.

Rugger barked and he jumped from the bed, grabbing his gun off the nightstand.

Fuck!

He moved out of the door, sticking to the shadows. Rugger let out another quiet bark. He saw movement to his side and turned as he saw Tom walk down the passage.

"Rugger, what is it? Arianna? You okay?" Tom asked.

Bain moved forward and saw Arianna standing at the top of the stairs. Rugger was next to her. She was wearing a large T-shirt. One he guessed belonged to Tom since it was swimming on her. And didn't that just rile his protective, possessive instincts?

Fuck.

Then he noticed that Rugger had the bottom of the T-shirt in his mouth. He tugged on it with a soft growl.

"Ari?" Bain called out quietly, having guessed what was going on. Although how the hell Rugger knew was beyond him.

"Is she okay?" Tom asked.

"She's sleepwalking. She's done it before." He moved carefully forward. Fuck. How had she gotten past his door? He thought he'd been on alert for her.

"Don't think Rugger wants her going down the stairs."

"She's not used to stairs." And she could have fucking hurt herself if she'd taken a stumble.

His heart raced with fear just thinking about it. Fuck. Somehow, she'd gotten under his thick skin, slipping through the barriers he'd erected.

And all the snarling and snapping in the world wasn't going to make these feelings for her disappear.

"Shouldn't we try to get her back to bed?" Tom asked.

"Angel, you need to go back to bed now." He gently grasped hold of her shoulders and turned her towards her room.

As soon as he let her go, she turned back.

"No." She stomped her foot on the floor.

"Okay, seems she doesn't want to go to bed," Tom said with amusement.

They both watched as Arianna stuck her thumb in her mouth.

"Shit," Tom said. "She regresses when she sleepwalks?"

"You never saw this," Bain growled at his oldest friend.

"Jesus, you shithead, like I'd ever tell anyone this."

"Sorry. It's just. . .I don't even know if she knows. . ."

"Fuck. You haven't told her?"

"How the hell do I tell her?" Bain snapped.

Tom ran his hand over his face. "Yeah, I can see the problem. But man. . ."

"I know, all right," he snapped. "I know how it fucking looks.

I'll tell her. Just let's get through tonight. She's been through enough today."

"Yeah. Agreed. Everyone has their breaking point. All right, what do you need?"

"Ice cream and a stuffed toy if you have one."

"Yeah, Jen has a teddy bear Mac gave her one year for Valentine's Day. How are you going to get her downstairs? Should she walk down them?"

He stepped around the other side of Arianna. He positioned himself in front of her, so if she did try to step forward, he'd be able to catch her. He looked back down the staircase with a shudder. Long way to fall. His stomach dropped at the thought. Reaching out, he patted the dog's head. "Good job keeping our girl safe."

Our girl. He was fucked.

Tom returned with the soft toy and Bain took it with a nod of thanks.

"Angel, it's me. Bain." He wanted to say Daddy. But he didn't dare.

"Got a teddy for you. You wanna hold him?"

She looked down at the toy and for a moment he wondered if she was awake but then she grabbed the huge, stuffed bear by the paw. She hugged it with one arm and stuck the thumb of her other hand in her mouth.

"Want some ice cream?"

Ari nodded.

"There's stairs. You can't walk down them."

She frowned, her thumb slipping from her mouth. She shuffled forward a step, a stubborn look crossing her face. The defiance in her move was clear. He actually felt his lips twitch. Oh, she was being a bit naughty tonight, was she?

"You're too little to walk down them on your own, angel," he said firmly. He was all too aware of Tom's gaze on him. But the other man knew what he was. Bain knew Tom would never tell anyone about this.

She stomped her foot and shook her head. It kind of surprised him. She was usually very sweet and obedient in Little mode. Then again, he generally gave her what she wanted.

"Yes," he said firmly. "You got a choice. I carry you and you get ice cream. Or you go to bed without any ice cream."

Her lower lip dropped and then she held her arms up. She was so short, that even standing on a lower step, he was still taller than she was. Very carefully, he lifted her into his arms. She burrowed in against him. So trusting. Her small arms wrapped around his neck; her legs went around his waist. He placed one arm under that round ass.

Fuck. Thought this through, didn't you, asshole?

He took a second, closing his eyes and breathing in the scent of her. He could smell the soap she'd used from her recent shower. But under all that was her scent.

A mix of citrus and vanilla. Which sounded like an odd combination, but it seemed to work.

"Good girl. Hold on."

"Do you want any help?" Tom asked.

Bain shook his head. Tom called to Rugger, who looked from Arianna to Tom then back again.

"He can come," Bain said then he turned and walked with his precious bundle downstairs. He settled her at the island on a stool.

She made a protesting noise and climbed off. Then she shocked him by wrapping her hand up in the back of his T-shirt, one he'd borrowed from Mac.

"Shh, Angel. Just getting your ice cream."

Another whimper of protest. He looked down at her, but she was staring off into the distance. He decided to just go with it. It seemed she felt better being close to him. He opened the freezer door and found a tub of ice cream. Cookies and cream.

It would have to do. He searched through the cupboards with her still clinging to the back of his shirt. He pulled out a bowl and a spoon then scooped some ice cream out.

He set the bowl down then tried to turn and grab her. She just kept moving with him. If she wasn't sleepwalking, he'd think she was playing with him.

"Ice cream's ready. It will melt." She didn't move. Shit. "Let go of my shirt and come sit on the stool." He made his voice sterner and it seemed to do the trick as she let go of his shirt.

She moved around to the stool; Jen's teddy still held in one hand. He lifted her onto the stool. She sat and stared at the bowl of ice cream, not moving to grab the spoon. Her thumb moved into her mouth.

"Baby, what's wrong?" he crooned, sitting on the stool next to her. He turned to her and she leaned into him, her side resting against his chest, her body between his open legs. He ran his hand up and down her back as she sucked on her thumb and held the teddy tight.

"Poor baby, you had such a rough night. Not surprising you're out of sorts. Everything will be okay. I won't let anything bad happen to you."

Fuck. He meant every word too. Christ. He knew he needed to talk to her about her sleepwalking. And sooner rather than later.

She buried her face in his chest. He ran his fingers gently through her thick hair which had once again become tangled. "Do you want me to feed you?"

She nodded and turned her face.

He helped her sit and spooned up a small mouthful of ice cream. She opened her mouth comically wide and he had to grin at the sight. He placed the spoon into her mouth, and she wrinkled her nose, giving him an upset look.

"I know, but it's all Tom had."

She sighed. A long, drawn out sigh that was filled with her

displeasure but then she opened her mouth again. So she wasn't happy that it wasn't caramel, but not so upset that she wouldn't keep eating.

He fed her the last few mouthfuls. Then put the bowl in the sink. He turned, not really surprised to find her right behind him. He was getting used to the way she kept managing to sneak up on him.

He lifted her against his hip, and she clung to him like a little monkey as he made his way up the stairs, Rugger on his heels. He set her down and she walked into the bedroom, yawning, the bear in her hand practically dragging on the ground. She moved to the bed then stood there. He stared at her in puzzlement. What was she waiting for?

Then it struck him. He shook his head, his lips quirking in amusement as he wrapped his hands around her small waist and lifted her into bed.

Little minx.

He settled her on her side, facing him, her thumb already in her mouth. He tucked her in, unable to stop himself from kissing her forehead. Longing filled him. What if things were different? What if he'd met her under other circumstances? Where she wasn't Arianna Silvers, famous rich singer and he wasn't just her bodyguard?

Where he could be her Daddy and she could be little Ari?

He turned the light on in the connected bathroom and kept the door open. Rugger jumped onto the end of her bed and settled in with a deep sigh.

"Don't wake her," he warned the dog. Then he tried to leave.

And found he couldn't.

"Shit."

He moved to the other side of the bed and climbed on top of the covers. He probably still wouldn't sleep, but he knew he couldn't leave her side tonight.

9

Smelly, hot air brushed against her face.

She screwed up her nose. Eww.

She opened her eyes, right into a pair of dark brown eyes. She gasped. Then the owner of those eyes reached out and licked her. Right across her face.

Gross.

She giggled. She loved dogs. She loved all animals, but she thought she might love dogs most of all. She wrapped her arms around Rugger's thick neck and rested her head against him. A low-grade headache thumped behind her temples.

She was kind of surprised she'd slept. She'd expected to be woken with nightmares. She shuddered as she remembered last night. She held on tight to Rugger, who just lay there and let her cuddle him. Maybe she should get a dog. It no longer mattered that her mother was allergic to dog hair, she didn't live with her.

And maybe it would stop her from visiting.

Bonus.

She sighed, knowing she had to get up. Last thing she wanted was Bain coming to wake her up. It would no doubt just add to the negative opinion he had about her. Staying in bed and hugging Rugger wasn't going to fix her problems. She forced herself to sit up. She had to get back home, check on Joe and Estelle.

Rugger gave her hand a slobbery kiss. She patted him then got up and dressed. She took a look in the mirror, sighing at the state of her hair before pulling it back and twisting it into a bun. It was a total rat's nest that was going to take her a ton of conditioner to untangle.

Later.

She wandered downstairs, Rugger trailing after her. She followed the scent of coffee and found Tom at the stove in the kitchen.

"Well, good morning," he said with a smile. Then he looked down at Rugger. "Thought that must be where you were, Rugger. Hope he didn't annoy you."

She shook her head with a smile. "No, not at all."

"Coffee?"

She nodded. "Please." He poured her a cup. "Creamer and sugar are on the counter already. Bain's in the living room, he's watching news reports about last night."

She wrinkled her nose. She knew she had to face reality at some stage. But not right now.

"Would you mind letting Rugger out? Just open the sliding door, the backyard is fully fenced."

"Sure."

She walked towards the back door, coffee in hand, and slid it open. Some air sounded like a great idea. Rugger slammed into her on his way out and she dropped the cup of coffee, watching with horror as it fell onto the tiled floor, smashing and spilling hot coffee on her bare feet.

Oh no. Oh no.

"Rugger!" Tom yelled, making her jump.

"I'm so sorry! Let me clean it up."

You clumsy idiot, Arianna.

"Hey, it's fine. It was Rugger's fault for bumping into you. Just a broken cup. No issue," Tom soothed.

"What's going on? Ari? Are you okay?" Bain walked in.

She stared down at the mess she'd made. Her feet were stinging from the hot coffee.

"What happened? Shit! Don't move!"

Bain strode towards her and operating on instinct she moved away from him, hissing out a breath as she stepped on a piece of sharp ceramic, cutting her foot.

"Rugger bumped into her and she dropped a cup of coffee. She might be burnt," Tom told Bain.

His face darkened. Shoot. She was always causing him trouble.

"I'm so sorry," she muttered. She crouched down to start picking up the broken pieces.

"Nothing to be sorry for, sweetheart," Tom soothed her. "Please leave it. I don't want you cutting yourself."

"No. . .no, I'll clean it up."

Bain picked her up. She let out a cry of surprise. Rugger barked, then growled.

"Rugger," Tom scolded as Bain carried her over to the counter.

"Bain! I can't sit up here," she worried.

"You're fine." He grabbed her cut foot, inspecting it.

"Put her feet in the sink, run the cold water over them," Tom directed.

Bain picked her back up and set her down next to the sink. She shook her head; she couldn't put her feet in the sink. She could just go upstairs to the bathroom. It was just a few small burns and a cut. Although she guessed Tom didn't want her traipsing blood through his house.

No, that would just cement her role as the worst houseguest ever.

"I'm so sorry, Tom," she said. "You've opened your home up and I broke your cup and made a mess—"

"Just a mug," Bain told her. "No big deal."

Maybe not to him, but if she'd done that growing up, her mother would never have let her hear the end of it.

But you're not in your parents' house. And it was just a cup. Although the coffee...

"I should mop up the coffee so it doesn't stain."

"I got it," Tom told her with a gentle smile. He probably thought she was a complete twit. He left the room.

Bain had her feet in the sink by now and had turned on the cold water. Water splashed the bottom of her sweatpants.

She frowned. Damn man could have given her a chance to roll them up at the ends. She tried to pull her feet back out. That water was cold.

"Keep them in there," Bain snapped.

"I'm sorry I'm such a bother," she told him.

"Not a bother."

She had to hope that Tom would lend her another pair of pants. Tom walked in with the mop and started cleaning up.

"I'll do that," she told him, trying to move.

"Stay where you are," Bain commanded. He looked at her feet again. "Gonna take you to the Emergency Room."

She shook her head frantically. Nope. No way. "No."

He grabbed hold of her chin, his grip firm but not painful. "Yes. We're going."

She narrowed her gaze at him, glaring at him stubbornly. No, they were not. "No."

He growled. Actually, growled at her! What the hell? Was the man part wolf?

She crossed her arms over her chest and gave a fair imitation of his growl then shook her head back at him.

Tom barked out a laugh, then patted Bain on the back. "Good luck with that, buddy."

BAIN TURNED and scowled at Tom. "She never argues."

He couldn't believe that she'd growled at him. What the fuck? And she was giving him that stubborn-ass look.

She was not in charge of this, though. This was her safety. And she would be going to the hospital to get checked over.

End. Of. Story.

"She's sitting right there, man. One thing I know that will piss a woman off, it's talking about her like she's not even there and capable of making her own decisions."

"This isn't her decision. It's mine." He spoke to Tom, but he kept his gaze on Arianna, making certain that his face was firm. "You are going. I'm responsible for you. You'll do as I say."

"Because every man who ever said that to a woman kept his balls attached to his body," Tom muttered.

"You're not fucking helping," Bain snapped at Tom who leaned back against the counter with his arms crossed over his chest.

"Good," Tom replied. "'Cause I'm on Ari's side."

Arianna sent him a big smile. What the fuck? "You're on her side? There aren't any sides. I've said what's going to happen and there will be no arguments, understand me?"

Bain gave Arianna a stern look.

"How about you have a look at her feet and see how bad they are before you rush her off to sit in an emergency room for God knows how many hours, with people bothering her all the time, hmm?"

Fuck. Bastard had a point.

He sucked in a breath then let it out slowly. Maybe he was overreacting. Slightly. But he didn't like the idea of her being hurt. Especially not after last night.

"All right, fine," he muttered.

"Might be an idea to get her feet out of the water before she starts turning blue," Tom said quietly.

Christ. She was shivering. How had he missed that? He turned off the tap. Then he picked up the foot with the cut. It was only small. There were patches of red on the top of her foot, but nothing too bad.

Okay, so he'd definitely overreacted.

"Arianna? How are your feet?" Tom asked calmly as he reached for her other foot. No cuts. Burns looked the same. He'd put some cream on them to help with the sting.

"They're fine," she said quietly.

"I'll get some cream. Sweetheart, don't worry about the cup and mess, okay?"

"Okay."

Bain lifted her, carrying her over to the kitchen dining table. He sat with her on his lap. Yep, it was fucking unprofessional as hell. And he knew that he was going to have to call Kent today and tell him. Probably get himself reassigned.

Fuck.

"Here you go." Tom walked in with a first aid kit then smiled gently at Ari before heading out again.

Bain stood and picked her up, setting her on the counter again. He grabbed the foot with the cut and put some antiseptic cream on it. He grabbed a Band-Aid and put it over it even though it wasn't bleeding much anymore.

She took in a long slow breath. He calmly dabbed cream on her burns, wincing as she let out a small pained noise.

"Sorry, baby. I'll find some painkillers for you in a moment."

Baby. Shit. He was in such trouble.

"Thank you," she said quietly.

"I'll get Tom to find you some new sweats."

"You keep having to rescue me."

"My job." As soon as he said the words, he wished them back. This was so far beyond his job it wasn't funny.

That cold mask came back over her face.

"I appreciate you doing your job so thoroughly," she told him very politely.

Damn it. He'd far rather have the Ari who called him an ogre than this formal, closed-off version.

But a bit of space was probably a good thing as he was finding it harder and harder to not touch her.

"Didn't mean it like that," he said gruffly. "Aren't just a job."

She blinked, looking shocked. Shit. What was he doing?

He clasped her around the waist to lift her down, when she wrapped her hands around his neck, leaning in to kiss him.

Shock filled him, making him freeze. Her kiss was innocent. Just a press of lips against his. But it sent waves of arousal through him. He didn't move. Couldn't move. He wanted to deepen the kiss.

But. . .

She's the client.

Suddenly, she pulled back, staring at him, her breath coming in fast pants. He opened his mouth to say something. Closed his mouth. Then opened it again.

Say something, man.

Your fish impression isn't exactly attractive.

Suddenly, Arianna shoved against him. Caught off guard, he moved a step away. She quickly slid off the counter and raced out of the kitchen.

What the. . .fuck!

"Arianna! Ari!" he yelled out. What the hell was she doing? She shouldn't be running on her cut foot.

She's running because she kissed you and you just stood there like a dickhead. Fuck!

Tom walked into the room; his eyes wide. "What's going on?

Arianna just raced past me like she had hellhounds chasing her. What did you do?"

"She kissed me."

Tom grinned. "Good for her."

"She's the fucking client, Tom."

His gaze narrowed. "You're not interested in her? Certainly, hasn't seemed that way to me. The way you look at her. . .the way you take care of her. . .I haven't seen you act that way. Ever."

Bain glared at him. "Still the client."

"But she won't be a client forever, will she?"

"Then what? Don't think she'd be happy living on a ranch in the middle of Montana miles away from the nearest shops."

"Woah, there's some judgment right there. How the hell do you know what she'd be happy with?"

"She's a famous singer. Worth millions. Lives in some fancy apartment. Her shoe collection probably cost more than I make in a year. I live in a fucking two-bed cabin that I don't even own. Just recovered financially from my divorce. Don't need to get involved with another woman who. . ."

"Who what? Will lie to you? Will spend all your money on shoes and jewelry while you get further and further into debt? Jillian was a bitch, man. I get why you'd be wary about getting involved with another woman. But it's been five years. You got to let down that guard."

"I don't think Arianna is Jillian." The two were nothing alike.

"No? Have you ever asked her whether she likes her life? She could still have her career and be with you. If you were willing to compromise a little. Or does it hurt your pride that she makes more than you?"

'Course it fucking didn't. He was proud of how talented she was. "Why the fuck we talking about this? I barely even know her. I was hired to do a job and soon I'm heading home. That kiss should never have happened."

A gasp had him turning. Fuck. Him.

She stood there, gaping at him. Her face pale, eyes wide. She looked exhausted. Stressed. And here he was being a complete prick.

"Way to go" Tom muttered.

"Ari, whatever you're thinking, stop." He ran his hand over his head.

"Real smooth man," Tom muttered. "I'll leave you two alone for a moment." Then he walked out.

Which left Bain facing Arianna. Fuck. How did he apologize for this? What could he even say to make it better?

"Arianna, I didn't mean—"

"Bain! You might want to get in here! Now!" Tom yelled.

Bain moved past Arianna, aware of her darting away from him as he grew closer. Regret bit deep.

He moved into the living room just as Tom rewound something on the T.V.

"Fuck. Is that Larry?"

"Larry? What is he doing?" Arianna asked.

He glanced back at her, noting how much distance she was keeping between them.

Why had he said what he did? And now she couldn't even look him in the eyes.

And he hated that he'd been the cause of that.

"Ari—"

"I am alarmed and horrified to tell you that we have received credible evidence that the fire set last night was indeed a threat against my client and friend, Arianna Silvers."

"What the fuck?" Bain exploded. "What evidence? And if he has fucking evidence what the fuck is he doing holding a press conference about it!"

Bain turned on Arianna. "Did you know about this?"

Her eyes went wide. She shook her head. "N-no."

"What the hell does he think he is doing? Got no fucking business going to the press with this. Fuck. Where's my phone. Got to call Dominic. Get him contained."

"It's too late, man. It's everywhere."

Bain watched as headlines moved across the bottom of the television.

Singer Arianna Silvers receives death threats.

Charity concert ended when firebomb started by stalker.

Arianna Silvers' life in danger. Concert goers speak of their terror.

"There's no taking any of this back." Tom looked over at him then to Arianna.

He cursed as he saw the way she'd wrapped her arms around her middle. She looked so lost and scared.

He should say something reassuring. But Dominic was the one who was good at talking to people. Bain got called in when someone needed intimidating.

He attempted to look reassuring. "Ari, it will be okay."

She just stared at him for a moment. "We need to go." They did need to go, but he didn't like how closed off she was.

"Ari—"

"I'll get my shoes on." She turned away and raced out. He winced as he realized she was still running around on her injured foot.

Fuck.

Tom whistled. "Man, you better practice getting down on your knees because you have got some fucking groveling to do."

"Why the fuck am I friends with you?"

"We became friends before you grew into a grumpy, cynical bastard. Also, no one else will be friends with you." His face grew serious. "Stop hurting her, Bain. She might be strong in some ways, but she seems infinitely fragile in others."

Did he think he wanted to hurt her? He hated himself for the way he'd treated her. But he wasn't sure what he could do to make up for being a complete prick.

WHY HAD SHE KISSED HIM?

She'd thought he was leaning in to kiss her. Turns out, she'd totally misconstrued that look on his face.

Surprise. Surprise.

Once again, she'd proven that she had no fucking idea about the opposite sex.

Idiot.

And then he'd said it meant nothing. It shouldn't have hurt as much as it did. This is what she got for letting people in.

"Arianna?" he murmured. He'd put the privacy screen up so Joe couldn't hear them.

She kept her gaze down on her fuzzy-clad feet. She was wearing the cutest bunny slippers. When he'd realized that she couldn't stand to put her high-heeled boots back over the small burns on her feet, Tom had given her these. He'd told her they were brand new, that he'd bought them for his wife. She'd objected to taking them, but Tom had assured her he could get a new pair.

She loved them. Tom had been so kind to her. She'd have to do something for him.

She sighed. She was so lonely. Maybe that's why she'd made the mistake of kissing Bain. It couldn't be that she was attracted to the asshole.

Except, he wasn't always an asshole. That was the problem. Sure, he could be a bossy, arrogant prick. Then other times, he could be funny and kind.

Which was the real Bain?

"Arianna, look at me."

Nope. Nuh-uh. No way.

"You can't ignore me forever."

Just try me.

Wasn't like he'd be around forever, anyway. He was leaving soon. Sooner the better as far as she was concerned.

Right. You keep telling yourself that, Ari.

"Fine. Guess we can have this talk without you looking at me. Might be easier anyway."

She stayed scrunched up against the door, staring down at her fuzzy slippers. She wondered if they made puppy ones.

"I was married. Her name was Jillian."

Why was he telling her this? What happened?

"We were childhood sweethearts. I was the quarterback for our football team. Jillian was a cheerleader. It was meant to be, everyone said. A perfect love story. I thought so too. When we left high school, neither of us were that interested in college. I joined the Navy. Jillian started working in a shoe store. I thought we were happy. Saving for a deposit for a small house. Then we'd have kids. It was going to take us a while to get there, but I thought we had shared goals."

She chewed her lower lip, wondering what went wrong.

"Seems Jillian didn't share those goals. Only she didn't let me know. I was away a lot. Training and overseas deployments. Left all our accounts in her hands. If she went out and bought some pretty things, I didn't mind. Wanted her to be happy."

"What happened?" she whispered.

He let out a small sigh. "The money I thought we'd saved for a deposit didn't exist. She'd been running up credit cards and personal loans and never told me. She rang me, told me she'd been laid off, in tears worried about what would happen. Told her it would be all right, I'd take care of her." He tapped his fingers against his leg. "First of many lies as it turns out. Seems she was always late getting to work. And there was money missing out of the till. No proof it was her, but she was fired. Once she was gone, the money stopped disappearing."

"Oh no. What did you do?"

"Confronted her. That's when I discovered the true state of our accounts. And all the lies. Jillian didn't want the small house with the two kids and the dog. She wanted a mansion. She wanted flashy cars and expensive shoes. A life I couldn't afford to give her."

Oh no.

"She wanted a divorce. Took me years to get myself out of debt. Credit cards had been in both of our names. She'd forged my signature. Ended up leaving the Navy, taking a job at JSI. Gave me back a family. A home."

He cleared his throat. "I don't talk to anyone about that. About her."

So why had he told her? Because he wanted her to understand why he wasn't interested in her? She guessed to him she must represent everything he hated. Everything that had cost him his wife.

Thing is, she'd give all of this up in a heartbeat just to be happy. To have someone who loved her just for her.

Maybe he thinks you're like Jillian. Maybe he thinks you only care about material things.

"Thing is. . . reason I pushed you away before when you kissed me is—"

"I'm not your type, it's all right I get it."

He shifted, turning towards her. "No. Don't think you do. I—"

"I'm sorry I kissed you," she said quickly. "It won't happen again. I promise. I misread the situation. I thought you wanted to kiss me and I'm more embarrassed than I can say, so you don't have to worry I'll force myself on you."

"Force yourself on me? Arianna, that's not—" he growled as

his phone rang. He pulled it out and looked at it. Then he put it down. "I—"

"I know you probably think I'm like her, but I'm not. I—"

His phone went off again and he answered it. "What? Yeah. . .right. . .thanks." He ended the call and pressed the button to slide down the privacy screen.

"Joe, that was Dominic. He's had to call in some extra security to clear the entranceway for us."

"The vultures are circling. Might be able to catch one or two on my grill."

"Joe," Arianna scolded gently.

"Aww, come on, Miss Ari. You never let me have some fun. After they published that stuff about you having wild orgy parties, I've been dying to get a hold of a few of them."

Arianna blushed, shaking her head at him. "Joe, you know no one believes that stuff anyway."

"Wouldn't be so sure of that, Miss Ari. Lots of crazies out there that will believe anything."

He drove towards the entrance to the underground garage and she groaned at the crowds that had gathered. Not just paparazzi but fans as well.

She sat back, rubbing her temples as a headache gathered. She was probably going to have to make a statement. She hated this part.

Joe moved slowly along while Bain watched the crowd. "What the fuck was Larry thinking?"

"Larry was thinking what Larry always thinks. About himself," Joe commented as they finally made their way underground.

"Rob is going to have a fit about all the people in front of the building," she muttered. "All the other people who live here are going to be upset. I need to send them all something as an apology."

"You're worried about the other people in the building?" Bain asked incredulously.

"Miss Ari always worries about other people," Joe commented casually. "Always puts everyone else first. Haven't you figured that out yet? Or are you like everyone else and think just because she's shy and quiet that she must be a bitch."

"Joe," she scolded. She quickly climbed out of the car before either man could help her, embarrassed at Joe's words.

Bain quickly moved to her side. "Don't do that again."

"What?"

"Don't climb out of a car before I'm there. I'm your protection. Use me."

"You think someone could get in here? But this is a secure garage."

"Not that secure. Don't do that again. Understand?" His tone was short, gruff. Not like the man who'd been talking to her earlier in the car. The ogre was back.

He kept close to her as they made their way up to her apartment. When they got inside, she expected to feel relieved that she was home. Instead, she kind of wished she could walk back out the door and never return. Everything felt like it was weighing down on her. Making it hard for her to breathe.

She rubbed at her chest.

"Ari? You all right?" he asked quietly.

This softer side of him was almost harder to take. Because it made her wish she could have more. That he found her attractive.

She couldn't believe she'd forced herself on him like that.

So embarrassing.

"I'm fine." She turned to Joe. "You and Estelle head home, Joe. Take a few days off."

Joe nodded but wouldn't meet her gaze for some reason. She frowned. She knew she should insist that both he and Estelle retire. They were staying on because of her and it wasn't fair.

Before she could ask him if anything was wrong, though, Estelle came storming down the passage. "Did you tell her, you old fool?"

Joe shuffled his feet. "No."

"Tell me what? Is everything okay?"

"No, it's not okay. At all." Estelle glared at Joe with a mix of anger and hurt.

She frowned. She couldn't remember Joe and Estelle ever fighting. "What's going on?"

"What's going on is that this asshole took money from Larry to spy on you!" Estelle pointed at Joe.

"W-what?" Why would Joe do that?

Pain engulfed her. Joe and Estelle were hers. She'd hired them. Not her parents. Not Larry. She'd thought they were loyal to her.

"I'm so sorry, Miss Ari," Joe turned towards her. "Got myself into a bit of trouble betting on the horses. Needed some money quick. Larry made me an offer a while ago that he'd pay me to keep an eye on you. I thought, what was the harm? It was me who told him about Dominic and Bain arriving."

"Oh." Oh? That was all she could say considering his betrayal?

"And the rest," Estelle urged.

"Last night he paid me to take him home rather than follow the plan to pick you up at the second spot. I'm so sorry. He did tell me that you knew I was taking him home. But I kind of knew he was lying."

Estelle sniffed. "I'm so sorry. We've betrayed your trust and I know you don't trust many people."

"It's not your fault," she said to Estelle. She couldn't believe this. How could Joe do this to her?

"No, but I'm married to this old coot. I'm afraid we have to hand in our resignation. At least, before you fire us. I have all our stuff together. We'll leave now."

Tears welled but she forced herself not to let them free. She felt Bain move up behind her.

"I'm going to miss you," she whispered.

Estelle blinked back her own tears. "I've thought of you as a daughter."

She moved to the older woman, hugging her gently before stepping back. She couldn't look at Joe.

"I'm sorry, Miss Ari. Maybe someday you'll forgive me."

She didn't say anything. Couldn't say anything. What else could possibly go wrong?

"Ari?" Bain asked after they were gone.

She shook her head. She couldn't look at him right now. If she did, she might break. And right now, she didn't have time to lose it. Maybe later. . .when she was alone, she could deal with all of this.

Joe and Estelle were gone. She had a stalker. Larry had done what Larry usually did. Exactly what he wanted.

He'd paid Joe to spy on her. Anger filled her. She started striding down the passage, following the sounds of voices coming from the living room.

"I don't know what the problem is here!" Larry yelled as he paced up and down the room. "I made a call and I stick by it. Arianna's fans deserved to know what happened last night."

"You don't know that the fire had anything to do with Arianna." Dominic was standing across the far end of the room, his arms folded over his chest as he glared at Larry. "And you had no right to talk to the press about those threats. Especially when you didn't even show us this latest threat first."

"Oh, so your nose is out of joint because I didn't come to you first," Larry sneered. "Or is it because last night just highlighted how incompetent you are! How did you miss whoever set that fire last night? How did that get past your security measures?"

Dominic's scowl deepened.

"Larry!" she snapped.

He whirled around. "Arianna, darling! There you are! Where have you been?" Larry waved his hand. "That doesn't matter. Amazing news! Your song sales are through the roof. I've had so many calls from people wanting to do interviews with you. Talk show hosts. Don't worry, I'll only choose a couple. I know how much you dislike doing that sort of thing. But this is an amazing opportunity, darling."

Arianna just gaped at him.

"You're fucking kidding me!" Bain snapped.

She turned to look at him, shocked by the fury in his face.

"You're happy about the publicity she's getting because of these threats? Do you not understand that she could be in danger?" Bain demanded.

Larry glared at him. "Arianna needs this. Her sales have been dropping. If she wants to continue making money, we need the publicity."

"This is a publicity stunt. Was there even another threat?" Bain asked suspiciously.

"Yes! Of course, there is. Do you seriously think I'd make up a threat?" Larry glared at him.

"Where is it?" Bain demanded.

"Here." Larry pulled a piece of paper from his pocket.

"You're carrying it around in your fucking pocket?" Bain snapped. "What about fingerprints? Where is the envelope? When did you receive this?"

"It was in Arianna's dressing room at the venue," Larry said.

"You got it this morning?" Bain asked.

"Yes. The police let me in early this morning. I thought it was fan mail. Opened it up in my car. The envelope got thrown in a trash can, I'm afraid."

And he'd immediately contacted the press to arrange an interview.

Bain scowled as he read the note. "Fucking brazen bastard putting it in your dressing room."

"I'll get onto the venue to see if we can get hold of any footage of who entered Arianna's dressing room." Dominic pointed at Larry. "We warned you not to do this."

Larry sneered. "I don't take orders from you."

"What does it say?" she whispered.

He showed her the note, watching her carefully.

HELLO MY LITTLE SONGBIRD. *Soon you won't sing so sweet. When we die everything goes to ash. And so will you.*

"E-EVERYTHING GOES TO ASH? So he set the fire? It was my fault?"

Bain frowned. "Definitely not your fucking fault. Get that out of your mind now."

"If I hadn't done the concert. . ." She felt ill.

"Not your fault. His." Bain glared at Larry. "And this should have gone to the cops straight away. They'll be pissed." They'd insisted Arianna give the other notes to the police soon after they'd arrived for this job.

"Well, I'm sorry I wasn't thinking clearly," Larry said snidely.

"You were thinking clearly enough to call the press and tell them that Ari had been receiving threats though," Bain snapped back.

"Arianna, darling, I was only doing what I thought was best for you. I always have your best interests at heart. You don't look well. Why don't you go lie down and I'll take care of getting rid of these two?"

"Rid of them?"

"They've shown how incompetent they are. Why, you could have been hurt last night in that crowd."

"Because you had Joe take you home," Bain snarled, walking closer to him, his hands curling into fists. "You're trying to turn this on us. You just made it so much harder to do our jobs. She can't even walk out the door without paparazzi getting into her face. How fucking safe do you think that is? Her stalker could hide in the crowd, could pull a gun or knife and hurt her. You did that with your stupid stunt. If anyone is leaving, it's you."

"I. . .I. . ." Larry had grown pale.

She felt ill. Bain was right. How long was the press going to be hanging around? How long until she felt safe leaving her home again?

"Arianna, are you going to let him get away with talking to me this way? I hope you see why you have to get rid of him."

"Leave, Larry."

"W-what?"

"Leave," she said more firmly. Her hands were shaking, but this felt right. It was something she should have done a long time ago. "I can't have you near me right now. You. . .you. . .you paid Joe to spy on me. You went public with these threats. I can't have you around me right now."

"But. . .I. . ."

"Go!" she said more harshly.

He just gaped at her in shock. She guessed she'd never spoken to him like that before. She'd never really snapped at anyone like that before.

"Leave, Larry. Now."

The panic was weighing down on her. She didn't want to see him. Didn't want to see anyone.

"I guess I'll come back when you're being more reasonable," he snipped.

"Leave your access card as well," Bain demanded.

"Arianna," Larry wheedled.

"You heard him," she said. He didn't need it to get out of the building. And truthfully, she'd never liked that he had a card. He'd bullied her into getting one for him.

He scowled at her. "You're making a huge mistake." But he strode away, throwing his access card onto the floor.

"Arianna." Bain turned to her. "Are you—"

"I need some time alone. I don't feel well."

And knowing she was being a coward, she fled into her bedroom.

BAIN STARED after where Arianna had raced out.

Shit.

He hated how stressed she looked. Although he was proud of her for telling Larry to fuck off.

"Anything I need to know?" Dominic asked carefully.

"Other than the fact that I've fucked things?"

Dominic snorted. "We've all done that before. What matters is how you handle things now."

Bain wiped his hand down his face. "Need to give her some space and time."

"Yeah? That seems like the best idea to you, does it?"

Fucked if he knew.

"Seems to me everyone gives that girl space. She's got no one in her corner. In the time we've been here, how many visitors has she had? How often has she gone out? Met a friend for a coffee? How many personal calls has she had?" Dominic sighed. "Whatever you did, just apologize. Way she looks at you, I'm pretty sure she'll forgive you."

"She kissed me. I didn't react. I've already overstepped the bounds with her. She thought I didn't want to kiss her. That I'm not interested in her."

"Then go prove that you do want her."

"She's still our client."

Dominic frowned. "Caleb was supposed to be organizing something more permanent for her. We need to check on how that is going. I'll call Kent."

"No, I'll call him." He sighed. "I have some explaining to do."

"You know, there's one simple solution to all this."

"What's that?"

"Don't work for her anymore. Tell Kent that you quit this job. Then you can stay on and take care of her without this whole client issue." Dominic waggled his eyebrows suggestively.

Bastard.

But he wasn't wrong. All he had to do was make a phone call. Then he'd be free. Both to pursue her and to protect her.

But the real question was. . .was he prepared to take a chance? Or would he let what happened with Jillian hold him back?

10

No. No. No.

How could she have none? She searched through her bathroom drawers. There had to be some here. Somewhere.

She couldn't be that unprepared.

She sat on the bathroom floor. Awesome. Just awesome. This was just the cherry on top of a crappy day. She moaned and lay down on her back. What the hell was she going to do?

Put on your big girl panties, Ari. You're just going to have to demand that Dominic and Bain let you go out.

Christ. She pulled herself up off the floor, bending over as a cramp took her by surprise.

Ow. Crap.

She hadn't had a period in so long that this one had caught her by surprise. And just her luck, it had to be such a strong, painful one. She made it to the toilet and tidied herself up. She'd managed to find one overnight pad. Yay! Wasn't going to last that long, though.

She downed a couple of Tylenol in the hope that would kick in quick. She'd already changed out of Jen's clothes. She grabbed a jacket, hat and scarf. It wasn't that cold outside, but maybe it would help disguise her.

She hoped like hell that Bain and Dominic had managed to get the crowd downstairs to disperse. Because the last thing she needed was to get photographed going out to grab tampons with her two brawny bodyguards.

No doubt they'd twist it to say she was off buying condoms for an orgy. Or a pregnancy test. She groaned at the thought.

She opened the door to her bedroom, coming to a stop as she saw Bain standing on the other side. He looked just as shocked to see her standing there. Which didn't make sense since it was her bedroom.

"Ari. Can I talk to you?"

"Not now." Another cramp hit her, and she had to bite her lip as she held on to the doorframe.

"You all right? What's wrong?" He jumped forward and was reaching for her. She took a step back.

"I have to go out."

"What?" He stared at her in puzzlement.

"I've got to go out. Can you make it happen?" She knew she had to seem like a crazy person. And she was being rude. "Please."

She stepped past him and started walking towards the front door.

"We can't go anywhere," Bain called out to her.

She could feel him walking closely behind her.

"Arianna. Stop." He grabbed her arm just as Dominic walked out of the kitchen, eating a huge sandwich.

He chewed and swallowed his bite, watching them both warily. "What's going on?"

"You tell me," Bain growled. "Ari has gotten it into her head that she wants to go out."

"I don't want to go out." She scowled up at Bain. "I need to go out."

"What?"

"Arianna, why do you need to go out?" Dominic sent Bain a look as she fidgeted back and forth.

She could feel her face going bright red. "Is it not enough to know that I just really need to go out. Do you have to know why?"

"You're not going anywhere," Bain snapped. "It's not safe."

"Your job is to keep me safe, isn't it?"

"Yes, it is. But it will make our job easier if we know why you need to go out," Dominic told her gently. "We're going to be the ones taking you, so we need to know where we're going."

"I need to go to the pharmacy."

"Why? You sick?" Bain asked.

Crap. They were right. She was going to have to tell them. Otherwise they'd never take her. But this was so humiliating. She wasn't used to talking about this sort of stuff.

"I. . .I. . .shit!" She bent over as another cramp hit her.

"Ari!" Bain yelled out. Grabbing her, he picked her up into his arms. "What's the matter? What's wrong? Dominic, we need to get her to the hospital."

"No, no hospital!"

"You're in pain!"

"Because I have my period, you dense man!" Another cramp hit. She tried to wiggle her way out of his arms. Could her embarrassment get any worse? But he tightened his hold.

"Your period? Oh, baby. Why didn't you just say?"

What?

She sniffled and gaped up at him. Where had grouchy Bain gone? And who was this honey-voiced man?

"Don't cry, baby. Have you got bad cramps? Do you have a heating pad? Tylenol?"

"I. . .I. . .what? You. . .I. . ." *Spit it out, Arianna.*

Bain raised his eyebrows, then looked to Dominic. "Think I've shocked her into silence."

"Probably thinks you've been body-snatched since you're not scolding her."

"I don't scold her that often," Bain snapped.

Okay. There was her ogre. Well, not *her* ogre.

Bain shook his head as he looked down at her. He gently set her on her feet. "Why didn't you just say that was the problem? Do you need tampons? Pads?"

"Chocolate? Comfort food?" Dominic added.

"I. . .I. . .all of those things," she admitted. She dropped her gaze. Even though they were being super understanding she still couldn't help but feel ashamed.

"No need to be embarrassed," Bain told her. "We've both been married."

Well, now she felt like an idiot. If she hadn't made such a big deal of it. . .

"Why don't you write me a list of what you need, sweetheart and I'll go grab it for you," Dominic offered.

"You. . .you'll go buy me sanitary products?"

"Yep. Not the first time I've bought them. I was married for nineteen years before my wife died."

His wife died? Oh no. That explained the hint of sadness she'd often sensed around Dominic. "I'm so sorry."

"Thank you, sweetheart. It's been a few years since I lost Jane. Now, why don't you write me that list? I'll go grab you everything and you can let the grouch here coddle you and try to make up for being an ass."

"I. . .I thank you. But I don't need coddling." She sent Bain a wary look as she moved into her office to grab a piece of paper and a pen.

She handed the list off to Dominic. He took it with a wink. "Be back soon."

Once he'd left, she was acutely aware that she and Bain were alone.

"Come on. Let's get you comfy. You want to change into your pajamas?"

"I. . .um. . .yes."

He raised his eyebrows. "Everything okay?"

"F-fine." She took a deep breath and focused on her speech. "I'm fine. You're just. . .I'm not used to you being. . .like this."

He gave her a puzzled look. "Like what?"

"Umm, kind I guess."

His eyes widened. "You saying I'm usually mean?"

"What? No, that's not what I mean."

"But you don't think I can be kind." He crossed his arms over his chest and scowled down at her. Well, right now he kind of looked mean.

Way to go insulting the guy who was just being sweet to you, Ari. The guy you also practically mauled this morning.

"Maybe kind was the wrong word. Maybe I meant sweet."

"You don't think I can be sweet? I can be sweet."

"You can?"

WHAT THE HELL was he doing? Was he trying to argue that he was kind and sweet? 'Cause he wasn't. Except he sort of wanted to be for her. He didn't like that she thought he was mean.

"Have I been mean to you, angel?"

"Why do you call me that?"

He blinked, feeling his cheeks heat. Crap.

"You sing like an angel." That wasn't the only reason, though. She looked like an angel. And she'd had that nightie with a teddy bear angel on it the first night he'd found her sleepwalking.

"Oh." She blinked then sniffed. "That's really sweet."

Okay, yeah, he really wasn't used to being called sweet. Or

feeling this way. Fuck. He wanted her. Wanted to explore these feelings he had for her.

Christ.

He watched her warily. "You're not crying, are you?"

She wiped her cheeks. "No."

She dropped her head. Crap. He hated that. She looked so alone and sad. "I can't believe Joe did that to me."

"I know, baby."

"They were family."

God, she was killing him.

"Come here, angel." He pulled her close to him. "Let me take care of you tonight."

"Why?"

"Because I want to. Because I need to." It was a compulsion. He couldn't not take care of her. He couldn't stand the idea of her hurting. Of her being alone.

"I don't understand. I thought you didn't even like me. I remind you of your ex-wife, even though I'm nothing like her. I don't need all this stuff. It's just stuff. It doesn't give me a hug when I'm lonely or cheer me up when I'm feeling down."

He rubbed his thumb over her cheek. "Are you often lonely and sad, angel?"

She shrugged. "I don't really have any friends. My family only ever visits or calls when they want something. And the two people I thought were loyal are gone. Pretty pathetic, huh? No wonder you'd never be interested in someone like me. I think I'll go to bed now. Can you just get Dominic to leave the stuff by my bedroom door and knock so I know it's there? Thanks."

Never be interested in someone like her?

What nonsense was she spouting now?

She let out a small whimper and leaned against the hallway wall. For fuck's sake. What did she think she was doing?

He sighed and picked her up, carrying her in his arms.

"Bain! What are you doing?"

"Taking care of you."

"And that means picking me up and carrying me around?" She stared up in bewilderment.

"Yep." He walked into her bedroom and set her down on the bed. "Now, where do you keep your pajamas?" He strode into her walk-in closet.

He came to a stop. Woah. So that's why all those clothes were out in her bedroom.

"I use this as a music room."

He frowned and turned to find her standing behind him. "Why in here? Why not use one of the other rooms in this monstrous apartment?"

She shrugged, looking embarrassed. "I like it in here. No one ever comes in here. Larry thinks it's a waste of time to create my own songs when I can use what other people create."

"Larry's a jerk."

In the walk-in closet there was a guitar, and a keyboard. As well as a couple of pads and pens scattered around. Several big cushions sat on the floor. He could imagine her in there, creating music.

"This is why you spend so much time in your room?"

"Hmm. Oh yes. Oh no, did you think I was being rude?" She looked mortified.

"No. No one could think you rude." She wouldn't know how to be. In fact, she seemed to worry too much about looking after everyone else and not enough about herself.

"Where are your pajamas?"

"In the drawers in the bedroom."

He picked her back up. "Bain! You can't keep carrying me around!"

"Why not?" He set her back on the bed. "Now, stay put. I'm taking care of you."

"But I don't understand why!" She stared up at him as he sat her on the bed.

Right. He hadn't told her that part yet. He knelt in front of her then he rested his hands on her thighs. "I'm not great at communication."

"Okay," she drawled. "You're not actually telling me anything I don't know."

He sighed. "Sometimes I'll forget to explain things. Be patient with me. Make me talk. Point out stuff I'm doing wrong. Or where I'm being a bit overbearing."

"A bit?" She raised an eyebrow. "Bain, I'm not sure what you're talking about. This sounds like you want. . ."

"A relationship?" he asked gruffly. "Good, was worried I wasn't communicating clearly."

She gave him an exasperated look. "You're not! I think you've left out part of the explanation."

"Yeah. Think there might have been a misunderstanding earlier."

"You think?"

"Watch the sass," he growled, tapping his finger against her lips warningly. "Little girls who get too sassy get their butt spanked."

She just gaped at him; her mouth slightly open.

"When I didn't react to your kiss this morning, wasn't because I didn't want to kiss you. I wanted to kiss you too much."

"Too much. . .then why didn't you?"

"You're the client. There are rules. Procedures to be followed."

"And you never break rules or procedures."

He frowned. "Rules are there for a reason, Arianna."

"So what are you doing right now? Surely this isn't procedure?"

"You are right." He stood and walked out of the room. "Stay there."

11

Um. So what the hell just happened? He laid that all on her and then he just left?

"The man has more mood swings than a tired toddler in need of a nap."

"Speaking of naps, need to get you on a sleep schedule. Might help with the sleepwalking," Bain told her, walking back into the room with his phone in his hand.

She froze at those words. Sleepwalking? He knew she sleep-walked? But how? Why hadn't he said anything before now? When had he seen her?

And what was he doing, right?

She stood, groaning at another cramp. That Tylenol just wasn't cutting it. She needed more.

"Where are you going?" he growled. "Thought I told you to stay put."

"Bain, you can't just tell me to stay put and expect me to obey."

"I can't? Would make life so much easier."

He wasn't serious, was he? Then she noticed his mouth twitch. The ass!

"Sit down, baby. You're in pain. I don't like it." He watched her worriedly. Damn it! Now he was back to being sweet. She couldn't keep up with him.

"I don't like it either. I need more Tylenol."

"Haven't you taken any yet?"

"Yeah, I took a couple just before. But it's not cutting it." She hoped Dominic hurried back.

"You can't take any more," he told her.

"What? Why?"

"I'll read the instructions, but pretty sure you're not supposed to take more than two."

"I'm sure it's just a recommended dose," she muttered. "Um, Bain, how did you know that I sleepwalk?"

He fiddled with his phone then brought it up to his ear. "Kent. It's me. I quit."

Her eyes widened. Wait. Kent? As in Kent Jensen? And quit? Was he quitting his job? Why?

"No, not my job, just this job."

Her heart started again. Thank God for that. But wait. . .he was quitting his job as her bodyguard? He was leaving her?

Tears started to well.

"Nah, I'm staying on to protect her. Just can't do it while you're paying me. Yeah. No. Because she's mine. Got it."

He ended the call and placed it on her bedside table.

"You didn't say goodbye."

Okay, Ari. That is seriously not important. So his manners were atrocious. What did that matter?

He just said you were his.

"I'm yours?"

"You're mine." He watched her cautiously.

"You. . .did you seriously just claim me?"

"I did."

"That's really caveman. A bit like picking me up and hauling me around."

He just shrugged.

"You can't just claim me."

"I did. Ari, I have feelings for you." He looked slightly ill as he said that.

"And you don't want to?"

"No! I mean, I hadn't planned on it. I never planned on getting involved with someone again. Not after Jillian. But you. . .you're very different than I thought you would be. Tried to tell myself to keep distance between us. It hasn't worked. I can't stop thinking about you."

"Oh," she said quietly.

"Oh?"

She blushed. "I. . .uh. . .I don't really know how to do relation-ship stuff. I'm not always great with other people."

"We're a great match then."

She bit her lip worriedly. "Did you really just quit your job because of me?"

"Just this job. If I'm not getting paid by JSI, then I can still stay and protect you. But I can also do things like this." He cupped the back of her head and leaned in to kiss her. This kiss was far different from the kiss this morning. This time he was firmly in charge. She didn't have to think or worry that she was doing some-thing wrong because he completely dominated.

And she melted.

When he drew back, she realized she had her hands twisted in his T-shirt. She pulled them free, patting the material down. "Are you sure? You really want me?"

"Baby, wanted you since day I saw you. Was too damn pig-headed to admit it. Also didn't think there was any chance you could want me."

"Are you kidding?" she squeaked.

"I rarely joke."

No, she guessed that was right.

"Um. . .I. . .what does all this mean? Does this mean I'm your girlfriend?"

There was a beat of silence. Idiot. *Why did you ask him that?* She was such a dork. Why did they have to put a label on it? She wished she was more experienced at this sort of thing.

"You want to call me your boyfriend, you can. I'm going to call you mine. Should warn you. There's no half-measures with me. I'm all in. All the time. No doubt that will piss you off sometimes. I'm protective. I'm possessive. Stickler for following the rules. And don't ever, ever lie to me. That's really important."

"I won't," she squeaked.

He leaned in. "There's something between us, Arianna. Something I want more of. You feel the same?"

"Yes. Yes, I do."

"Then let's explore it."

Could it be that simple? She didn't think so. But right now, she wanted it to be. She wanted to be his. Despite the fact she thought they were likely to butt heads. A lot. He was stubborn. He was bossy. And he didn't understand the word compromise.

But the big butthead was all she could think about. All she wanted.

"Yes, let's explore it."

"Good," was all he said. "Dominic will be back soon. Let's get you comfy. Then see if I can give you more painkillers. You have a heating pad?"

"Umm, yes it's in the kitchen. How do you know that I sleepwalk?"

"Seen you a few times. So you know you do it?"

She picked at the bedspread. "Yes. It started when I was young. Now it only happens when I'm really stressed."

"Right. So we need to eliminate some stress."

She gave him a pointed look. "Kind of impossible right now, don't you think?"

"Did your parents ever take you to someone to help?"

She snorted. "Oh, yeah. They took me to the best therapists. Behavioral, cognitive, speech therapists. I saw them all. Anything to stop me from continuing to embarrass dear old Mom and Dad."

"What?" he barked. "They were embarrassed?"

"I embarrass them a lot. It wasn't just the sleepwalking. When I was four, I stopped talking. Selective mutism, they called it. At first my parents thought I was doing it for attention. Makes sense, I never got much attention from them. I was raised by a series of nannies and tutors. Can't go to school if you can't talk. Can't do anything to tarnish the Silvers name."

"They cared more about their reputation than their daughter?" He looked dumbfounded.

"My mother *only* cares about her reputation. All of her children had to be perfect. Nothing else was acceptable. I wasn't."

She took a deep breath then let it out, forcing herself to smile. "Listen to me complaining. It wasn't so bad. I had the best tutors, clothes, holidays. I have nothing to complain about."

He scowled. "Everything except their love and acceptance."

Yeah. Pretty much.

"Why did you stop talking?"

She shrugged. "No one knows. I've always had anxiety. I guess it was related to that. Same with the sleepwalking and nightmares."

"Nightmares?"

"Yeah, I used to wake the house screaming. My mother complained it ruined her beauty sleep."

"Bitch. Your dad?"

"He wasn't around much. He worked a lot. Which I found out later, was really just him fucking his assistant in hotels."

"Christ."

She shrugged. "When they got sick of the sleepwalking and nightmares, they put me in a downstairs room and would lock the door at night."

"Fucking hell." He ran his hand over his closely shaved head. "You didn't go to school?"

"Only later, after my father lost most of his money and they couldn't afford private tutors."

"What about social development? Friends? Other activities?"

She shrugged. "I never really had friends. Or did other activities."

He swore. "Those assholes."

"My parents have certain expectations of their children. My brother was captain of the basketball team. My sister was very popular. She was a cheerleader. And smart. I was none of those things. They didn't want people to know I was a failure. I was of no use to them until they learned I could sing."

"And then you weren't considered a failure anymore."

"No," she whispered.

"Those fucking bastards. When did you start talking again?"

"When I started singing." She smiled. "One of the therapists suggested it. When I'm singing, I'm not anxious. I don't worry. I just get lost in the music. I love it."

"I can see that."

"I wish I could just create music and sing. Without all the rest of it. Maybe one day."

12

"I'll help you get changed."

"You're not helping me get dressed, Bain." She glared up at him.

He scowled down at her. "What if you get light-headed and slip? You need my help."

"Bain. I'm twenty-six years old. I've been putting my pajamas on for years by myself. Now shoo."

"Did you just shoo me?" he growled.

"Yes. I shooed you. Shoo. We're not at a place in our relationship where you can see me. . .where you can help me. . ." She was blushing and he sighed. Now that he'd decided he was all in he wanted to be all in. But he had to remind himself that not everyone moved at his pace.

He needed to have a talk with her about her Little side. But that could wait for now.

Don't overwhelm her.

"Fine. Call out if you need help."

"I'll be fine. Wait out here." She turned and walked into the bathroom.

Bossy little thing, wasn't she? He kind of liked it. As long as she didn't think she got to be in charge. Ahh, hell, who was he kidding? She could completely wrap him around her little finger. It had been a long time since he'd been anyone's Daddy. He would have to make certain not to indulge her too much.

She would listen when it came to health and safety. He needed to get her eating more and sleeping better.

Listening to her childhood had nearly killed him. It also explained some things. Like the reason she got worked up over things like spilling food or breaking coffee mugs. He bet her bitch of a mother had liked to highlight every perceived flaw.

He hated that she'd grown up thinking she was less than fucking perfect.

There was a knock on the bedroom door. He walked over and opened the door. Dominic raised his eyebrows then his lips twitched.

"What?" Bain snapped at him.

"Nothing, man. Nothing at all. Just think it took you long enough. Unless. . .Arianna does know you're in here, right?"

"Course she does. We're in a relationship. I've quit my job as her bodyguard. But I'm staying on to take care of her. Now I can kiss her without breaking the rules."

He grabbed the bag Dominic held then shut the door in his face. He turned to find Arianna standing behind him. She was wearing a pair of soft-looking pajamas with puppies on them. Seemed to be a theme she had going on. Her mouth was open as she stared at him.

"That was kind of rude."

He just shrugged and started rifling in the bag. "Pads or tampons?"

"Bain! Give me the bag?"

"Why?"

"Bain! Give. Me. The. Bag."

He sighed and handed it over then watched as she pulled out the sanitary products.

"I'll be back soon." Her face was beet red.

He grabbed her wrist as she walked towards the attached bathroom. This wasn't acceptable. He couldn't have her embarrassed.

"Look at me, angel."

"Bain, I really have to—"

"Please."

She raised her head quickly, staring at him in shock.

"What?"

"You said please. You never say please."

"I say please."

She shook her head. "Never. I've never heard you say it."

"I'm mean and I don't have manners. I sound charming."

"Surprisingly, you are. In your own Bain-like way."

He had no idea what that meant. But this wasn't why he'd stopped her. "Don't know why you're so embarrassed. You don't need to hide any of this from me. You get a period. You have cramps. You need some extra care from me. Angel, whatever you need. I'm here. You need me to go get you stuff, I'll do it. You need me to massage your back, get you a heating pad, run you a bath. I can do that too. Just don't hide anything from me. I don't do well with that."

Understanding filled her face. "Right. Okay. I. . .just. . .periods weren't talked about in my house growing up. They were kind of a taboo subject. My mother didn't even explain any of this to me. She bought me some stuff and sent me a link to information online. I'm not used to talking about it. Or having anyone take care of me."

He pulled her close and hugged her tight. "That's all going to change. Now, I'll go warm up your heating pad and then meet you in the living room."

13

It felt kind of surreal.

She was tucked up in the corner sofa in her living room. Bain had placed a heating pad over her tummy. He'd also grabbed a blanket from his closet and was currently tucking it around her.

This nurturing side of him was a surprise, she wasn't going to lie.

He handed her a bowl with some of the ice cream she'd asked Dominic to get. Yum. Rocky Road. Caramel was her favorite. But in times like this nothing would do but Rocky Road. She spooned up some.

"Where's your ice cream?" she asked.

"Don't eat ice cream."

She froze and stared up at him as he grabbed the remotes for the T.V. "You don't eat ice cream?"

"Nope."

"What's wrong with you?" she blurted out. Then she winced. That wasn't very polite.

"Lots of things apparently. According to you, I'm mean. I'm not sweet. I'm too rule-driven. I'm. . ."

"Okay, but besides all of that. Really? You don't eat ice cream?"

"Nah. I'm not big on sweet stuff."

"I love sweet things." She took a mouthful, and something crunched in her mouth. "Did you put sprinkles in this?"

He sat next to her, wrapping his big arm around her shoulders. "Sprinkles make everything better, right?"

"How did you know that?"

"I saw you decorating cupcakes the other day with Estelle."

She bit her lip. "You did?"

"Yep. It was the first real sign I had that you might be a Little. You looked cute with icing all over your face, your tongue out as you concentrated on spreading your sprinkles."

"A Little?" she asked with trepidation.

"Oh, right yeah. We're going to wait and talk about that tomorrow."

"We are?"

"Yeah."

"Why?"

"Needs to be talked about. Need to talk about limits. How young you think you are. Do we need diapers? Are you comfortable with spanking being used as a punishment? Is there anything about your health I have to be aware of? And that's just the Little stuff. Need to talk about sex too."

"I. . .we. . .we do?" she managed to get out. Go her. Because he had quite literally blown her mind. Seriously. She wasn't sure how she was still breathing right now.

"Yeah. Are you okay with bondage? With anal sex? Is there anything I need to be aware of with your sexual history?"

Well, that part would be a short conversation.

"So are you. . .are you a Daddy Dom?"

"Yes."

Caleb had warned her.

"But we're not talking about this tonight. Everything is too new. You need time to adjust. We'll talk tomorrow."

"And by tomorrow, I would have adjusted?"

He shifted, lowering his free hand to rub her belly. Okay, that was bliss. "I thought so. Do you need longer? We could schedule this talk for the day after?"

"Do you think it's kind of a bit odd to schedule a talk like this?"

"How else will we know to have it?"

"We could have it right now."

"You're meant to be relaxing. You shouldn't be stressed before bed. Might affect your sleep. You don't sleep well as it is."

"When you saw me sleepwalking how did I act? I didn't do anything embarrassing, did I?"

She put the empty bowl down on the floor.

"No. What would you do that was embarrassing?"

"I don't know. . .I don't really know what I do when I sleepwalk. It's kind of terrifying. What if I wander out of the apartment? What if the person who is sending me these letters is watching and saw me?"

"Won't let that happen."

"But how would you even know? You could be asleep. You'd have no idea."

"Ahh. Yeah. After the first time caught you sleepwalking, I put a monitor in your room."

"You. . .you what?"

"It has these pads that go under your mattress. You can buy as many as you like. Normally, they go under a child's cot, so you just need a couple. But I put around twelve under your bed. Then when you get out of bed, it sets an alarm off on my phone."

She couldn't believe it. "You. . .you've been monitoring me?"

"Yeah. . .that a problem?" He sounded confused. As though he couldn't understand how that could possibly be an issue.

It should be. It was a total breach of privacy. And yet, all she felt was relief. She slipped her arms around his waist. Their position was kind of awkward and he ended up lifting her onto his lap.

"Thank you."

"You're thanking me?"

"I know I should probably yell at you. That's seriously not something you do without a person's permission. I mean that's my bedroom and you just—"

He placed his hand gently over her mouth. "Let's just stick with thank you."

She poked her tongue out and licked his hand.

"Did you just lick my hand?" he growled. She was getting used to those growls though. They didn't intimidate her anymore. Well, most of the time.

"Yep."

"Were you poking your tongue out at me? You know that's naughty, right?"

Her heart raced, her insides heating at his low, dominant voice. Was it messed up that she liked that? That she wanted to be naughty just to have him speak like that to her again?

Another cramp hit her, and she let out a low, pained noise.

"Still hurting, baby?"

"Yeah."

He rubbed her tummy, kissing the top of her head. Despite the fact that she was in all kinds of pain and feeling bloated and awful, this was hands down one of the best experiences of her life. Had anyone ever held her on their lap and just cuddled her like this?

"Know what's good for period cramps?"

"More Tylenol?" Bastard still hadn't let her take any more.

"An orgasm."

She stilled. Was he offering to. . .

"I don't think I'm ready for that," she squeaked out. "I mean. . .we've just started to. . .and I'm not exactly feeling sexy and I have my period!"

"That's why I suggested an orgasm to help with your cramps."

Right. Way to act like an idiot, Arianna.

She buried her face in his chest.

He rubbed his big hand up and down her back soothing. "Nothing to get all stressed out about. If you don't want me to help, you could do it yourself."

"I can't do that with you here!"

Holy shit.

"Well, I guess I could leave. Give you some privacy. How long do you need? Five minutes?"

"What, no!"

"Longer?"

"No, Bain. I'm not. . .I'm not going to. . .with you. . .and Dominic."

"What's Dominic got to do with anything? You don't want him to help, do you? Because I don't share. Ever."

"What? No! But what if he were to walk in?"

"He won't," he told her. "He's giving us alone time."

Right now, maybe she could do with less alone time with Bain.

"Do you have something you use? I can get it for you."

"Something I use?" she asked.

"Like a vibrator?"

"No!" she squeaked.

He tilted up her face. "Talking about this stuff embarrasses you?"

"Yes!"

"But why? Told you nothing was taboo between us."

"Yes. . .but, Bain. . .I feel like you move at the speed of a bullet and I'm a tortoise. In my family, we didn't talk about sex or periods. My mother didn't even like us to say toilet, we had to say powder room."

"Fucking weird. Okay, I understand."

"You do?"

"Yeah. No more talk of masturbation and orgasms."

She slumped against him. Thank God for that.

"But just saying, in the future, you can have that on tap when you have cramps."

Interest filled her. "What about the rest of the time?"

"Well, that depends how good you are." His voice was low, seductive and a shiver of pleasure raced up her spine.

"What do you want to watch?" he asked.

"Is there an action movie? I'm in the mood for watching stuff being blown up."

"Wasn't quite what I had in mind. But okay."

They settled in when he found a re-run of an old classic. She snuggled in against his wide chest with a contented sigh.

She didn't realize she'd started to doze off until she was suddenly moving.

"You're really strong," she mumbled as he carried her out of the room in his arms. "I like that. I didn't think I would. But it's sexy."

He snorted. She yawned as he carried her through her bedroom to the bathroom. He set her down. She swayed.

"You gonna be okay in here by yourself?"

"Sure. Been peeing on my own for a while now."

He turned her towards the toilet. "Go. Do what you need to. I'll be in the bedroom."

She stumbled through her routine then walked out to find he'd already turned down her bed. She practically fell into it. His soft laughter filled the room and she smiled.

He tucked her in then ran his fingers through her hair. "Where's your stuffy, angel?"

"My. . .my what?"

"Your stuffy. Where do you keep it? Assume you sleep with it, since you were carrying it the first night I saw you sleepwalking."

"How many times have I done it?"

"Three that I know of. Twice here. Once at Tom's. Jen had a stuffed teddy that we gave you."

"Oh God. That's so embarrassing."

"What have I told you about being embarrassed?"

"Yes. . .but you might be a Daddy Dom, however Tom. . ."

"Has known me a long time. He knew my ex-wife. He knows what a Little is. He's also involved in a long-term ménage relationship. Takes a lot to embarrass him."

"Jillian was your Little?"

"No. Sometimes she tried to be in order to manipulate me. Not that I realized it at the time. But she wasn't a Little."

"Have you had many?"

"Nope. Just you. Your stuffy?"

"In the drawer under the bed," she whispered, surprised at his answer. "Her name is Patches."

"Right. I should have guessed." He pulled the puppy out and handed her over. She snatched the stuffed puppy close.

"This really doesn't worry you."

"Baby, I think it's cute as fuck. I'd tell you if I thought differently." He leaned in and kissed her forehead. "You like dogs, huh?"

"Yeah. I always wanted a puppy, but my mother is allergic."

"You had a cat instead?"

"No, she's allergic to them as well."

"Donkey?"

She snorted. "Right. I could just imagine a donkey running around the sterile house I grew up in. The lawns were manicured, no weeds dared to grow in the garden. A donkey? No."

"A goldfish?"

She shook her head.

Jesus.

"How can someone be allergic to a goldfish?" he asked.

"She said I'd just get sad when it died, and she couldn't deal with that."

What a cow. His poor baby. "I'm sorry, baby."

"Not your problem."

"Would you like a light on?"

"Um, yes. If you could turn on my lamp then switch off the main light, please."

"Of course." He turned the lamp on, creating star shapes over the walls and ceiling.

"You like stars, huh?"

"Yes. They remind me of the time that Caleb's family took me on vacation with them," she said sleepily. "It was my first real family vacation. Oh, my parents took us on holiday. But it was all for show. They'd take photos with us that they could use to show off to their friends. Then they'd send us off with the nanny and we wouldn't see them again. That vacation with Caleb's family, it was so much fun. We camped out. Roasted marshmallows. His parents spent time with us. And one night, I snuck out and slept under the stars. It was so peaceful. It was one of my happiest memories."

He kissed her forehead gently, aching for that little girl. He wanted to climb into bed beside her, to hold her in his arms. But even he knew that would be moving too fast. Instead, he leaned in and kissed her forehead.

"You'll have many more happy memories. I promise."

14

She wasn't quite sure how to act the next morning. He'd repeatedly told her not to be embarrassed by anything that happened between them. But she had no idea how to do any of this. She'd never had a boyfriend before. She'd only had sex once.

At least her cramps were mostly gone this morning. She wandered into the kitchen, following the scent of something sweet and delicious. She came to a stop as she saw Bain at the stove. Dominic was sitting at the island, sipping coffee while looking at his phone. He glanced up and smiled at her.

"Hey, there, sweetheart, sleep okay?"

"Yes. Thank you." Surprisingly, she had.

Bain turned at his words, running his gaze over her. She stiffened. What was wrong? Did she have toothpaste down her front? Was her top on back to front? Wouldn't be the first time. Or even the fifth. She didn't always notice things like that. Which drove her mother nuts.

"What is it? What's on me?"

His gaze narrowed. "Nothing's wrong. You look better than last night. Got color in your cheeks. Cramps still bad?"

"Bain!" she protested, not able to even look at Dominic. "You can't ask me that."

"Why not? Need to know if you need some Tylenol this morning."

"I've taken some already, thanks. And Dominic's sitting right there. I'm sure he's not interested in this conversation."

She didn't even want this conversation and it was about her body.

Bain flicked his gaze over to Dominic. "Dominic doesn't care."

"But Arianna might," Dominic said. "Go easy, man. Not everyone appreciates total, brutal honesty."

Bain gave her an assessing look then to her surprise he nodded. "Sorry. I'll try to be more discreet."

She moved over to Dominic. "Teach me your ways, oh wise one."

Dominic grinned at her. "Just be firm with him. Show him where the boundaries are and stick to them. Much like dealing with a child."

Bain turned and scowled at him. "You want waffles for breakfast or not?"

"I'm shutting up now." Dominic grinned at her. "Bain's waffles are the best and I can't cook for shit."

"How many waffles you want, angel?" Bain asked, grabbing some plates and setting them out. "Thought you might like waffles, seeing as you're after a donkey sidekick."

What did that mean? Then she clicked on and grinned. "And in the morning, I'm making waffles."

Dominic groaned. "You two already have your own weird language going on, huh? Now I really feel like an awkward third wheel."

"I'm sorry," she said hastily. "I didn't mean to make you feel like that."

Dominic waved his hand with a smile. "I'm teasing. I'm glad the big fella finally pulled his head out of his ass and realized what a treasure you are."

She blushed. "Wouldn't be so sure of that."

"It's not a weird language. It's from *Shrek*," Bain informed him.

"Oh right, I've never seen it."

"We're going to have to rectify this situation," she said to Bain.

He gave a nod. "Definitely. Tonight."

Dominic groaned but smiled.

"Are there still reporters outside?" she asked.

Dominic's face grew serious. "Yeah. A few. They'll disappear after a while if you refuse to talk to them. Probably be a good idea to stay in the apartment for a while."

That she could do.

"How many waffles?" Bain asked.

"One, please."

"You'll have two."

She sighed but didn't argue as she sat beside Dominic. Bain disappeared into the butler's pantry.

"You're good for him," Dominic told her quietly. "He's always been intense. But it's his way of showing he cares. Taking care of you. Just fight the big things, the things that are really important to you and let him have the small victories. He'll calm down."

"Yeah?"

"Yeah. Maybe. Eventually."

Right. That sounded hopeful.

Bain came back out and plated them up some waffles. Dominic ate quickly and left.

"Is he all right?" she asked Bain.

"He's just giving us some privacy to talk."

"Uh-oh, sounds ominous." She gathered up the plates. He rinsed everything, while she stacked them in the dishwasher.

They worked in companionable silence. It was so normal that it made her feel kind of sad. Normal was all she'd ever wanted and yet it seemed so unattainable.

Stupid, huh?

"More coffee?" Bain asked.

"Yes, please, but I can get it."

He shook his head and gestured back to the counter. "You sit, baby. I'll get it."

"What did you want to talk about?"

He set her cup of coffee in front of her. She took a sip and sighed. Perfect.

"About rules and limits. And about your Little."

"Right into it then, huh?" she said nervously.

He leaned across the counter and placed his hand over hers. "Communication is important."

She raised her eyebrows.

He grinned. "Know that it's not always my strong point. But it is important in a relationship like this. I'm not a mind reader. I need to know what's going on in your mind. I'll try to be much better at making my expectations clear. All right?"

"Yes. Okay. I don't really know how any of this works. I've never been in a relationship."

"With a Dom, you mean?"

"No, at all," she whispered. "I've only had sex once. Does it disappoint you?"

"Disappoint me? Why the hell would it?"

"Because I don't know what I'm doing." She stared down into her coffee.

"Angel, look at me."

She shook her head.

"Angel. Look. At. Me."

"Nope."

"Testing me so soon, huh, little bit?"

Testing him? No, she wasn't testing him. She just didn't want to look at him. But she raised her gaze anyway. She wasn't ready yet to see what happened if she tested him.

She'd probably have to endure another scolding.

"Good girl." He cupped the side of her face. "There is nothing to be embarrassed about."

"The paparazzi would have a field day with this. I'm meant to be up here having orgies. Not sitting around in my pajamas watching *Shrek*."

"Who cares what other people think? Only matters what we think."

But she'd been raised to worry about what others thought of her. Especially her family. But she knew he was right. And who would even know?

"You're right," she told him.

"I'm always right."

She snorted.

"This goes as slow or as quick as you want. You have the reins. At least in this. While I'll have rules for you and I'll be in charge when you're Little, you always have the ultimate control. This is your choice. You choose to trust me with your Little, to gift me your submission. You agree to obey my rules and submit to my discipline. You'll have a safeword to use if you ever feel uncomfortable or scared."

"You won't get mad if I use it?"

"I'd never get upset with you for using your safeword. I would never retaliate against you, understand? You use it, we stop and talk about what scared you. All right?"

"All right. What should be my safeword?"

"That's up to you, angel. Something that you wouldn't normally say in that situation."

"Donkey."

His lips twitched. "Good choice."

She sighed with a smile.

"When you feel comfortable with showing me your Little, with trusting me fully, I will be in charge. And there might be some special rules for your Little. Understand?"

"I think so. I don't know when I'll be able to. . .to let her out."

"That's okay. Got some ideas to help. But that's your choice. There's no pressure. Things move at your pace."

Damn. He was being so amazing. She'd almost expected him to push her because he was so pushy in other areas.

"You've already got some rules for your protection. They haven't changed. They might get adapted once this threat is past. But what has changed is how you'll get punished if you break them."

"Punished? I was going to get punished before?"

"With a firm scolding. Now, you'll get your butt roasted."

Her eyes widened.

"Any triggers I should know about when it comes to discipline? Hard limits? Soft limits?"

"Umm. I don't know."

"You know what I'm talking about though, right?"

"Yeah. I've seen some movies." She blushed.

"Okay. The punishments I'll use will depend on what rules you've broken. Corner time, lines, spankings are pretty standard. A paddle or similar when you've been very naughty. Any issues with that?"

"I. . .I've never been spanked."

"Never? Hmm. Could explain a few things." He winked.

"Hey! I'm a good girl."

"That's what all Littles say, angel. Usually right before they go over Daddy's knee and get their bottom spanked." He tilted her face up. "A lot of Littles don't like being punished. . ."

Did that mean there were some who did like it?

"But they feel more secure with boundaries. Rules. With knowing their Daddy or Mommy cares about them, about their safety and health and won't hesitate to correct any naughty behavior. Especially when it puts them at risk. Then after a punishment, everything is forgiven. Slate wiped clean."

"Really? It's never brought up again?"

"No. I would take you in my arms, cuddle you close and remind you that you're my special, good girl."

"That sounds nice," she murmured.

"It is."

She blushed. "I'm okay with all that. I always have my safeword."

"Always."

"Now, other rules. You know how I feel about lies. No lying. Ever. You can tell me anything. All right?"

She nodded. "I know." She got it. She didn't like lies either.

"No putting yourself down."

That might be a bit harder, but she'd try.

"When you're Little, I expect you to call me Daddy."

"Okay." She felt her cheeks go red.

"We need to talk about adjusting your sleep. Sleepwalking can be due to fatigue. You need to get more rest."

He'd been doing research into sleepwalking. Damn, that was sweet.

"We'll start off with some afternoon naps."

"What? No! I don't need to take naps."

"Baby, you're exhausted. There are dark smudges under your eyes. You don't sleep well. Naps will help." He gave her a stern look.

Well, that just sucked.

"I don't want you exercising to the point of exhaustion like the other day. I'd prefer you exercise with me so I can keep an eye on you, but I won't go that far. Yet. I find out you've pushed yourself too far, we're going to adjust that, understand?"

"Yes." She didn't push herself that hard very often so she didn't think it would be a problem.

"Any questions for me?"

"Umm, yeah, should we talk about sex?"

He tilted his head to one side. His lips tilted up at the corner. "Yeah. We can do that. You might not have much experience, but have you had fantasies?"

"F-fantasies?"

"Yeah." He ran his thumb over the back of her hand. "Ever dream of being restrained? Of role play? What do you think about when you get yourself off?"

"Bain! I can't talk about that!"

He raised his eyebrows. She squirmed on the stool.

"Tell me," he said huskily.

"I guess I've thought about being restrained," she said, sounding slightly breathless. "And dominated."

"Good." His grin was almost wolfish.

Oh hell. She thought she just might be in trouble here.

"Arianna, stop running through the house!"

Whoops. Caught. She sighed. She turned to find Bain glaring at her. He folded his arms over his massive chest. She actually had to resist the urge to lick her lips. These past two days since Bain had told her that he wanted her as well had been the happiest of her life. They'd spent most of their time together. They'd included Dominic, but he seemed to be happy doing his own thing. Although they forced him to watch a *Shrek* movie each night.

There hadn't been any more threats, at least. She'd noticed how quiet everything was. She knew that Bain had taken her laptop and phone. She should demand them back. She couldn't just cut herself off from work like this.

But it was so nice to have a break. She hadn't realized how tired and stressed she'd been until that had all been taken off her shoulders.

Of course, the biggest source of her stress was gone. Larry. She hadn't heard from him since she told him to leave. But she knew it wouldn't last. No doubt he was plotting something.

She just didn't know what.

The good news was, the fire the other night at the concert had nothing to do with her. The police had arrested a disgruntled employee who had set off a small explosion. All of the reporters had disappeared from outside her apartment. She guessed they had moved on to something else. Thank God. The bad news was that the cameras hadn't caught anyone suspicious entering or leaving her dressing room. So they had no leads on who left that last letter.

"But if I don't get up speed, I can't slide across the floor."

His eyes widened. "What?"

"I get up speed on the carpet then once I hit the marble, I can slide with my socks on. It's fun. You should try it."

"Now that, I'd pay to see." Dominic came up behind her. She turned to look at him with a grin.

"You want to try, Dominic?"

He held up his hands. "No thanks, sweetheart. I'm too old for those sorts of shenanigans."

She snickered. Shenanigans? "You're not *that* old, Dominic."

"Thanks, sweetheart. But I certainly feel old."

"No one is going to be doing any sliding along the marble," Bain grumbled. "It's too dangerous."

She rolled her eyes at Dominic.

"And I saw that."

Considering that she hadn't yet felt comfortable enough to

fully let her Little out, he sure didn't seem to have the same problem with letting out his Daddy side. He'd been showing her more and more of that part of himself. It was intriguing.

"Have to go out for a while," Bain said abruptly. "Dominic, you're in charge of her."

"Uh-oh," Dominic muttered.

"Where are you going?" she asked nosily.

"Just to run some errands. You stay here. Listen to Dominic. Behave yourself. No sliding on the marble."

He walked forward and kissed her gently on the lips. They were still tingling as he left.

"The boss man has spoken," Dominic told her with a grin.

She smiled back. "What he doesn't know won't hurt him, though, right?"

Dominic held up his hands. "Oh no. I'm having no part of that."

"Wimp."

"I prefer to think of it as older and wiser. I also don't want to endure his grumpiness' wrath. The man can hold a grudge."

"His grumpiness? I bet you don't say that to his face."

He widened his eyes comically. "Good Lord no. See this pretty face? I like it just where it is, thank you very much."

"I call him an ogre," she confessed.

He nodded. "Bet you don't say it to his face either."

"Oh no. I like to be able to sit."

15

"Ari, what are you doing?"

She started, closing the laptop with a screech. "Oh God, I didn't hear you come in. You move like a ghost."

Bain frowned down at her. "Why are you looking up things about yourself on the internet?"

"Because I'm a masochist?"

"If you're truly a masochist, I can help with that." He sat on the desk facing her.

She leaned back in her chair, gaping up at him. "What. . .no. . .umm. . ."

He grinned.

"You're teasing me. Since when do you tease people?"

"I tease all the time."

Uh-huh. Sure he did.

"How did you get your laptop, little miss?" he asked sternly.

She squirmed on her seat. Uh-oh. "I found it in your room."

"You snuck into my room and searched through all my stuff. That was very naughty."

She bit her lip, feeling bad. Until she remembered that this was her laptop. And he'd taken it without her permission.

She straightened. "You went into my room without my permission when you put that monitor in."

"That was different. I was taking care of you."

She gave him a skeptical look. "You stole my laptop and phone and hid them from me."

"Because you needed a break. Last thing you needed was to be hassled by reporters, wanting the juicy details. You can't tell me that you don't feel better for it."

She rubbed her aching head. She wasn't truly angry with him. If she'd wanted her stuff back, she could have gotten it at any time. It had been sitting on the dresser in his room.

"I guess I did need a break. But I have to go back to work sometime. I can't hide forever."

"Give it a bit longer. And stop reading stuff online about yourself. Ninety-five percent of it is rubbish. Don't want you getting upset by what you read."

"You can't protect me from everything."

"I can try," he replied stubbornly. "Come on. I have a surprise for you." He stood and held out his hand. She slipped her hand into his and let him lead her out of her office and down the passage, into her bedroom. She froze with surprise as she saw the picnic that had been set up.

"You did all this?" she asked as he tugged her gently forward. He'd laid out a blanket on the floor and set out some plastic plates and cups. In the middle of the blanket there was a large platter filled with sandwiches with all the crusts cut off. Then there was a bowl of grapes and some cheese and crackers.

"Yep. Wasn't hard. Can I pour you a sparkling grape juice?"

She giggled. "Yes. Please. How did you know I like picnics?"

"You told me, when you said I needed to cut the crusts off my sandwich."

She blushed. "Oh yeah."

"I'd take you outside for a picnic, but it's not safe. Also a bit cold out there. Got to keep my baby warm."

She smiled shyly.

"You can have your juice in a big girl cup, or you can have it in this." He pulled a sippy cup out of the basket.

Her breath caught in her chest. "Where did you get that?"

"Got it this morning."

"That was the errand you had to run?"

"Yep. Also grabbed a few other things." He stood and walked out of the room, returning with a bag, which he handed over to her.

The first thing she pulled out was a puppy onesie. It was so soft, and she immediately rubbed it up against her face. "Oh wow, I love it!"

"Thought you might. It will keep you warm and it's cute. Added bonus, it's got a butt flap. When you're naughty, I can just flip you over my knee, pull down the butt flap and spank you."

She gaped at him. Then she shook her head. Had he seriously just said that? "That's not what a butt flap is for."

"Sure it is. Or if it's not, it should be. Found it at a store for Littles that's not that far from here."

"Really? There's a store that sells things for Littles?" Come to think of it, that sippy cup was kind of adult sized.

"Yep. Was a good find."

She reached into the bag and drew out an oversized pacifier. She immediately went bright red. "I don't think my Little is that young."

"You were sucking your thumb when you were sleepwalking. Not great for your teeth. That one is orthodontist approved."

"Seriously?" An orthodontist actually approved this over-sized pacifier that could only be for an adult?

"Yep. I asked the woman at the desk. She was very helpful."

She cleared her throat. "I'm still not sure. . ."

"Don't have to use it right away. But I catch you sucking your thumb, I'll replace it with the pacifier."

She wrinkled her nose but moved on to the next item. She squealed as she pulled out the pen. It was bright pink with a huge, sequined heart at the end of it.

"I love this! How did you know I love sequins!"

"Saw your notebook. It's cute. This is cute." He shrugged, looking slightly embarrassed. "I like cute things."

Oh my God. He was so adorable sometimes.

She drew out the next thing. It was a set of pastel coloring pens. Followed by a coloring book. Holy crap. He was spoiling her.

The next item shocked her. Well, items, but they were all packaged together. Her face grew hot. "Is this. . ."

"Anal plugs. Trainee anal plugs. Did you decide anal play was a hard limit?"

"I guess I'd like to try it but if I don't like it. . ."

"Then we wouldn't do it again."

"But you like it?"

"Yeah. But I won't enjoy it if you don't. Angel, look at me." He leaned forward and waited for her gaze to meet his. "Listen carefully. Don't ever want you to agree to something or do anything that you're not comfortable with because you think I might want it."

"But I won't know until I try, right?"

"Some things you'll try and won't like. Some things you will enjoy. You always have a safe word. We start something and it hurts, or you don't like it, or you get scared, say your safeword and everything will stop."

She nodded and squealed at the next thing she brought out. "Dolly!" He'd bought her a doll along with a collection of dolls clothes.

"You like?"

"Yes, thank you, Daddy!"

She froze as she realized what she said. But Bain just gave her a smile. In fact, it was the most unguarded she'd ever seen him. Like a screen had come down and she could see the man underneath.

Maybe he needed this as much as she did. She hugged the doll tight.

"I like hearing you call me Daddy," he told her. "But don't force it, all right? You need more time, that's fine. This is all at your pace."

Back was her honey-voiced man. This sweet side of him was going to kill her.

Had she really only known him for a few weeks? Was she ready to be this vulnerable with him? To completely let down her shields?

Then again, hadn't she already shown him her vulnerable side? When she was sleepwalking, she could easily be harmed. Anything could happen to her. He'd taken care of her. Like he'd done while she had her period. Like he was doing now.

She drew out the last item in the bag, staring at it in puzzlement.

"It's a sleep sack," he explained. "Ever heard of them?"

She shook her head.

He opened it up to show her. It was a pale green color. And it looked snuggly and soft.

"You sleep inside it. Feels a bit like being swaddled. It applies gentle pressure, meant to help with sleep issues and anxiety."

"You shouldn't have bought me so much."

"Why not? I can afford it." He frowned.

Shit. Why hadn't she thought before speaking? "No, I didn't mean it like that. I just. . .I'm not used to anyone buying me things. Not without a reason. And that you bought me something to help with my anxiety and sleeping, it's so thoughtful. I wasn't saying that I thought you couldn't afford it. Sorry."

He ran his hand over his face. "No, I'm sorry. That was me being defensive."

"I get it," she said quietly.

He gently grasped hold of her chin. "Such a sweetheart. I'll try to do better."

"I don't. . .I don't care how much money you have. All I ever wanted growing up was my parents time and love. Not the things they could buy me."

"Ari. I know you're more than your money. You're smart, kind, creative and generous. I see you. And seems to me you need to be spoiled. Gonna give you all the time and attention you need. Maybe more than you even want." He grinned. "You might get sick of me."

She was pretty sure she wouldn't.

"I find it hard to let other people close to me. I was never able to make friends. I was always that weird, quiet Silvers girl. Now, I never know whether someone is being nice to me because they like me or they want me to do something for them."

"People have done that? Gotten close to you to use you?"

She smiled sadly. "Yeah. More often than I care to admit. That's why it's so surprising how at ease I feel with you. I think part of it is because you're so honest. Sometimes perhaps a bit too honest. But I know you'll always tell me the truth. And you've opened up to me as well. About your ex-wife. Your life."

"I don't like secrets. Arianna, you're safe with me. Your safety, happiness and protection is the most important thing to me."

"I know." She licked her lips and took a steadying breath. She knew he wouldn't make fun of her. She just had to lower that final barrier and let him in. Let him be everything she needed.

"Can I have my juice in a sippy cup, Daddy?" A weight truly lifted, and she found herself smiling. It felt so right.

"You sure can, baby girl. Here's your juice. Daddy wants you to drink it all, okay?"

She held her new doll close to her chest, feeling nervous. She reached out for the cup.

"What do you say?" he asked.

"Umm."

"Thank you, Daddy."

"Oh. Thank you, Daddy." Kind of ironic that he was teaching her about manners when he pretty much had none. But the smile he gave her was everything.

"Good girl. What's your dolly's name?" He lay on his side.

She tipped back the sippy cup and drank before putting it down. "I don't know." She peered at the doll. It was soft bodied with dark brown hair and light brown eyes.

"She looks like a Melly. I'm going to name her Melly."

"Sounds good, baby. I'm going to put some food on your plate, and I want you to eat it all, understand?"

She frowned. She wasn't sure about that. She watched as he put two sandwich triangles on her plate along with a bunch of grapes. He picked up some cheese and crackers, just putting a few out.

"That's a lot of food, Daddy. I don't know if I can eat it all."

"Give it a good go."

There was a strict note in his voice that had her nodding her head in agreement. She could try, she guessed.

He filled up his own plate, which overflowed by the time he was finished.

"Daddy, are you sure you should eat all that? You'll get a sore tummy."

He raised his eyebrows. "I need all this food to fuel my muscles. Got to be able to carry my baby girl around. Even though she protests when I pick her up and put her places."

She had to grin. "Daddy, I gots a secret. Wanna hear it?"

His eyes danced with enjoyment. He really did like this. He looked more at ease than she'd ever seen him.

"What is it? Little girls shouldn't keep secrets from their daddies, you know."

She leaned over and whispered in his ear. "I actually like you picking me up and carrying me places."

His eyes widened and he let out a dramatic gasp. "No!"

She nodded enthusiastically. "Uh-huh. It's true. No lies."

"I would never have guessed." He grinned at her. Then he started eating. She had lost interest in the food, especially when Melly had come with all these cool outfits. Hmm, what to change her into first?

She began pulling off the clothes Melly already had on.

"Angel, eat your lunch or I'm going to have to put Melly away," he warned.

She paused with a gasp. "What? No! Daddy, you can't do that!"

"Can and will, little bit. Now eat something."

She studied him, trying to ascertain if he was serious or not. He gave her a stern look. She let out a dramatic sigh but picked up a couple of grapes and ate them.

Yum. She did love grapes.

She pulled off Melly's top then turned her over to undo and tug off her jeans. She gasped as she saw her doll's bottom.

"Daddy!"

"What's wrong?"

"Somebody spanked Melly!" She turned her doll around to show him her doll's bottom.

His lips twitched into a smile.

"Daddy! It's not a smiling matter."

"She was bought from a Little store. Guessing lots of people who shop there have had red bottoms at some stage. The dolls are probably modelled on them."

She scrunched up her nose. "That's not very nice, is it, Melly? What did you do that was so naughty, hmm?"

"She probably didn't listen to her Daddy and eat her lunch.

That seems to be a problem going around."

Okay. She got it.

"Do you want some sandwich, Melly?" She grabbed one and held it up to her doll's mouth. "Nom, nom, nom."

"How about Ari eats some food, huh?" Bain prompted.

She wrinkled her nose. "Ari isn't hungry."

"Ari hasn't eaten since breakfast. And Ari needs to listen to Daddy. Last warning."

The urge to push was there. To see exactly what would happen. But caution held her back. With a big sigh, she picked up a sandwich and dutifully ate it.

"Good girl," he said warmly.

Happiness bubbled inside her. She liked being a good girl. She continued to play with her doll, feeding her bits of food and chatting to her.

"Eat again, Ari," Bain prompted.

"I already ate, Daddy," she replied.

"Hand over Melly please," he said firmly.

She looked up at him and hugged her doll close to her chest. "No!"

His gaze narrowed. "Yes. Now. No more warnings or it's corner time for you."

Don't be a bother, Arianna. Just do what Daddy wants.

She reluctantly handed over Melly, her lower lip trembling.

He shook his head. "Adorable, angel. But not going to work."

She sniffled. "How comes I can't have Melly? Was she naughty?"

"No, Melly wasn't naughty. However, she was distracting Ari from using her listening ears."

"I'll put them on, Daddy and then I can have her back." She smiled cheerfully. Problem solved. She picked up an imaginary pair of ears and secured them on. "Got them on. Now I can have Melly."

She reached out, but he stood and placed Melly on the bed. "No, you already had your chance to eat and play. I can see there needs to be a ban on toys at mealtimes. It's difficult enough to get you to eat as it is."

She gave him big puppy dog eyes.

He just shook his head. "Nope. New rule. No dolls or other toys while Ari is supposed to be eating. You can have Melly back after lunch."

"But what if she gets hungry?"

"I'm sure she can wait," he said dryly.

"Daddy! That's not very nice."

He grinned. "Daddy never claimed to be nice."

"I think Daddy might be the naughty one. I think Daddy might need a spankin'."

"Oh, it's not Daddy who gets spanked around here for misbehaving. Now, come here, little bit." He crooked a finger at her.

She was immediately suspicious. Oh no.

"Why?"

"Arianna Marie, come here right now."

She practically threw herself at him. What was she doing? She needed to behave. She wasn't sure what to make of this side of herself. She didn't want Bain to get tired of her.

"Sorry, Daddy," she muttered.

"That's okay, baby." He kissed the top of her head. "Daddy's fault for letting you have Melly before eating." He settled her on his lap and picked up a sandwich, feeding it to her. She didn't think she'd ever had anyone feed her since she was a child. It was a bit odd, but as she settled into his lap, she kind of started to like it.

He was taking care of her.

"I really loves her, Daddy. Thank you."

"You're welcome, baby. Here, have some juice." He held the sippy cup up to her mouth.

She reached up to grab the cup and he pulled it away. "Uh-uh, if Daddy is feeding you then he helps you drink as well. Just keep your hands on your lap, please."

His voice was firm, and she dropped her hands as he held the sippy cup to her mouth.

"Good, baby?" he asked after he took away the cup.

He turned her further into his chest and started rubbing her back. She let out a small burp and immediately gasped, horrified.

"I's sorry. I didn't mean to do that!"

He grinned down at her. "It's okay, baby. I don't know how, but even your burps are cute."

She rolled her eyes. He was crazy. She settled her face into his chest, her eyes fluttering shut. "I like this. I wish it never had to end."

HE STILLED, staring down at her. End? She was already thinking of when this would end? She yawned and he continued to rub her back, liking the way she nestled into his lap.

"Somehow, it seems easier to always be Little, but I know I can't."

Ahh. That's what she'd meant. That knot in his stomach unraveled. He didn't know what the future would bring. They both lived very different lives. But he'd gone into this relationship knowing that. Compromising wasn't something he was used to doing.

But for her, it would be worth it. Even if he only got a fraction of her time, it would be worth it.

He'd half-expected her to throw a tantrum earlier when he'd taken Melly away to help her focus on eating. So he'd been surprised when she'd pulled back.

He had to judge where the line was. How hard or easy to go.

"Come on, baby. Time for bed."

"It's not bedtime!"

"It's naptime."

"Nuh-uh. I'm a big girl. I don't need a nap."

"You're not a big girl. You're my baby. And you very much need a nap. You were nearly asleep on my lap."

"I was relaxin', Daddy. I'm all better now. See? Wide awake." She pushed her eyes open with her fingers.

He snorted. "Nice try, angel. But it's naptime. Go use the bathroom, then I'll help you put your PJs on."

"But I don't wanna nap, Daddy." Her face grew mutinous.

He pointed at the bathroom, making sure he kept his face stern. "Bathroom. Now. Or do you want to have a nap with a red bottom?"

Her eyes narrowed. Here it came. He was certain she was going to refuse and end up over his knee. But she stood and stomped her way towards the bathroom. "Come on, Melly. Daddy says we gotta take a nap even if we don't think we need a nap. Yeah. . .I know. . .silly, huh?"

He shook his head at her antics then he got her pajamas ready. When she moved back into the bedroom, he was sitting on the bed. He crooked a finger at her. She dragged her feet as she moved towards him.

He tilted up her face. "Daddy just wants you healthy, all right? Don't like that you sleepwalk because I'm worried that something might happen to you. I also don't like how tired you look. All right?"

"Yeah, Daddy. I'm sorry."

"Good girl. Now, put your arms up. Let's get you changed." He stood and whipped off her sweater. She was dressed in just a tank top underneath. Then he sat and started to pull down her pants. He heard her indrawn breath, but she didn't say anything as he drew her pants off. Then he grabbed her pajama bottoms. He figured she could sleep in the tank top comfortably.

"Hold onto my shoulders, angel. I don't want you falling over."

He helped her into the pants. Then he stood and walked over to grab her sleep sack. "Want to try it?"

She nodded eagerly. He laid it out on the bed and helped her climb in. She mumbled something happily.

"You like?"

"Uh-huh, feels like my whole body being hugged."

He kissed her cheek gently. "Good. You can sleep in it each nap time and at night."

Her eyes closed as he started to lightly massage her scalp.

"If you need to go potty, you can get up but otherwise I want you to stay in bed until I come get you, understand?"

"Yes."

"Yes, Daddy," he prompted.

"Yes, Daddy."

"Thank you for trusting me. I haven't enjoyed a picnic so much in my life."

She smiled up at him. "Me either, Daddy."

"Now, close your eyes and I'll stay with you until you go to sleep."

Her eyes fluttered shut and her thumb crept into her mouth. Nope. Couldn't have that. He walked over to the bag of stuff he'd bought her and drew out the pacifier. He'd already washed it. He slid her thumb from her mouth.

"No, Daddy," she grumbled.

"Yes, little one. Try this." He pressed the pacifier into her mouth. She screwed up her nose and spat it back out.

"Yuck, Daddy."

"Daddy wants you to try this for him. Let yourself get used to it. No spitting it out."

She sighed then opened her mouth. "Good girl. Go to sleep. Daddy is watching over you. That's my little angel."

16

"Yay! I won!"

She jumped to her feet and did a dance. Dominic and Bain just gave her indulgent smiles.

"Another game?" she asked, sitting down.

"Nope," Bain replied as he and Dominic started packing up Candyland. It was her favorite. Although, she loved most board games. "It's bedtime."

"Bedtime? It's early."

"You need sleep."

"You made me take a two-hour nap today."

"You're playing catch-up."

"I had to take one yesterday as well," she pointed out. After breakfast, she and Bain had joined Dominic in the gym and then she'd spent most of the day in Little space, playing in her bedroom, before Bain made her nap.

And she'd been an angel all day. She was proud of herself even though there had been a few times when she'd had to rein herself in. She didn't want to be a bother or give him any cause to reject her.

"Bedtime," he said firmly.

"But, Daddy," she wheedled. Then she froze. Shit. Shit. Shit. It had just slipped out.

But it had slipped out in front of Dominic. Mortification filled her.

"I'm sorry. I'm so sorry," she muttered to Bain.

"Angel, it's okay—"

She jumped up, her face burning.

What an idiot! What if Bain didn't want Dominic to know that about them? What if she'd just horribly embarrassed him?

What would he do?

Would he decide she wasn't worth the effort anymore?

She raced out of the living room, down the passage and into her bedroom. She started pacing. She was barely aware of the door opening and Bain stepping inside.

"Angel, what's going on?"

"I'm so sorry. Did I embarrass you? I didn't mean to. It just slipped out. It won't happen again, I promise. Please don't leave." Tears dripped down her cheeks. She wiped at them, forcing herself to stare at him.

"Whoa, okay, angel. You seem to have jumped to some rash conclusions." He studied her, carefully moving forward as though he thought she might bolt.

"Angel, I'm going to pull you into my arms, all right? Shh. It's all right. Everything is fine." He tugged her close and she buried her face into his chest.

"Sorry. Sorry."

"Angel, you have nothing to be sorry about."

"I called you Daddy in front of Dominic," she wailed. Hadn't he heard?

But he didn't pull away from her, he simply kept rubbing her back with slow, firm strokes.

"Angel, calm down. Calm down so Daddy can talk to you. Good girl. Let's get Patches, I bet she'll make you feel better."

He settled her on his lap on the bed and picked up Patches. She held the dog tight and buried herself back into his arms.

"Tell me what just happened."

"I embarrassed you."

"You did? How?"

Why did they even have to talk about this? "You were there."

"I was. Want you to explain why you think I'm embarrassed. Sure as shit don't feel embarrassed."

"You. . .you don't?"

"Nope."

"You don't care that I called you Daddy in front of someone else? Does Dominic. . .does he know?"

"Haven't told you about Sanctuary Ranch, have I?"

What did that have to do with anything?

"No."

"You said Caleb is a Daddy Dom, right?"

"Yes," she whispered. "He, uh, he told me that your boss was one and that a lot of the men that worked for him were too. Does that mean Dominic is?"

"He is. Many of the men who live on Sanctuary Ranch are Daddy Doms. All of the men believe in protecting and treasuring the women who live there."

She breathed a sigh of relief.

"Just so we're clear, even if he wasn't, I wouldn't have cared that you called me Daddy in front of him. Call me Daddy in front of whoever you like."

"I. . .I can?"

"Yeah, baby. Nothing you could ever do would embarrass me."

"You don't know that," she whispered.

"This is about your parents."

She really didn't want to talk about this. "I'm tired, Daddy."

"I know you are. But communication, remember?"

"Maybe you should tell me more about where you live," she suggested.

"I'll tell you anything you wish to know. But right now, we're talking about you. And why you freaked out."

"How come you always wanna talk when it's stuff about me."

"I want to know everything about you," he told her. "More I know, better I can take care of you. And baby, that's what I was put on this Earth to do."

She sniffled. "Damn. Just when I didn't think you could get any sweeter."

He snorted. She fidgeted on his lap.

"Talk. Now." And there was her bossy ogre again. The honey voice was gone. In its place was firm steel.

She wasn't getting out of this.

"I'm weird. The Silvers don't do weird. The Silvers are the epitome of social breeding. The Silvers don't fall over their own feet. Or spill food while eating. Or snort while laughing."

"I think that snort is cute."

"A Silvers is never less than perfect," she said in a voice that imitated her mother.

"Those fucking assholes. Listen to me." He raised her chin up. "Imagine if we all had no flaws, nothing that made us different? Am I perfect?"

"Umm."

He grinned. "Honesty."

"No."

"No, I'm not. I don't give a fuck. Am who I am. Abrupt, sometimes brutally honest, don't care much about social niceties. Do I embarrass you?"

"No! Never. You're loyal and smart and I kind of like how honest you are. I never have to worry about what you're thinking or saying behind my back."

"You are smart, kind, talented and beautiful. They couldn't see all that then that's on them. So you stumble and snort when you laugh? Who are they to say that's a fucking flaw?"

She cupped his cheek with her hand. "You're a special kind of guy, Bain Grady."

"Heard that before."

"I mean it. Can't believe you're here. That you want me."

"Feel the same fucking way about you." He leaned his forehead on hers. "You're not getting rid of me easily. I warned you. Once I'm in, I'm all the way in. You don't have to be perfect for me."

She sighed.

"Give me all of you. Not going to be annoyed or get sick of you or expect you to behave in a certain way. Know you've been holding back on me."

"You do?"

"Seen you pull back a few times when you're Little. Usually right before I'm about to hand down some discipline. Just be yourself, angel. Don't want who you think you should be. I want the real Ari. Because she's amazing and kind and worth far more than she could ever imagine."

17

"Oh drat! I'm so stupid! Why can't I do this?"

"Arianna, that's enough."

She heard Bain call out a warning in a low voice. But she ignored him. This was a child's crossword. It should be easy. Why couldn't she get it? She was procrastinating. She knew she should ask Bain for her phone back. There had to be messages and emails she needed to deal with.

But instead, she was trying to figure out this stupid game that even children could do.

"Urgh!" She thumped the crossword down on the floor where she was sitting. "I'm such a moron!"

"Enough." Bain rose from his seat then walked over and grabbed hold of her around the waist, pulling her onto her feet.

"What are you doing?" she asked.

He sat on the sofa then drew her over his lap.

"Daddy?" she asked.

"What's your rule about putting yourself down?"

"I'm not allowed to say bad things about myself. But I wasn't!"

"Heard you call yourself stupid and a moron."

"But you didn't give me any warnings! Shouldn't you give warnings?"

"Gave you one warning. From now on, that's all you're getting, little miss. You should already know not to call yourself names. I'm going to pull your pants and panties down because this is a serious transgression. Understand me?"

To her mortification, he tugged off her pants and underwear. This was the first time she was going to be partially naked around him. And she was not expecting it to be like this.

"Want me to hold your hands?" he asked.

"No! Daddy, don't spank me!"

"Sorry, baby. Putting yourself down isn't acceptable. Ever." He smacked his hand down on her bottom. "Don't want to hear you speak about yourself like that again."

Smack! Smack!

"My girl does not call herself a moron."

Ouch.

Smack! Smack!

"Or stupid."

Smack! Smack!

Ow. That hurt!

"If she gets frustrated, then she can ask her Daddy for help."

Two more smacks. By now her backside was throbbing. And this was just from his hand! What would it feel like if he was to use something else on her poor bottom?

He stopped, rubbing her butt.

"I'm sorry, Daddy," she said, guessing that was the end of it. Thank God! That was awful.

"Glad to hear that, baby girl. How are you doing?"

"I'm sore! That was horrible!"

She tried to push herself off his lap. But he kept a heavy hand on the small of her back, keeping her in place. "Stay there, angel."

"But. . .but. . .isn't that the end?"

"No, afraid not. Just paused to check in on you since this is your first spanking. This is in no way the end. If it's too much for you in one go, we can finish up tonight before bed."

Wait for the rest? That sounded even worse than taking it all once.

"I don't want any more!"

"Of course, you don't," he soothed. "This is punishment. It shouldn't be easy."

It certainly wasn't that. He rubbed her cheeks again. "Continue or wait?"

"Continue on." She sniffled. Waiting would be awful. At least now he might feel slightly tired. If she gave him until tonight, then he'd probably regain some energy.

His hand landed again without warning. Over and over until she was kicking her feet, her cries so loud she had no doubts that Dominic could probably hear them.

Which made it all even more embarrassing.

"D-daddy, no! Please!"

"Sorry this first punishment has to be such a strict one, angel. But you were very naughty."

Shit. Shit.

Tears flooded down her face, dripping on the wooden floor. Her bottom was hot and throbbing painfully. Sobs racked her body, making it hard to catch her breath.

She vowed to never, ever say another bad word about herself again.

Then the spanks slowed, and he stopped, laying his hand on her lower thighs. Thank God, because she didn't want anything touching her backside. Ever. Again.

Bain let out a small chuckle. "That's a shame. I'm quite fond of touching this bottom. It's so cute."

"It hurts!" Whoops. She hadn't actually meant to say that out loud.

"Good. It was meant to. I never want to hear such words coming from your mouth again, understand me?"

"Y-yes, Daddy."

"Good girl." He turned her over then lay on his back on the couch with her sprawled over him on her stomach. She continued to quietly sob as his hands rubbed up and down her back, careful not to touch her hot butt cheeks.

"Cry it out. You'll feel better if you get it all out. That's my good girl."

"That. . .that was m-mean."

"I wasn't being mean. I was correcting you for saying terrible things about my girl. Who is certainly not stupid or a moron."

She sobbed in another breath before rubbing her face against him. There, that was better.

"Did you just wipe your face on my shirt?" he asked

"Yes." He deserved it. He'd caused the tears after all.

His chest moved as he chuckled.

"What's so funny?"

"Nothing." He went still.

She leaned up, resting her forearms on his chest so she could stare down at him. "Daddy."

He ran a hand over his face, looking sheepish. Okay, now she really had to know.

"When we first came here, you seemed so untouchable. An ice princess. Like you'd never even have a snotty nose let alone wipe it on my shirt."

"I didn't wipe my snotty nose on your shirt!" she protested. "It was my tears."

He grinned at her.

"I'm not an ice princess. I'm just not very good at meeting new people. I'm awkward. And you're gorgeous and intimidating and I didn't really know what to say to you. I was scared of saying something weird."

"I know. You're my quiet, sweet princess." He leaned up and kissed her nose. "Now that you've calmed down, it's corner time."

"What?" She gaped at him. "But you just punished me."

"I also want you to stand in the corner and think over all the—"

A knock on the door interrupted him and she gasped, trying to reach back to cover her bottom with her hands.

"It's okay. He won't come in."

"Bain?" Dominic called out.

"Yeah?"

"I'm sorry to interrupt, man. But I need you to come out here. We've got visitors."

Bain helped her stand and pull on her panties and pants. Ouch. She was going to have to start wearing skirts if he was planning on spanking her often.

Funny thing was, as painful as it was, she actually felt a bit lighter. He didn't like her calling herself names. He really did think she was special.

"Who do you think it is?" she asked. She never had visitors.

"I don't know, but I want you to stay behind me until I give you permission to move."

Permission? Seriously?

She just shook her head at him as he opened the door and stepped out into the corridor with a nod at Dominic. "Who is it?"

"Ahh, well, it's Caleb Pierce and a couple of other guys. They were entering the building when I was coming in, so I brought them up with—"

"Arianna!" Bain snapped as she flew past him. But she ignored him in a rush to see her best friend. She raced around the corner and opened the door, throwing herself at the big man standing in the foyer. He caught her, turning in a circle with her held tight against him.

Caleb was tall, just a few inches shorter than Bain but not

nearly as wide. He had white-blond hair and a fair complexion. He was her best friend, pretty much her only friend growing up, and she'd missed him so much. She sunk into his embrace.

"Arianna!" Bain growled. "What do you think you're doing!"

She turned her head. "It's all right. I know these guys. It's just Caleb."

"Just Caleb?" the man in question asked.

She smiled up at him then kissed his cheek, ignoring the rumbling noise from the big man behind her.

"Hey, what about the rest of us? Got some sugar for us?" Aleki asked, stepping forward. She leaned out of Caleb's embrace and Aleki caught her easily.

Aleki's mother was Samoan and he had black hair that curled when he let it grow. A big, tribal tattoo wound its way from his hand up his arm. He was the shortest of the three, but the most muscular. And he always had a grin on his face.

Wolfe stepped forward. He was quieter. More thoughtful than the other two. He always made her feel calm and centered. She entered his embrace, and just breathed him in. With his glasses, lean build and messy, blue-black hair people often underestimated him. But that's the way he liked it. The man could move like a ghost when he needed to.

"So, Arianna," Caleb said, turning her back to him. "Want to explain why you haven't been answering my messages? Why there's a big dude glaring daggers at us? And why the hell you've been crying?"

BAIN WAS LIVID.

About to breathe fire, livid.

And it was all aimed at the three men who were daring to

touch his woman. Caleb actually pulled her behind his back while the other two moved in to surround her.

"Easy, man, calm down," Dominic told him. "They're Ari's friends. Caleb knows Kent, remember?"

"Someone better fucking explain to me what is going on," Caleb demanded. "We've been trying to get hold of Ari for days. We've been traveling for over twenty hours. I'm on a very short fuse and getting here to find she's been crying; the match is about to be lit."

"I don't fucking care," Bain snapped back. "Hand her over now."

"It really would be best if you let Arianna out before he explodes," Dominic said calmly.

"Aleki, let me go. You guys all need to calm down. I'm sorry I worried you. It was inexcusable of me. I just needed a break, but I should have called you. I'm so sorry. And now you've made a long journey for no reason. I feel terrible."

"It's okay, Ari," Caleb told her soothingly. "Calm down, sweetheart. We're not mad at you. I've never known you not to answer the phone, so yeah, we were freaked. But I'm guessing there's a reason you didn't have your phone on."

"I took her phone and laptop," Bain told him. "She was stressed. She needed a break. Let her go. Now."

"No. The two of you can now leave. You've done the job I hired you to do but we're here now. We'll take care of Arianna."

"Over my dead fucking body," Bain snarled, taking a step forward, his hands clenching into fists.

"All of you stop it!"

It was obvious Arianna was getting more upset, which just fueled his anger. Aleki let out a small grunt.

"Ouch, Ari, what'd you kick me for?"

"Out of the way!" She slid past him, but Caleb grabbed her as she went to go past him.

"Let her go!" Bain yelled.

"Bain! Stop!" she snapped at him. Then she turned to Caleb. "And you stop too!"

"You wouldn't turn off your phone unless they made you. And you've been crying! You never cry!"

"I was crying because. . ." she paused and took a deep breath. "Bain spanked me, okay?"

"What?" Caleb roared, stepping forward.

"He's my Daddy!" she yelled out before he could reach Bain.

Caleb froze. "What?"

He turned towards Arianna. She pressed her hands to her cheeks with a groan. "I can't believe this is happening. You wanted me to find a Daddy Dom? Well, I did."

"Him?" Caleb gestured to Bain.

"He's a good guy, Caleb."

"What was he spanking you for?" Aleki demanded to know.

"Do we have to talk about that?" she asked.

"Yep," Caleb drawled, crossing his arms over his chest.

Bain stared back at him. "She was putting herself down. Calling herself unacceptable names."

Caleb continued to stare at him, then to Bain's shock, he stretched his arms above his head with a yawn. "Yeah, she does that. What happens when you grow up with her fucking pitiful excuse for a family."

"Caleb," Arianna protested.

The other men all started to relax. Caleb walked over to him, holding his hand out. Bain scowled down at it but shook it.

"Just so you know, I'm still gonna be calling Kent for information on you both. You hurt her, at all, and we will hunt you down and make your life hell. It won't be a quick kill. It will be torture. For years."

"Caleb!" she said, looking horrified.

But Bain just grinned. "We're gonna get on just fine."

~

SHE COULDN'T BELIEVE that they were all basically best friends now. They seemed to have bonded over their shared beliefs about her. And her tendency to misbehave.

It wasn't that she didn't want them to get along. It was just that after that little performance earlier; she hadn't expected them to do a one-eighty.

Now they were all gathered around the kitchen counter while Bain fixed them all some food, because apparently there was a game coming on soon.

"So, anyone want to tell me what's going on with these letters Ari has been getting? And why the fuck did Larry give a press conference on them?" Caleb asked. "Who thought that was a good idea?"

"He did it without consulting us," Bain growled. "Fucking prick. Never even told us about the other letter before he did it."

"I hope you damn well fired him, Ari," Caleb said to her. Before she could answer, though, he turned back to Bain. "I've never liked that asshole. Her parents hired him. So that they could control him and Ari."

Bain frowned at that piece of information.

"He's good at his job, Caleb."

This was an old argument.

"He's not good for you, Ari," Caleb insisted. "He pushes you too hard."

"That's the industry."

"Yeah? So it's normal to collapse after doing ten concerts in less than three weeks across five different states? You were dehydrated, you hadn't been eating properly and you were completely exhausted. You spent five days in the hospital, Ari."

"What?" Bain barked. "When was this?"

"Last year." Caleb took a sip of beer. "Larry pushed for that many concerts. And Ari, not wanting to let him or her fans down, drove herself to breaking point."

"That won't happen again," Bain growled.

Caleb smiled, looking entirely too smug. Bastard did that on purpose. She glared at him before kicking him in the leg.

"What! Ari, that wasn't very nice. You shouldn't kick people. Especially when they've flown halfway across the world, terrified out of their minds that something has happened to their best friend, only to find she's holed up with her new man and getting her ass spanked for being naughty."

Her face flamed hot even as guilt filled her. "I'm sorry. Really. I feel terrible."

"It wasn't her fault," Bain told Caleb, giving the other man a look.

It was, though. She should have realized Caleb and the others would be worried about her. It was inexcusable.

Aleki placed his arm around her shoulders, ignoring Bain's possessive glower.

"Don't let him fool you. Truth is, Kassim has been dying for an excuse to visit the states. He got himself a new private jet. More lux than any five-star hotel you've been in. He was only too happy to fly us over here."

"You flew on a private jet?" she asked Caleb. He'd conveniently left that part out.

He crossed his arms over his chest, looking stubborn. "It still took forever. And I was worried about you the whole time."

"I know. I really am sorry."

"Enough," Bain said firmly. "She said she was sorry."

Caleb nodded then pulled her off her stool and into his arms. "Just don't do it again, yeah? I don't think you realize how much I love you, Ari. You're precious to me. To Aleki and Wolfe. We don't want anything to happen to you, understand?"

She hugged him tight. "I love you guys too. Prince Kassim came with you?"

"They all came," Caleb told her. "Aric wanted to go shopping, apparently. Matek, well, Matek does what he wants. And Tavi. . ." he looked over at Aleki then Wolfe, "he wants a private concert."

"What?"

"He's a big fan, apparently. He was super pissed to learn that we know you and hadn't yet introduced you. You don't have to say yes."

"Of course I will. I feel like I know them from hearing you guys talking about them."

"Yeah. . .well. . ." Caleb ran the back of his hand over his head. "Don't be surprised if he gets a little possessive of you."

"What does that mean?" Bain asked.

Caleb shrugged. "These guys, they're rich, they're royalty, no one ever tells them no. And when he talks about Ari, well, I've told him that he can't steal you."

"S-steal me?" She watched him with wide eyes.

"He won't," Caleb said quickly. "It's just. . .they have this tradition in Escana. It's called bride stealing."

"But I'm not their bride."

"Their?" Bain asked. "They share?"

"Ah, yeah, it's common practice in Escana for a woman to have a harem of men."

She hadn't believed it when he'd first told her. She'd thought he was pulling her leg.

"But the men are very much in charge," Aleki told them. "And bride stealing is acceptable."

"However, you're taken, which is good," Caleb said with relief. "Because Tavi is really obsessed with you."

"He'd need the others approval before stealing her as they would all share, anyway," Aleki said.

"Yeah, but do you really think the others would object once they met her?" Caleb answered.

"Nah. Anyone would be damn lucky to get Ari." Aleki winked at her.

"Guys," she protested. She knew they had to say such things since they were her friends.

"She never believes us when we say nice things about her," Caleb said to Bain. "Crazy, that she doesn't see how amazing she is, right?"

"Yep," Bain rumbled.

"She's definitely Kassim's type," Aleki said. "Sweet and submissive."

"With enough bite to suit Arik," Caleb added. "And Matek, well, who the hell knows what he likes."

"Game's starting," Dominic called out from the living room.

Aleki and Wolfe headed out of the kitchen, leaving her with just Caleb and Bain.

"Maybe this private concert isn't a good idea," Bain grumbled.

Caleb whacked him on the back. "Relax. They won't steal her. Well, not unless they think she wants to be taken. And you don't want that, do you, Squirt?"

She shook her head. "No. I'm happy."

"Glad to hear it," Bain said, still not looking thrilled.

She wrapped herself around his arm as Caleb wandered away to join the others.

"You're not really worried, are you?"

He leaned in and kissed her gently. "No. Because I'll watch over you. You can be damn sure I won't let you out of my sight. But you will do everything I tell you."

"I will. I promise."

He turned then picked her up, setting her on the counter. "Like you promised to obey my orders when it came to safety."

"Yes," she replied, sensing a trap of some sort. But not knowing what it was.

"Did I not tell you to stay behind me earlier?" His voice had grown cold. Stern.

"But there was no danger. Dominic told us it was them. They're my friends."

His face didn't soften. He had hidden it well, but it was obvious now he was really unhappy with her. And she was already having a hard time sitting on her bottom as it was.

"Doesn't matter. I didn't know them. Didn't know their intentions. And it's my job to keep you safe."

"But it's not your job anymore. You quit."

"Protecting you is now my permanent job because you are mine."

The statement was completely possessive. He'd told her before he was all in.

"I had one relationship and it was toxic. Our relationship is not like that. You are not Jillian. She was never really my Little. She tried to use my needs to manipulate me. To get what she wanted from me. You are everything I ever wanted or needed. You come first with me. Over everyone else. You are to follow all my rules for safety, understand?"

"Yes, I will."

He kissed her forehead. "Good. You're still getting spanked, though. And don't think I've forgotten about your corner time."

"But I just got spanked! I'm still sore."

"You should have thought about that before you disobeyed me."

"But Daddy," she wheedled.

He tapped her nose. "If you want, we can go take care of it right now."

"No!" she squeaked. "Later is fine."

THE GUYS STAYED THROUGH DINNER. She ordered them all in pizza, which she nibbled on. She noticed Bain giving her a couple of looks and she forced herself to eat two slices.

Damn it.

How could she have gone from never having been spanked in her life to getting two spankings in one day?

She sighed. As the guys left, they all kissed her on the forehead.

"I'll let Tavi know you're willing to give a private performance, yeah?" Caleb asked, giving her a big hug. "He'll be thrilled."

"I'm happy to. Just warn him about Bain. Because he's a bit on edge."

Caleb chuckled. "A bit? If you weren't already his, I'd be worried he was going to steal you, take you away to his cabin in the woods and keep you tied to his bed."

"Idea has merit," Bain said from behind her. "Now let my woman go before I have your head mounted on a wall in my cabin."

Caleb just grinned. Then he gave her another hug, obviously to piss Bain off, before he left. They were all staying at The Plaza. Apparently, they had some friends guarding the princes while they were here.

She turned to face Bain. "You don't have animal heads mounted on a wall in your cabin, do you?"

He shook his head. "But he doesn't know that. And I'm damn good with a rifle." He drew her into his arms. "Come here. I've hardly gotten you to myself since they invaded. And they keep touching you."

She giggled at his grumbles. He kissed her gently, then he deepened the kiss, pressing his tongue into her mouth. Her body heated and she wound her arms around his neck. Her clit was throbbing, her nipples hard as she rubbed them against his chest.

So good.

He drew away and she whimpered, wanting more.

"Damn, baby. I want to keep going."

"So why did you stop?"

"Because we have other things to take care of." He raised an eyebrow at her pout.

"We could just forget about that."

"No. We could not. Get ready for bed. Then put just your nightgown on, no panties. Stand in the corner of your bedroom with your nose against the wall, your feet spread wide and your bottom pushed out. Hold your nightie up over your bottom."

Her mouth dropped open and she stared up at him in horror. "You can't be serious!"

"I am. Very serious." He tapped her nose. "I take your safety seriously. And what you say about yourself. Want you to think about what you did wrong today and what you could have done differently. You'll wait in the corner until I come in and tell you that you can move." He turned her around and slapped his palm against her ass. "Now, go!"

18

The music flowed. She hadn't ever felt this invigorated. This driven. This creative.

And she knew the reason for that.

A smile stole over her face as she thought of her stubborn, crabby, gorgeous man. Who'd have known she could have gone from being so nervous, she ran when she saw him coming, to wanting to climb him like she was a monkey and he was a tree. Now she felt like she wouldn't be whole without him.

She wasn't quite sure what would happen in the future. Caleb and the others were interviewing some bodyguards for her while they were here. That felt wrong. She didn't want anyone else. But Bain had his own career.

He'd never be happy here. She wasn't even happy here. Maybe there was some way she could move to Sanctuary with him.

Excitement filled her. All she wanted to do was to create music. She could do that in a cabin in the woods. Sure, she would probably have to leave sometimes, but maybe Bain could come with her those times. She wouldn't need a new bodyguard then.

She jumped to her feet, ready to race off and find him. Maybe she could tell him she loved him as well.

It wasn't too early for that, right?

The bedroom door opened, and Bain stepped in.

"Bain! I've got something to tell you!" She reached for him, noticing the frown on his face.

"Ari," he rumbled.

Then he said the one thing that could bring her happiness crashing down. That could make her remember that she couldn't live the life she wanted.

Because her life wasn't her own.

"Your family is here."

HER FAMILY WERE demons dressed in Prada.

Honest to fucking God, he was pretty sure there wasn't a piece of clothing on her mother's stick-thin body that didn't have fucking Prada written on it. And her sister wasn't any better. Except she wore slightly less clothing.

Didn't she know it was fucking 65 degrees out there? And she was wearing a skirt so short that if she bent over, they were all going to get an eyeful.

Please, God, don't let her bend over. He didn't really trust her to have underwear on.

The thought made him feel queasy.

The father wasn't any better. He was dressed in a three-piece suit, sitting in an armchair in Arianna's office, the look on his face colder than an arctic breeze.

As soon as he'd told her that her family was here, she'd closed down on him. And he hated it. He wished he could walk over to where she was perched on the edge of an armchair, pick her up and carry her the fuck away from these people.

"Really, Arianna, is the bodyguard necessary? We're your family, we're hardly going to attack you." The mother looked him up and down dismissively.

Suited him fine. He didn't want any attention from her. Her hair was dyed a honey-brown and pulled back severely from her face. A very-unlined and stiff-looking face. Obviously, no stranger to plastic surgery. She pursed her lips, which was an unfortunate look for her. Her legs were crossed, her hands resting on her lap. Diamonds glinted from her ears, neck and fingers.

Everything about her screamed money.

Arianna's sister, who he knew was several years older, was just as thin as the mother. She had darker hair which she wore down. Her shirt was too tight with several buttons undone, showing off a lot of cleavage. If he had to guess, the boobs were fake and so were her pouty lips.

She didn't look at him with disdain as she sat next to her mother. Oh no, her gaze ate him up.

The father tapped his fingers against the arm of his chair, glaring at Arianna who sat opposite him in the other armchair. Bain stood behind Ari and to the right.

She didn't even look back at him as she answered her mother. "He stays."

"Arianna," her mother replied, looking shocked. "There's no need to be so snappish."

That was snappish? He'd heard far more attitude coming from her mouth than that. But then, maybe that was because she wasn't afraid to give him sass. Did these people even know the real Ari?

"He's my bodyguard, mother," she said coolly. "He goes where I go."

"But there's no danger here right now," her mother replied. "And this is a private, family matter."

"He stays," Arianna replied firmly.

"For God's sake, Bernadette. Let the damn bodyguard stay. He would've signed an NDA. He's not going to talk to anyone."

"Fine. I was just trying to protect you, Arianna," her mother drawled. "I wasn't certain you'd want a member of your staff hearing about all your issues."

All her issues? What the fuck? Only years of training and control allowed him to keep his face from displaying his disbelief at what this bitch just said.

"What are you talking about?" Arianna asked warily.

"Why did you hire bodyguards without consulting us, Arianna?" her father snapped. "Larry had possible candidates lined up who I am certain are much better qualified than these buffoons."

Buffoons? Seriously?

"Dominic and Bain work for JSI. They are both ex-Navy SEALs. There is no one better than them."

The father's gaze flicked to him for the first time. "JSI, huh? They work for Kent Jensen?"

"Yes," Arianna said slowly, as though uncertain at her father's change of tune. He didn't like it either.

"JSI? Never heard of them," her mother said snootily. "Larry wanted to hire that dead actress's bodyguard. He would have been far better suited to deal with Arianna."

Deal with her? Were these people for real?

"I think he looks just fine," the sister said. "If Arianna no longer needs him, I'll take him."

"What? Of course, I need him," Arianna said. "Why are you here, Gabrielle? I thought you were in San Francisco with Julian."

The sister waved her hand. "I ended things. He was so demanding. I'm now free again." She licked her lips while staring at Bain.

Something in Arianna's façade cracked and she shifted around on the chair. "Bain is mine."

"Yours?" her mother snapped. "What do you mean by that? You can't be involved with him, surely, Arianna?"

"That's none of your business."

"He's an employee." Her mother held a hand to her chest. "A bodyguard. We raised you better than that."

What the fuck? First of all, they hadn't raised her. And secondly, were they saying he wasn't good enough for her? These people were unfucking believable.

"What I do is none of your business."

The mother's mouth dropped open. Then she turned to her husband. "Frederick, say something."

"Arianna, you cannot and will not get involved with your bodyguard. That's just. . .that's. . ."

"Trashy," her mother replied.

Arianna turned to Bain and that blankness in her gaze hit him hard. The need to protect her, to wrap her up in safety and love slammed into him.

"Bain, maybe you should—"

"I'm not going anywhere." He stepped closer and put his hand on her shoulder. It was then he could feel the fine tremor running through her body. It wasn't visible in the way she held herself. But it was there. This was affecting her far more than she was letting on.

"I'll have your job for this!" Her father leaped to his feet. "You cannot sleep with a client."

"Arianna isn't a client. I'm not being paid by JSI to guard her," Bain said in a low voice. "If you're only here to berate your daughter, then it's time you left."

Arianna placed her hand on his and squeezed.

"Arianna, this is completely unacceptable," her mother said. "Think of our reputation. Your father is a respected businessman. We cannot have you slutting around with the help."

"Oh, leave her alone," her sister spoke up surprisingly. "So she wants to fuck the bodyguard. Look at him, who wouldn't? It's not like she's gonna marry him. Even though she's weird, she still has needs. Truthfully, I was starting to think you were a lesbian, sis."

"Gabrielle!" her mother protested.

"What? Ari's always been weird. She never had any friends. Just that stuck-up asshole that lived next door and that weird little kid who belonged to one of the maids."

"Frederick!"

Arianna's father ran his hand over his face. "I told you it was a mistake to bring Gabrielle. You're the one who insisted she come."

"I thought she could do some sisterly bonding with Arianna."

Gabrielle shrugged. "I came because I need Arianna to give me some more money."

The trembles rocking Arianna's body had grown stronger and he knew he needed to get these people away from her. Now.

And just what did the sister mean, she needed more money? Surely, Arianna didn't support her?

"You all need to go," he told them.

The mother spun; her face twisted. "Is it your fault she isn't answering Larry's calls? She needs to get back to work. If she doesn't, Larry will drop her, and we need him. He brings in the money. Arianna has obligations. She needs to remember that." She turned to Arianna. "Answer Larry's calls. And finish up with the bodyguard."

Arianna stiffened.

"Come, let's go. We're not getting anywhere. We'll come back another day and speak to you alone, Arianna," her father said stiffly. "We're staying at the Four Seasons for the week. We will expect you to make time to see us."

"Your father had to leave important business meetings to come and deal with you, Arianna. The least you could do is meet with us alone," her mother spat. "And for goodness sake, start dressing like a proper Silvers. This mess you have on isn't becoming. And whatever diet you're on isn't working. You've put on weight and it doesn't look good on you."

Her mother and father stormed out. Gabrielle stood and smoothed down her skirt. The entire time she eye-fucked him.

Christ, all of them were a piece of work.

"So, about that money?"

"I'll put some into your account," Arianna replied dully.

"Great, thanks, sis. Love you. Go get yourself some. I know I would." She winked at Bain then flounced out.

Bain turned to Arianna. "I'll make sure they're gone. Wait here."

He didn't want to leave her. But he also didn't want those assholes wandering around freely. Dominic was out on an errand so he couldn't make sure they went.

Arianna didn't say anything and unsurprisingly, when he returned, she was gone.

19

She pushed herself to go faster on the treadmill.

She didn't pay attention to the fact that her breath was growing labored. Her legs were tiring. That sweat coated her body. She just wanted to run until she couldn't think anymore. Until she couldn't feel the pain of their words like slashes against her soul.

Her parents had left over an hour ago. Bain had tried to talk to her soon after. She winced as she remembered how cold she'd been to him. How she'd told him to leave her alone.

That she wished everyone would leave her the fuck alone.

It hadn't been true. Inside, she'd been crying out to him to pull her into his arms and cuddle her. To help heal the pain that had opened up her insides and made her feel like she was bleeding.

She was screaming silently.

Why couldn't he see that? Why could no one ever see that?

Tears blurred her eyes, but she didn't stop. She couldn't stop. The pain could be numbed. If she just pushed herself hard enough, it could all go away.

And she could be blessedly numb.

That is not the way a Silvers acts.

That is not the way a Silvers speaks.

Don't embarrass the family, Arianna.

She shouldn't have let Bain into that meeting. Then he wouldn't have seen how much her family truly didn't care about her.

All they did was use her.

A sob broke free. No, this was meant to stop her from feeling. She needed to be numb.

"Arianna, stop now."

A hand reached out towards the treadmill, pressing on the button to slow the speed.

No, no, no. She wasn't there yet. She wasn't so completely spent that she couldn't feel a damn thing. That she could slip into oblivion and sleep.

"No!" She tried to push his hand away. The treadmill slowed.

"Yes.".

"I don't. . .I'm not ready to stop."

"You are ready. Fuck, if I knew you were gonna sneak in here I would have ignored your need for space. What were you thinking? Why didn't you come to me?"

He stopped the treadmill and lifted her to the floor. Then he drew her close. She tried to pull back. She had to smell something awful. But he didn't care that she was sweaty and disgusting. He held her tight against his chest, one hand rubbing up and down her back while he rocked her gently.

"I'm sorry."

"For what? For telling me to leave you alone when clearly you didn't want that? For breaking a rule and running until you were past exhaustion? For trying to hide from me how you really feel?"

"Ah, well, I guess all of that."

She wrapped her arms around his waist, resting her weight on him knowing he could easily take it. She thought Bain could take anything. He was strong. Tough. So different from her.

"What are you thinking?"

"I wish I was as strong as you."

He leaned back and cupped her face between his hands. "The hell are you talking about? You're stronger than I am."

"Um. Have you taken a hit on the head or something?"

"Come here. You need to stretch, or you'll seize up." He drew her over to the mat. She began stretching out her legs obediently. "And you're far stronger than me, Ari. Don't know many people who would face their fears like you do. You hate all the publicity, yet you still do it all."

"I don't want to," she whispered.

She got down on the floor, laying on her back as he helped her stretch her quads and glutes.

"And that's why you're fucking strong."

She shook her head. "I'm sorry for how they treated you before."

"Don't apologize for them," he growled. "Your family is fucked up, angel. They should treat you like the fucking treasure you are, not belittle or hurt you."

"They've been like that for as long as I can remember." She sat up and took the bottle of water he handed her. "No, that's not true. When I was a kid, they ignored me. That was far better. I think most of the time they forgot I even existed. Until I became useful to them."

He sighed and sat next to her.

She ran a finger down the bottle. Her hand shook. She hoped he didn't notice that.

"You need to drink that. You're dehydrated. You also need something to eat."

Drat. Too much to hope he hadn't seen her shaking.

"You're not in here exercising because of that bullshit your mother said about you putting on weight are you, because—"

"No. No." She shook her head. "I mean, it hurts, I won't lie. When she says things about how I look or dress or act. No matter how I try to block it, it always hurts."

He got up and grabbed her a bottle of electrolyte and a protein bar that was kept in the fridge. "I want you to eat all of this and drink that water."

She unwrapped the bar. "I learned that I can't let them see how they affect me. It makes it all worse. When I'm unsure or scared or angry, I just kind of shut down. That's what happened earlier."

He nodded and pulled her onto his lap.

"Bain, I'm all sweaty and smelly."

"I'll give you a bath soon."

He would give her a bath? What did that mean exactly?

"I should have asked you to leave us. You shouldn't have to put up with them insulting you."

He cupped her chin, raising her face. "Your job ain't to protect me, angel."

"But it is. Because I love you. I know I'm probably meant to wait a prescribed amount of time before I tell you that. I know you might not feel the same and you don't have to say anything—"

Her words were cut off as he pressed his lips against hers. His kiss stole her breath, her ability to think as he ravaged her mouth. He took full control, kissing her until she was mush in his arms. Then he drew back to look down at her, his eyes blazing with lust and need.

And something else. Something deeper.

"Arianna, I—"

"Bain, you really don't have to—"

"Shut up," he told her fiercely. Her eyes widened. He'd never told her to shut up and maybe she should be offended. But there was something in his voice, in the intense look on his face. "Don't give a shit about what is normal or correct. I fucking love you too.

Probably have from the moment I found you under your damn desk, hiding from me."

"Not my finest moment."

"Don't like you hiding from me. Not physically or emotionally. We're going to work hard to make sure you don't do that, got me?"

He brushed back her hair. "You don't need to hide anything from me. Because I can take all that you are. Not going anywhere. Never gonna be embarrassed by you. Or try to change you. Sometimes it would be easier if you were instantly obedient, but it's not like I'm ever gonna get my wish on that."

She snorted. "You like me challenging you."

"As long as you know that I'm always going to follow through with consequences if you risk yourself. Put yourself in danger and you're going over my knee."

"I know," she whispered. "Whenever I did something wrong, my parents would ignore me. Even more so than before. That was after a lecture on how much I disappointed and shamed them with my weirdness." She clenched her hands together. "When they finally noticed me, I was so happy that I did anything they wanted. Including taking my career places I didn't want to go. All in the name of more money. For them."

"You support them, don't you?"

She sighed. "Yeah. When we were growing up, we lived in this big, flashy mansion. It had columns and a sweeping drive. Very Scarlett O'Hara. My parents had lots of parties, people over, they had the best of everything. My father lost it all. Lost all their money. We had to sell that house and move. I didn't care. But they did. My brother had left for college by then. I think my sister was in her last year of school. There was no money for tutors, so I had to go to school. It was terrifying. I'd never been around kids other than my siblings, Caleb and the staff's kids. Funny, I forgot about Jerome until Gabrielle just mentioned him. But I was young when his mother was fired and left."

He ran his hand up and down her back and she snuggled into him.

"I thought school would be better than being stuck at home, but it wasn't. I spent most of my time trying to just figure out what the hell was going on." She shuddered. "I was bullied because I was quiet. I was just anxious about saying the wrong thing. I knew the consequences of speaking up when I shouldn't. But the one good thing was music class. My music teacher seemed so gruff and ancient, but he was very kind. When he heard me sing, he encouraged me to join the choir. He would let me sneak into the music room at lunchtime and practice the guitar. It was the only thing that got me through. Until the night of the concert for choir. I was freaking out. I didn't think I could do it. My parents didn't even come."

"Bastards."

She shrugged. "I didn't much care. I got up there and I did it for my music teachers. Someone loaded a video of me singing online and it took off. I guess my parents even heard about it."

"And they decided you were their cash cow."

She winced. It was harsh but accurate. "I guess so. For a start, I was just so happy they were noticing me. I was no longer a burden. Someone to be ignored. I went along with everything they wanted."

"Even though you didn't want it."

"Stupid, huh?"

"Not stupid. You were starved for attention and affection. But why do you keep doing it?"

"I don't know. I support all of them. Except my brother. They need me."

"They don't need you. They use you. Time for them to stand on their own two feet."

"They like to remind me of how much they sacrificed for me. All the money they spent on therapists and tutors to make me normal. Sometimes if I push myself enough, it can stop me from thinking. It can stop me from stressing. I go numb. That's why I was running. The drugs kind of do the same thing, but I don't want to take them."

"Why do you keep supporting them? Why keep putting yourself through this for people who never cared about you?"

"I don't know. Out of a feeling of obligation. Or maybe loneliness. If I didn't have them, as awful as they are, who would I have?"

"You're not fucking alone anymore. You have me. And I would never use you. Never allow anyone to use you again."

"Before they arrived, I was coming to tell you. . .to ask you. . ."

"Spit it out, angel," he said in his usual blunt way.

"I was wondering if I could come with you when you go back to Montana," she rushed out. "I still have contracts to fulfill so there will be times I'd have to leave to do that. But maybe I could spend most of my time creating music, the way I always wanted."

"Nothing I would want more. But are you sure that's what you want? I don't want you giving up everything for me."

"I'd give it all up for you. Every last cent."

"Angel—"

"But the beauty of it is I don't have to. I don't want any of this. I want you, a small log cabin in the woods, and music, laughter, love. I want to be yours. In all ways. I want you as my man, my protector, my daddy."

She sucked in a breath. She'd laid it all out there. Was it really what he wanted too?

"Angel, nothing would make me happier to be all of those things, to love you for the rest of our lives."

She leaned up and kissed him.

"But you might want to see that log cabin in the woods before you agree to live there."

She narrowed her gaze. "It does have running water and an

indoor toilet, right?"

"Has all the modern amenities. But it ain't all that close to civilization."

"Yeah, well, civilization isn't all that it's cracked up to be. I can live without the lattes and bright lights. Can't live without you."

"Just don't want you to regret it—"

"I won't."

He studied her. "If you can't live there or you regret making the move then I'll move here with you."

Her eyes widened then she burst into laughter.

"That was a genuine offer. You weren't supposed to laugh."

"Sorry. Sorry. It's just. . .Bain, you hate it here."

"Yeah, and you might hate it there," he grumbled.

She shook her head. "I really don't think I will. As long as I have you, my music and a coffee machine, I'll be happy."

"Nobody will ever hide you away again. No one will ever treat you like you're less."

She leaned into him, letting him surround her with his safety and heat. "Larry is gonna be so pissed."

She looked up to see Bain grinning. It was a dark, wicked grin. "That's a bonus."

She giggled.

"I've got a better way of shutting off your brain than exhausting yourself."

She stared up at him curiously.

"Little Ari doesn't have to worry or stress or think about anything. Do anything. Well, other than obey Daddy. You're owed a punishment for pushing yourself so hard. That was a rule, wasn't it?"

"Yes, I'm sorry."

"If you're ever feeling anxious or worried or scared, come to me, Ari. You have me now. I'm always in your corner. I'll always fight for you. Got me? No more hurting yourself to cope."

She bit her lip. "I don't hurt myself."

He raised an eyebrow. "I've seen the marks you put on yourself. Pushing yourself into exhaustion is hurting yourself. You could fall off the treadmill and hit your head. You could injure yourself. You could become so exhausted that you faint. That's all stopping, Arianna. Which is why you're getting punished for breaking that rule."

She nodded.

"I think we'll take care of that right now."

"Now?" she squeaked.

"Yes. Now." He set her down then stood and held his hand down to her.

She took hold and let him help her up. He walked over to the door and locked it.

She licked her lips nervously. "Maybe we should go somewhere more private."

"Nobody can walk in. I think it's fitting your punishment should be here." He pointed at a weight bench behind her. "Pull down your pants and panties. Spread your legs as far as you can and then bend over and place your hands on the bench."

She licked her dry lips as he walked around the room, looking as though he was searching for something. When he picked up a wide-cut, rubber resistance band she blanched. He wouldn't.

He grabbed hold of both ends in one hand, so it was doubled over and whacked it against the palm of his hand.

"Not as much sting as a paddle but it will do nicely."

"Can't you just use your hand?"

"Not this time. Unless you're saying your safe word, get into place."

His voice was stern. Hard. And she knew then exactly how upset he was with her.

"I'm sorry I broke the rule about not pushing myself too much when running."

"I'm sorry too. But you know why I have to punish you, right?"

"I guess."

He walked over and cupped her chin, raising her face up. "I let this go, then you'll start to believe I'll let other things slide. You won't believe me when I say there are consequences for breaking a rule. You might do this again, thinking there won't be a punishment, not knowing exactly how much I love you and want you to be healthy and safe. Something might happen. You might collapse and hit your head and I might not be around. I want you safe, Ari. Always."

She leaned in and wrapped her arms around him. "I understand."

He kissed the top of her head. "Good girl. Now push your pants and panties down then turn and bend over for your spanking."

Christ. Even though she was nervous as hell, there was still a small part of her that was turned on by this. She guessed his dominance just did something for her. You'd have thought that after years of feeling out of control of her own life, of doing as she was told, she'd hate it. But the opposite was true. Because she knew everything he did was for her. Because he loved her. Wanted the best for her. Not because he was ashamed of her or because he wanted to use her.

She pulled her pants and panties down. He hadn't even slept with her, but he'd already seen her privates up close and personal.

"Nothing to be embarrassed about, angel. You're gorgeous. Now turn around and bend over."

She shuffled around and placed her hands on the workout bench before moving her legs apart as far as they would go with her pants caught around her ankles.

"Good girl. Not going to lecture you or count. Going to give you as many as I think you need. You'll get a hand spanking first then the rest with the resistance band, understand?"

"Yes."

"Say your safeword if anything becomes overwhelming or too painful. What is it?"

"Donkey."

"Good girl. Love you, Arianna. Want you safe. Want you to share what you need to with me. You don't need to deal with all the shit life throws you on your own. I'm here now. I've got big shoulders. I can take on as many demons as you need me to."

She knew that. But she wanted to tackle them together. "We can."

"We can," he agreed.

Then his hand landed on her butt and she let out an embarrassingly high-pitched squeal. But he didn't pause. His hand landed again. And again. It wasn't long until her bottom was hot and throbbing. Tears welled in her eyes, spilling down her cheeks. And this was only the first part of her punishment.

Holy shit.

She turned her head, staring into the mirror at the sight they made. The slight girl bent over the workout bench with her bare butt in the air, her face stained with tears.

Over her stood the sexy man. His hand swinging back, landing against her bare bottom. She was a direct contrast to him. Small where he was large. Pale to his dark. Fragile to his strength.

And yet, they seemed so perfect together. She couldn't imagine herself without him.

"I'd look away now, Ari," he rumbled.

She closed her eyes, directing her gaze down as the rubber resistance band hit her already burning ass cheeks.

Okay. That wasn't as bad as she'd thought.

Then it landed again. And again. And the sting became a burn. The burn became fire. Sobs wracked her body and she had to lean her forearms down on the bench to balance herself.

Finally, he stopped. But the fiery pain in her backside didn't dissipate one bit. Bain grabbed hold of her, swinging her up into his arms. He held her cradled against his chest, rocking her back and forth and placing kisses on her head.

"Angel, I love you. I love you."

Funny, she'd always imagined he'd have trouble saying those words to her. But he continued to say them over and over. He sat on the bench with her in his lap, turned into his chest so she was leaning on a hip rather than her aching butt.

She didn't know how long they sat there, with him holding her, soothing words being murmured to her quietly. But she started to stir when she realized she urgently needed the bathroom.

"I gotta pee."

Her mother would kill her if she ever heard her say that. But she was tired of worrying about what her mother thought.

He stood her up between his open legs and dressed her like one might a small child. She rubbed at her eyes. God, she was exhausted. She winced at the feel of spandex over her poor butt. It felt like the darn thing had doubled in size and the damned spandex seemed to hold the heat in.

"Ouch."

"Sorry, baby girl. Soon as we get into the bathroom, you can take them back off."

She nodded, cuddling in as he picked her up in his arms

He held her carefully, like one might a new-born babe.

She was even more precious to him. She meant everything. And she was his. He couldn't believe she was willing to give this all up for him.

Weren't you willing to do the same for her?

Yeah. He'd do whatever was necessary to keep her. Even if that meant staying here.

He set her down in her bathroom, and crouched before her, undoing her sneakers. "Hold onto my shoulders, angel."

She held on as he first took off her sneakers and socks then drew down her pants and panties. Then he turned and put the plug in the bath, before turning on the taps.

"Go potty, little bit. I'll be back in a minute." He went and gathered up some pajamas for her to get dressed into. When he returned, she was washing her hands. She'd pulled her panties back up but left her pants off. He didn't blame her. The spandex wouldn't feel too nice against her hot ass.

"Daddy, it's not bedtime yet."

"You're tired. I thought you could have a bath and get into your jammies. I'll get us some dinner and we can make a nest in front of the T.V. in your bedroom, eat our dinner and relax."

"Oh." A smile crossed her face. "That sounds perfect actually."

He kissed her lightly. "Have you got any bubbles?"

"Of course! Can't have a bath without bubbles! I gots some bubble bath in here." She opened the cupboard doors and pulled out a big container of strawberry-scented bubble bath. He took it from her and poured some in the bath.

"More, Daddy! More!"

"I think that's enough," he said firmly, putting the container away. He noticed that her lower lip was poking out and he gave it a light tap with his finger. "Put that away. I don't want to lose you in all the bubbles, do I? You might slip on out of my grasp if there are too many bubbles."

"Silly Daddy. I can't slip out of the bath."

"Let's get you stripped out of these clothes." He reached for her tank top. She bit her lip, but she didn't say anything as he took off her top and bra. He made certain not to stare at her bare breasts for too long. Which wasn't easy. They were plump and topped with pink nipples that he longed to take into his mouth.

And he was pretty certain he'd been wrong. They weren't fake at all.

He drew down her panties before testing the temperature of the bath water and turning off the taps. He looked at her hair. "Got a tie for your hair, little bit?"

She nodded and pointed to a drawer. He drew out a dark blue tie. "All right, turn around."

She gave him a skeptical look. "Do you know how to do hair, Daddy?"

"Daddy knows everything." Not really.

But she turned dutifully, giving him quite the eyeful of her gorgeous ass which was pink from her spanking.

He managed to get her hair up into some sort of loose ponytail. It looked terrible, but it would keep the majority of her hair out of the water.

Grabbing hold of her, he lifted her into the bath.

She winced as she sat down and immediately moved onto her knees. "Ouchie."

"Poor baby," he crooned. "Have you got a sore bottom?

"You're the one who made it sore, Daddy," she said accusingly.

"Because you deserved it." He tapped her nose warningly. "Got any toys to play with?"

He reached into the cupboard and picked up one of the wash-cloths he'd spotted, wetting it in the bath.

She bit her lip. "Umm, there might be a rubber ducky and some other squirty toys. They're in a small basket with a lid on it."

He drew the basket out. You'd never know what was in there unless you went through her stuff. He opened the lid and then poured the toys into the bath. She let out a surprised squeal as the toys hit, splashing up water.

"Daddy!" she said with a laugh. But her embarrassment was gone.

He started washing her with the cloth, aware of the way she

tensed. He got it. This was her first time being completely naked with him. But he was going to show her she had nothing to be ashamed about.

She was beautiful. She was his. If she let him, he'd do this for her every day for the rest of their lives.

"So do your bath toys have names?" he asked to distract her.

She giggled. "No, Daddy."

"Well, why not? Maybe we should name them. How about Ducky, Flippy and Slippy?"

"Those are silly names." But she relaxed and started to play as he moved the cloth down her back.

"That was my best work," he protested as he washed her arms.

"Hmm, you can do better."

"Why you cheeky monkey." He started tickling her. She giggled, splashing water at him. By the time, he pulled back, his T-shirt was soaked.

He drew his T-shirt off, aware of her small gasp. He had to grin. He admitted he liked the way she stared at him. With awe and no tiny amount of arousal in her eyes. But he needed to get her clean and settled in her room. She needed more food than that protein bar she'd eaten. She also needed him to look after her. To show her care after how her parents treated her.

"Lie back, baby, so I can clean your front and legs."

She bit her lip but lay back without a word. He started at her feet. "Daddy, no more tickling."

"No more tickling, I promise. What movie do you want to watch?"

"I dunno. We can watch what you want to watch, Daddy." He moved the cloth up towards her pussy. Without giving her a chance to worry about it, he wiped it between her folds. Then he placed one hand under her lower back and lifted her bottom up so he could slide the cloth between her cheeks.

It was all done quickly and without a word.

"Daddy!" she let out a protest.

"Yes?" He threw the cloth in the hamper and picked up a towel.

"I...you...you just cleaned my butt!"

He had to grin. "You don't usually wash your butt?"

"What...yes...I mean...oh dear Lord."

"Come on, little bit. Out you get. Let's get you dried. Then you can pick what movie to watch."

THEY ENDED up settling on *Despicable Me*. One of her favorites. Bain set up what he called a nest. Which was a pile of pillows and blankets on the bedroom floor. She lay on them, under the duvet from her bed and he fed her little tidbits of food that he'd collected from the kitchen. There was cheese, crackers, meat, grapes and even a few bits of chocolate.

About halfway through the movie, she felt her eyelids drifting closed. She yawned and tried to force herself to stay awake. Bain got up and grabbed her sleep sack, laying it out on her bed.

"Come on. Time for sleep." He led her into the bathroom and helped her get ready. She climbed into her sleep sack and he grabbed her quilt, putting it over her.

Bain brushed his lips across her forehead. "Go to sleep, little bit."

"I don't want you to leave."

"I'll stay here as long as you want me to. I'm not planning on going anywhere. Never again." He climbed into bed next to her.

She snuggled in against him and he wrapped an arm around her. "I've never slept with anyone before."

"I'm glad to be your first then. Go to sleep, angel. I'm right here, watching over you."

20

She woke up alone, surprised to see she'd slept in. Had Bain stayed the night as promised?

Of course, he did. Bain always did what he said he would. She rolled to her side and caught a hint of his scent. Yum, delicious.

With another stretch, she stood and walked into the bathroom to pee and brush her teeth. When she walked back into the bedroom, she was surprised to see Bain lying on her bed. A tray of food sat in front of him.

"Good morning," she said quietly, taking him in. He was shirtless. His gorgeous, cut chest on display with rippling abs. A thin line of hair led down into his sweatpants.

Oh Lord. Was he trying to kill her? Seriously. She felt like she was about to self-combust.

"Hi, yourself," he murmured back with a heated look in his eyes. "Sleep okay?"

"Better than okay. I can't remember the last time I slept so good."

"That so? Wonder why that was."

She walked slowly forward then picked up the tray of food, noticing the bowls of muesli and strawberry yogurt. Along with two glasses of orange juice and some blueberry muffins.

Yummy.

But not what she felt like eating right now. She set the tray down on her bedside table and then climbed onto the bed.

Bain lay on his back, one hand tucked behind his head. But he watched her every move, his eyes devouring her.

"Hmm, I wonder. Maybe it was because for the first time ever I didn't sleep alone."

His eyes narrowed into slits. "Is that right? You think you'd sleep as good with just anyone?"

She straddled his hips with her legs then tapped her chin, pretending to ponder that. "I don't know. I suppose I could test that out. Find someone else to sleep with me tonight. Compare snuggle buddies."

He flipped her over and she cried out with surprise as suddenly he was lying between her spread legs, his hips pressed against hers, his forearms resting on the bed on either side of her, supporting his weight so he didn't crush her.

He wasn't a small guy.

"I'm the only damn snuggle buddy you'll ever have," he growled.

She had to bite her lip at those words to stop the surge of laughter. He must have spotted the amusement on her face. He shook his head. "Brat."

"Your brat."

"You are. All fucking mine." Leaning in, he kissed her. Devoured her. She wasn't sure how long he kissed her for, but by the time he pulled back her breath was coming fast, her insides burning with need.

"Bain," she murmured. "Please."

"You want more, Ari? You want me to touch you? Pleasure you?"

"God yes. Please. So much."

"You sure? We can do as little or as much as you're comfortable with."

"I want it all."

He groaned. "Fuck. Have you got any protection?"

"Oh. No." She bit her lip. "Do we need it? I have an implant."

"Damn. You're killing me here. I'm clean, baby. We get check-ups regularly and I always use condoms."

"Oh, I am too. I haven't had sex in a long time."

"Nothing I want more than to take you bare but are you certain? We can do other things. Fun things. If you're not ready to take this step."

Not ready? Was he insane? She was more than ready. "I want you, Bain. Please. Take me. Claim me. Make me yours."

"You already are. Ain't anything going to change that."

But he slid his mouth down to her chest, tugging at the neckline of her tank top. He drew it down over her breasts, freeing them to his gaze.

"Fucking prettiest breasts, I've ever seen." He scraped his teeth over her nipple, and she arched up, crying out. The sensation of his teeth against her sensitive nipple was almost too much. Just this side of pain.

And she fucking loved it.

He moved to her other nipple, but rather than giving it the same treatment, he sucked the tight nub into his mouth, then ran the flat of his tongue over it.

"Bain. Bain, please."

He sat on his knees and pulled her up, drawing her top off. "Please, what?"

Christ, she didn't know. *Please don't stop. Please give me more.*

She wanted it all. She wanted to lose herself in him. Already her mind was clouded in a fog of arousal.

"Please more," she finally managed to get out.

"You only had to ask."

Well, if she'd known that she might have asked a long time ago. He drew her bottoms down, pulling them off, leaving her completely naked. His gaze took her in, studying her until she started to feel slightly self-conscious.

"Bain? I..."

"Fucking beautiful," he muttered. He ran his finger down between her breasts, over her tummy to her mound. "I don't always have the right words, angel. Probably never will. But just know you're the most gorgeous thing I've seen in my life. And a lifetime of having you won't ever be enough."

She thought those words were perfect.

"Want you sitting up," he told her gruffly, reaching for her hands to help her sit. "Shuffle back so you're leaning against the headboard. Hands up, grabbing hold of the top."

She leaned against the padded, velvet headboard and reaching back with her hands.

"Keep your hands there," he commanded.

Her heart raced. She'd never had someone take control in the bedroom. Then again, she didn't exactly have a lot of sexual experience.

"You okay, angel?" he asked.

"Uhh, yeah, like I told you, I don't have a lot of, umm, experience. With sex," she added lamely. "I only had sex once, and it was bad. So bad. I didn't even get to come. It was over in a few pumps. Not that I actually wanted much more, 'cause it was kind of sore and the grunting noises he made were weird and I'm gonna shut up now," she said as he gaped at her.

"It was sore? Did he make you come first? Did he ensure that you were nice and wet and ready for him?"

She knew she was bright red. Just knew it. "I. . .umm. . .no."

"Fucking bastard." He studied her for a moment. "Don't worry, baby. You're going to be ready for me. I'll make sure of that. You okay with me taking control? We can go slower. Like I said before, we can go as far as you are comfortable with."

"Oh, I'm comfortable with it all," she blurted out. "More than comfortable. I want this. Badly. I just don't want you to be disappointed."

He snorted. "Not a fucking chance in hell. I'll be fucking ecstatic if all you're comfortable with is me eating you out."

"You. . .you want to do. . .that?"

"Fuck. Yes."

"What if I don't like it?"

"Pretty sure you will, but if there's ever anything you don't like, you just tell me. Or you say your safeword, got it? I'll stop. But baby, I hope to fuck you like this because there is nothing, I want more than to bury my tongue in your pussy."

"Ohh. . .well, I'd quite like to try that."

He grinned and just shook his head. "Bend your knees for me. And put your feet flat on the mattress. Spread them nice and wide. Fuck, yes, baby. You follow instructions so beautifully. Do you know how fucking hard I am for you?"

"No. Could you show me?"

She really wanted to see how hard he was. Even more to touch him. Maybe she should take him into her mouth. She'd never done it before, but it couldn't be that hard, right?

"Soon, angel. Keep your hands and legs where they are, understand? No moving or you'll have to be punished."

Her heart raced even faster at the thought. But then he lay down on the mattress, his head between her open legs. He used his fingers to part her lower lips then ran his tongue along her slick folds, circling the tight nub at the top before pressing his tongue over her entrance. Again, and again. Until she was trembling from need, her breath coming in sharp pants.

She had a tight grip on the headboard as he finally penetrated her with his tongue. His thumb moved to her clit, flicking it gently as he drove his tongue in and out of her passage. Her orgasm built. She was so close.

She cried out as he replaced his tongue with two fingers.

"Please! Please!"

"Do you need to come, angel?" he crooned.

"Yes. Yes, please!"

"Then come for me." He circled her clit with his tongue slowly. Too slowly. Then he flicked it firmly. His fingers moved in and out of her passage and she screamed, clenching down, her orgasm washing through her with a ferocity that was almost terrifying. She had never felt anything like this before. Hadn't even known it was possible to feel this amazing.

"Good girl," he murmured, kissing her inner thigh. "Fuck, you taste delicious. And those sounds you make when you come, I'm gonna hear those in my dreams."

She bit down on her lip. Maybe she should be embarrassed by that. But she wasn't.

"You can let go of the headboard now," he told her as he stood and started stripping off his sweatpants. "Still want to keep going?"

She nodded. Oh yes. She wanted more. She was feeling decidedly greedy. She watched as he drew down his jeans and boxers, revealing a thick, long cock. He was erect, the fat head glistened with pre-cum. She licked her lips as she crawled to the end of the bed.

"Can I taste you?" she asked.

"You sure you want to do that? You don't have to. It isn't something you have to do just because I had my mouth on you. 'Cause, baby, after tasting you I can tell you I'll be wanting to do that every day."

"You do?" She glanced up at him in shock.

His eyes were set at half-mast and he took hold of his cock, moving his hand up and down the thick shaft. "Hell, yes. You are fucking delicious. You just became my favorite treat."

"Bain!" she protested

Secretly, though, she kind of liked it.

He continued to pump his hand up and down his thick shaft. All that gorgeous skin on display made heat rush through her body. She wanted to touch every inch. To taste him. To lick her way down those abs to where that small trail of hair led to his shaft.

"I want to taste you," she said firmly.

He stepped closer and held his cock for her. "Then taste me, angel."

She ran her tongue over the fat head. "Tell me what to do."

"Not much you can do wrong, baby." He wrapped his hand in her long hair. "Just take it nice and slow to start. That's it. Lick me. Explore. Fuck yes, baby girl. You got it."

She licked her way down his shaft, learning the feel of him, delighting in his taste, his scent.

"Now take just the head into your mouth and suck. Fuck. So damn good. Your mouth is so hot and wet. That's it. Take more of me. Nice and slow. You don't do anything you don't want to. You never do anything again you don't want to do, you hear me?"

She knew he wasn't talking about just sex. She hummed her agreement and he groaned. "God, baby. That feels fucking good."

It did? Hmm. Good to know.

"The vibration when you do that is fucking amazing. Make as much noise as you like. Yeah, that's it. Now look up at me. Fuck."

She glanced up, met his dark gaze with her own, saw the tension in his neck and jaw, the heat in his gaze and it added to her own pleasure. She took as much of him as deep as she could. He still had his hand wrapped around the base of his shaft and she knew she'd never take all of him.

She moved slowly back up his shaft. Then she swirled her tongue around the head.

"That's it. Jesus. You're too fucking good at that." She took him in deep once more, a bit faster, sucking harder and then she let out a hum of enjoyment, smiling as he cursed.

Oh yeah. A girl could get addicted to this sort of power. She continued to play with him, even feeling brave enough to lightly touch his balls with her hand. His hips started to thrust, his hand in her hair tightening. He tugged on her hair and she looked up at him once more.

"Enough, baby. Enough. I don't want to come in your mouth."

She pouted. Well, why not?

He tapped her lower lip. "Don't pout. Next time, I promise. But right now, I want to come in your pussy, and I don't want to fucking wait. Get onto your back."

Okay. She guessed she could live with that. She rolled onto her back and he grabbed some of the cushions they'd used for their nest last night. He slid them under her hips, propping her up so she was at the perfect height for him to take her while standing up. He grasped hold of his cock in one hand and held her hip with the other while he pressed his cock inside her.

"Tell me if anything hurts," he gritted out. It was obvious he was trying hard to go slow and she appreciated it. Really, she did.

But right now, she didn't want slow. She wanted fast. Hard. Furious.

She wrapped her legs around the back of his hips and tugged him closer, thankful for all those workouts that had given her strong thigh muscles.

"Arianna!" he snapped. "I'm trying not to hurt you."

"You're not going to," she told him. "Unless it's from you going too slow. Please, Bain. I need you inside me."

He glowered down at her. "We do this at my pace."

"But your pace is so slow." She raised her hips up, taking more of him inside her. Their groans mingled together.

"Little brat, your butt is going to pay for that," he warned her in a dark voice.

Bring. It. On.

He grabbed hold of her hips and pressed himself deep. She let out a sigh of satisfaction. So damn good. He pulled back. Thrust in again. His pace grew faster. Harder. His face was dark. Intense. It might have scared her if she didn't know him so well.

He drew his cock free and she let out a cry. "No! Come back."

He shook his head and grasped her by the waist, pulling her up and turning her. "Bend over the pillows. Feet wide apart. Rest your weight on your forearms."

She bent over, spreading her legs wide as she rested on the cushions. He pressed his cock inside her. She let out a whimper. Felt so good. So fucking good. His pace was faster this time.

"Reach down and touch yourself, angel," he commanded, his hands once more around her hips, driving her back onto his cock. Fuck, she'd never felt so full, so on fire in her life.

"W-what?" she asked, certain she'd misheard him.

"Touch yourself."

"I can't do that," she said, shocked.

"You can. I want you to come when I do."

"But...but..."

"You got a problem touching yourself, baby? Don't you masturbate?"

"Do we have to have this conversation right now? Or ever?"

"Yep. Because I want you to touch your clit and make yourself come." He gave her ass a slap. Then another one. The sting was sharp and deep. "Touch yourself, Arianna."

She couldn't believe she was doing this. She reached down, though, and circled her swollen clit with her finger.

Ohhh. That felt so good.

"Fuck, yes. That's it, baby. Clench down on me. I'm going to come soon." Smack! His other hand landed on her left cheek and it was all she needed to set her off. She soared over the edge, her pussy rippling around his wide cock.

"Fuck!" he roared as he sank deep, his weight partially resting on her as he slid forward, catching himself on his arms.

She trembled with aftershocks, her pussy still pulsating, his cock still seated deep. He nipped at her neck, making her giggle. "Damn, baby. You are spectacular."

She really wasn't. But it was nice he thought so. He stood then slid free, leaving her empty. Then he turned her, picking her up and holding her against him, one arm under her bottom as he kissed her. He drew back and smiled down at her. That look he gave her was soft. Sweet. Not things you'd normally associate with Bain.

At least, not unless you knew him well.

And even then, she had this feeling that look . . . that look was hers alone.

21

She looked at the message on her phone and set it down with a sigh.

"Who was it this time?" Bain asked from where he sat across the kitchen counter from her, finishing off a mammoth sandwich. Her own sandwich lay mostly untouched on the plate in front of her.

"My sister. Again. Wondering when I'm going to put some more money in her account." She worried at her bottom lip. Her phone had been going non-stop this morning ever since she'd decided to call Larry and tell him that he was fired. She'd explained her plan to move to Montana with Bain, to take her career on a different path. To say he hadn't taken it well had been an exaggeration. He'd screamed so loudly that Bain had actually taken her phone off her and hung up on him. That had been about an hour ago.

Since then, her phone had been going non-stop with messages from her family. All of them growing increasingly more irate. Larry must have contacted them as soon as Bain hung up on him. She'd also called Caleb, before Bain had dragged her away from her office to have some lunch. He'd been guarded in his response, but she knew that was simply because he was worried about her. Because he wanted her to be happy.

She'd arranged for all of them, including the princes, to come over for dinner tomorrow night. That, at least, was something to look forward to. Unlike the upcoming confrontation with her family, because she knew she wouldn't be able to ignore them forever.

"You don't need to feel guilty about not bank-rolling them any longer," he said.

She raised her gaze to his. "I know."

"Your sister can get a job. You said that you bought her an apartment in L.A. so it's not like she's homeless."

All true.

She'd also bought her parents some ostentatious mansion.

"They need to learn to fend for themselves and not depend on you."

"I know."

"Then why do you sound so unhappy? You changed your mind about moving to Sanctuary with me?"

"What? No, of course not." She grabbed hold of his hand. "I want to do that. More than anything. Guess it's just ingrained in me to feel guilty, to feel like I owe them all something."

"You don't," he growled. "Anyone owes someone, it's them owing you for the way they've treated you all these years."

He was right. Of course he was right.

"I'll need to talk to them at some stage."

"Why don't you forget about all of that for a few hours? Turn off your phone. I have something for you. Got Dominic to pick it up this morning."

"Ooh, what is it?"

"Something that might help you relax. And stop worrying."

She clapped her hands. "Can I have it now?"

"No," he replied. "You can have it after you eat your lunch." He looked pointedly down at her sandwich.

She wrinkled her nose. "Not that hungry."

"Five bites. Big bites. Then you can have your present."

She sighed. That didn't seem fair.

"We can sit here all day until you eat it, little bit."

He wouldn't! Oh yeah, from the firm look on his face it seemed like he would. With a sigh, she took as small a bite as she dared. The sandwich he'd made her was actually pretty good, so she ended up eating half of it before setting it down.

"Ready!"

He shook his head, but he gave her an indulgent smile. "All right. It's in my room. Go wait in your bedroom and I'll get it." With a squeal, she jumped down and raced off to her bedroom, leaving her phone behind.

"No running," he barked. "Or you'll get a red bottom instead of your gift."

Oops. Well, that wouldn't do.

TWO HOURS LATER, she stepped back, looking at her masterpiece. It was missing something. It seemed too small for the space.

Hmm.

She looked down at the window crayons Bain had bought her. He was right. This had given her the break she needed. Concentrating on her piece of art on the window had slowly driven out all thoughts of her awful family and Larry. Her mother would be horrified if she could see the mess she'd made on the window.

Ari just grinned.

She tapped her chin. What did it need, though? The huge window in her bedroom was now covered in a picture of someone sitting under a tree, playing a guitar. Of course, she was no great artist, so it was a pretty simple picture.

Which is why it needed to be...

"Bigger!" she squealed. "That's it. I need to go up. I need something to stand on."

Bain had left her about ten minutes ago when his phone started ringing. She hadn't paid too much attention. She knew he wouldn't be long. She didn't want to leave to go find a ladder. She wasn't even sure she owned a ladder.

She looked over at the armchair in the corner of the room. Perfect. She strode over and grabbed hold of it, dragging it in front of the window. Darn thing was heavier than it looked. Grabbing a blue crayon, she started the top of the picture. She was so busy concentrating, she didn't even notice the door to her room opening.

"Ari! What do you think you are doing!"

She jumped, wobbling on the chair and probably would have fallen, had Bain not grabbed her by the waist and set her on her feet.

"Daddy! You frightened me!"

"I frightened you! What did you think you were doing standing on that chair?"

"I had to get up higher. My picture needed a sky." She thought it was pretty obvious why she'd been on the chair.

"What if you'd fallen? You could have hurt yourself."

The only risk of falling was when he'd given her a fright. But she decided it was best not to say that.

"Daddy, I wouldn't have fallen. And even if I did, it wasn't like I was high up in the air. I wouldn't have hurt myself."

"You don't know that. You could have broken your arm or leg. You could have hit your head. Furniture is not to be climbed on. You should have waited for me. I would have gotten a ladder and supervised you while you stood on it."

"I don't need supervision."

"That's where you're wrong, little bit. You obviously need more supervision than you've been getting."

"Daddy, you're over-reacting."

He crossed his arms over his chest and glowered down at her. Uh-oh. She bit her lower lip. "You got that look, Daddy."

"What look?"

"That look like you gonna start scolding, but I think I was already scolded enough. When you look like that, you reminds me of Shrek."

His eyes widened. Hmm. Okay, maybe she should have thought about what she was saying before she blurted that all out.

"Is that so?"

"Yeah, he was all grumpy and blustery on the outside. But on the inside, he was all squishy. Like you."

"I'm squishy?" He ran a hand over his face before letting out a bark of laughter. Then he surprised her by dragging her against him.

She leaned back and grinned at him. "Super squishy."

"Just gets worse," he muttered. Then his face grew stern. "No more getting up on furniture."

"Fine." She sighed.

She squealed as he leaned her over his left hip, his arm around her waist so she was bent over. He laid a series of smacks to her ass. They were hard and fast and over almost before she'd drawn breath to protest.

He stood her back up, his hands on her shoulders to hold her steady.

"What was that for?" she demanded.

"Just thought it seemed like something an ogre would do." His eyes twinkled with humor and she groaned. "Now, enough crayons today, I think."

"But Daddy, I'm not finished."

"You can do something else for a while." He picked up the chair and slid it back. "This chair is far too heavy for you to be moving."

She resisted rolling her eyes at his overprotectiveness. Just.

"What can I do now?" She looked out the window with a sigh. "I wish we could go to the playground."

"What's your favorite thing to do at the playground?"

"Swings, of course." Wasn't that everyone's favorite?

He slipped his arms around her from behind. "One day you'll be able to go play on the swings. Just not at the moment with this guy still out there."

She sighed. "What if we never know who it is?" That's what truly scared her. That she'd always have to worry about this threat hanging over her.

"That's not going to happen. I know we don't have any real leads. But he'll slip up."

"Maybe he's disappeared. Maybe seeing you guys around me scared him off," she said hopefully.

"Perhaps. Things will be easier at Sanctuary. You'll be able to have more freedom to move around. No one will get to you there."

She pulled back so she could look up at him. "Who called you?"

"Oh, I've got someone doing some work at the cabin."

"What?"

He tapped her nose. "You'll see, nosy."

A knock at the door had her turning. Bain walked over and opened it. Dominic said something to him quietly that had her man turning towards her with a frown on his face. "Dominic said your sister is here. She wants to talk to you."

She rubbed her forehead. "Oh. That's just awesome." She guessed she should have known that someone would turn up when she'd ignored them all day. She'd just hoped they would give her more time. "I guess I'll go talk to her."

She gave Dominic a small smile.

"I'll have her wait in your office, sweetheart," he told her warmly.

"Thank you."

Bain drew her into his arms, squeezing her tight. "I'll come talk to her with you."

"No. Thank you, but I've got to deal with my family at some stage." She did let him hold her for a while, though. Gabrielle could just wait. Finally, she drew back and took a deep breath.

Time to put on her big girl panties.

When she walked into the office, her sister was sitting behind her desk.

"Gaby?"

"It's Gabrielle, not Gaby."

"Right. Sorry."

"Surprised you agreed to see me. Did you need permission from your new boyfriend?"

"What are you talking about? Of course, I don't need to get permission from Bain. Why would I?"

"He's calling all the shots now, isn't he?" Gabrielle sneered. "Don't lie and tell us it's not because of him that you're moving to some dinky little cabin in the middle of nowhere."

Arianna sighed. "If you're only here to pick a fight then you need to leave. I know you're all upset with me for giving up my career—"

"You're so selfish, Arianna! Of course, we're upset. This affects all of us and you couldn't even call us to let us know. We had to hear about it from your agent."

"I was going to call you, but before I could, you and mother started sending me those awful messages."

"How can you do this to us, Arianna? We'll all be destitute."

Anger stirred in her gut. "Destitute? You're hardly going to be destitute. How much did that apartment I bought you cost? Over a million dollars, right? Sell it and you'll be set for years. Or better, yet, how about you actually get a job and support yourself. I bought mother and father a house. You've all had plenty from me over the years. You could have saved some of that money I gave you, instead you spent it on expensive trips with your boy-toys. Do you know the last time I had a vacation?"

Gabrielle looked taken aback. Arianna just glared at her. But inside, she felt lighter. As though a weight had been lifted off her. It was well past time she stood up for herself. That she forced them all to stop leeching off her.

"You make it sound like we were using you."

"You have been! That's exactly what you've been doing."

"Well, you let us. You've done it for years. Why?"

"Why?" It was a good question. "Because you were my family. I love you. And I guess I thought that if you all needed me then you might love me back. I get that this is my fault as well. I should have told you all a long time ago that this wasn't what I wanted. I hate doing concerts. I hate being in the limelight. I shouldn't have to support you all. It's not my job to do that. And you should love me regardless of what I do for you."

"You're so fucking weird, Arianna. Normal people don't think like this." Gabrielle scowled at her. But there was something in her gaze. Something like understanding.

Or maybe it was just wishful thinking.

"I...I have to go." Then her sister turned and stormed out of the room. Ari watched after her with a sigh. Then she slumped into the sofa, her legs hardly able to keep her up. She was so exhausted all of a sudden.

"Angel? You okay?"

She ran a shaky hand over her face as Bain walked into the room and crouched in front of her.

"No? Yes? Do you know, I'm really not sure how I feel? It felt good to tell her all that stuff, at the same time I'm not sure that she'll

ever speak to me again. I love her. But sometimes, I also hate her."
Tears dripped down her cheeks and he sat next to her, pulling her
onto his lap. "Why couldn't they just love me for who I am? Why
was I only worthy of being a Silvers when there was something I
could do for them? I just don't understand why I was so unlovable."

"You weren't," he told her harshly. "You hear me? That little
girl was not unlovable and the woman in my arms is most definitely worthy of love. I love you. And I swore I was never going to
love anyone again. Yet, you wormed your way into my heart."

She sniffled. "See you're a squishy, sweet ogre."

"Good Lord," he muttered. "Don't tell any of the other Littles at
Sanctuary that you call me an ogre. The name will catch on and
I'll never hear the end of it."

She grinned up at him. Oh, now she definitely had to let it slip.

He shook his head. "I'm in such trouble, aren't I?"

She nodded her head. Then her smile dropped as she thought
of another worry. "Will they like me?"

"The other Littles?"

"Yeah. I'm not used to interacting with other people much. I
don't really have any other friends—"

"No friends? So those three big bastards that flew halfway
around the world because you didn't answer your phone, what are
they?"

"Oh...well... Caleb is my friend and I guess Wolfe and Aleki
are too."

"You guess?"

"But they accept me as I am. They've known me for years.
They know I can be a bit different—"

"I know your mother tried to teach you that different is wrong.
That you had to fall into some sort of mold to be accepted. Not
true. There is nothing wrong with you. You're strong. You're smart.
Definitely creative. Sometimes a little crazy. But you're also scarily

kind. Scary, because you'd give everything of yourself if someone else asked for it."

"Just as well I've got a big, bad Daddy who'll make sure I don't do that anymore, huh?"

"Yeah? Where is he? Sounds like a good-looking guy."

"Hmm. I'm not sure. Are ogres considered good-looking?"

"Brat!" He laid her back on the sofa and started to tickle her mercilessly. He tickled her until she was snorting, trying to curl into herself in order to protect herself.

"Mercy! Mercy!" she cried.

He drew his hands away then pulled her onto his lap, taking hold of her chin to tilt her face up. He kissed her gently. Slowly. It was delicious. She drew back and opened her mouth just as she heard a loud noise coming from Bain's phone. He immediately jumped up and raced towards the foyer. She ran after him, noting Dominic racing down the other passage. Bain opened the door right as the elevator door slid shut.

"Ari, get back inside. Dom!"

"I've got her, go!" Dominic yelled back, tugging her back into the apartment as Bain raced towards the stairs.

Her breath came in fast pants as Dominic shut the door, locking it.

"What's going on? What happened!"

"Someone entered the foyer without our knowledge," Dominic said grimly. He reached down and using the bottom of his T-shirt, picked up a white envelope. "The alarm went off. Had it set to our phones."

"Someone? Like the stalker? Did he leave that? Oh God, and Bain's gone after him alone!"

She moved to open the door and Dominic wrapped his arm around her waist, setting the envelope down on the foyer table. "Ari! What do you think you are doing?"

"Bain's out there with the stalker alone! What if he gets hurt? We need to help him."

Dominic turned her, grasping her by the shoulders. His face was stern, something she'd never seen from the other man.

"You, little miss, are going nowhere."

Her eyes widened at his cold, commanding tone. Where had easy-going, understanding Dominic gone?

"Take a step towards that door and I'll lock you in your bedroom."

"You would not!"

"I would. Just try me."

"But Bain—"

"Can take care of himself. The worst thing for him right now, would be for you to race out there and get yourself hurt. This is his job. We are trained for this. You are not."

She glared up at Dominic. But she knew he was right. He must have seen something in her face because he eased up his hold on her.

"Ari, I let you get hurt and I'm a dead man."

She bit her lip. "What if he gets hurt?"

"Bain? Sweetheart, have you seen your man? He's built like a tank."

Didn't mean he couldn't get hurt. What if her stalker had a gun?

Dominic's phone made that same high-pitched noise and she jumped in fright. Her heart was racing so fast she thought she might be ill. Dominic moved to the small panel by the door which displayed a camera view of the foyer. They both saw Bain standing there, scowling.

Bain made some gesture with his hand and Dominic unlocked the door. As soon as he was inside, she threw herself at him. He caught her against his chest, rubbing his hand up and down her back.

"Angel, you okay? You're shaking."

"She was worried about you," Dominic told him dryly.

"About me? Why?"

"Because you chased after that guy without any sort of back-up." She drew away to frown up at him.

"She would have gone after you herself if I'd have let her," Dominic told him.

Bain's face filled with thunder and she glared over at Dominic. "You're a tattletale."

"I'd want to know if my Little was going to put herself in danger."

Bain grasped hold of her chin, tilting her face up. "Listen to me. You never, ever put yourself in danger, understand me? Especially not for me. I'm trained for this stuff."

"Yeah, that's what Dominic said," she said reluctantly.

"If you'd chased after me, you wouldn't have sat for a week."

Ouch.

Bain straightened. "Bastard seemed to disappear. I got down to the foyer but, elevator was empty. He leave us anything?"

"Yep," Dominic said. "It's on the table. I'll get some gloves and a bag for it."

She felt ill as she stared at the envelope. Dominic returned with his hands gloved and started to carefully open the envelope with a knife.

"Sure you want to see inside?" Bain asked her.

She nodded. She couldn't not know what it said.

Dominic pulled out the note and they crowded around to read it.

DON'T THINK *you can hide from me, songbird. I can always find you. I'll always come for you.*

. . .

"WHAT? WHAT DOES THAT MEAN?" she asked. "Does that mean he knows I'm planning on leaving? But how would he know that?"

"Don't read anything into it," Bain told her while Dominic bagged the note and envelope. "Could be because you've been keeping inside the apartment lately and he hasn't seen you."

Who was this guy? How did he keep getting so close to her apartment?

"I'll go down and talk to Rob. You get her settled," Dominic said to Bain.

Bain nodded and took the bag from him. He made certain the door was locked after Dominic left and the alarm was set.

"Get me settled? How am I meant to settle after this? You shouldn't have run after him! What if he'd had a gun!"

"Angel, this is what I'm trained to do. Guard you. I was a Navy SEAL. I know what I'm doing." He led her into her office and put the plastic bag down on her desk, by her laptop. Then he pulled her over to the sofa, drawing her onto his lap.

She wrapped her arms around him. "I don't want anything to happen to you."

He ran his hand up and down her back. "Nothing will happen to me. Sure as shit nothing will happen to you."

He held her until she stopped trembling, the adrenaline spike draining away, leaving her feeling awful.

Dominic appeared in the doorway. He was scowling. "Head of security is a fucking joke."

Her mouth dropped open. She'd never heard Dominic swear and this was as close to losing his temper as she'd ever seen.

"What? He wouldn't let you see the camera footage?" Bain asked.

"Said he'll set it up and let me see it when it's ready. Wouldn't surprise me if he fiddled with it."

"Think he could be our guy?" Bain asked.

"No way," Arianna said. "Rob is a weasel, but he wouldn't do that."

"He has access," Bain pointed out. "Would explain how this guy is getting up here. Also, how he disappeared on me as he would have access to all the floors on this building. He's tried to obstruct us at every turn. Either he's just an incompetent asshole or he's our guy. Just cause his record is squeaky clean doesn't mean he's not guilty."

"Well, the fucker doesn't know about the other camera we put in." Dominic walked out of the room.

"Will it have caught anything?" she asked.

"Hopefully," he told her. "Don't worry. Going to catch this asshole. Not going to let him do anything to harm you."

She knew he wouldn't.

Dominic returned with a large laptop. He set it down on her desk. "You gonna call the cops about that note?"

"Yeah. I'll give the detective we dealt with a call. Let him know."

"Here's the fucker." Dominic leaned in to watch the video. She moved around behind him, Bain standing over her.

A guy in a black hoodie slipped out of the elevator. She looked at the time stamp on the video. About fifteen minutes ago.

He moved quickly to the door, his head down and hidden. Frustration filled her. There was nothing new from this angle.

"There. See there."

She frowned, leaning it to see where Dominic was pointing.

"Is that a tattoo on his hand?" she asked.

"It sure is," Dominic said with satisfaction.

"Is that really going to help?" she asked skeptically. "Lots of people have tattoos on their hand."

"I'll send the video to Corbin," Dominic said. "See if he can enhance the image and whether or not he can spot anything else."

"Rob doesn't have a tattoo on his hand," Bain told him.

"Fuck," Dominic swore. "There goes that theory."

"It was a good one. I liked him for it. But definitely no tattoo on his hand. I'll go call the detective, see if he can come pick up this message and get that footage from that little asswipe." Bain turned to her, tugging her tight against him. "Don't worry, baby girl. We'll get him. This is another piece in the puzzle. Hopefully, the little fucker is in the system, since he wasn't wearing gloves and we'll get his prints."

She shuddered. She hoped so. She just wanted this over and done with. She wanted some peace in her life. To know she was safe. To be happy.

"Why don't you go watch some T.V. or something. I'll come let you know what's going on after I've spoken to the detective."

She shook her head. "I'm fine."

He leaned back so he could stare down into her face. Grasping hold of her chin, he tilted her face. "It's all right to not be fine, angel. Nothing bad is going to happen if you just take a bit of time to yourself. I've got this. I've got you. I'm here for you. No matter what."

She wrapped her arms around his waist, holding on tight. "This sucks. I hate having some weirdo sending me these letters, but at the same time I'm strangely grateful to him. Because if there wasn't this threat, I wouldn't have met you. And you're the best thing that's ever happened to me."

"I know exactly what you mean, angel. But this guy needs to be caught. This shit has got to stop."

She couldn't agree more.

22

The day had been shit.

She just wanted to lie on her bed and forget today had ever happened. But it seemed that wasn't in the cards for her today. With the call to Larry, her visit from Gabrielle then the note and the subsequent meeting with the detective, it felt like she'd been completely drained.

But now her damn phone was ringing. She looked at the name and knew she had to answer. She should have known she wouldn't just get away with sending him a text about what happened.

"Hey, Caleb."

"Squirt, you okay?"

"Yeah, I'm all right." Even to her ears, her voice sounded off. Devoid of emotion.

"Uh-huh, and I've got some nice magical beans to sell you. Tell me everything that happened."

She told him about the letter she'd just received and Bain running after her stalker. When she finished, she heard him swearing quietly and a deep voice asking him what was wrong.

This voice wasn't Aleki or Wolfe's, it had an accent. One of the princes?

Caleb said something back that she couldn't hear.

"So sounds like you had the day from hell," Caleb commented.

She let out a small laugh. "Yeah, you could say that."

"You're stressing. Stop stressing. Do the cops have any leads on who this asshole might be?"

"No. None. The letter has gone to their lab, they're hoping to get fingerprints from it so they can identify him."

"If he's in the system."

"Yeah."

"What about your family? Larry? They still hounding you?"

"Actually, they've gone weirdly quiet ever since Gabrielle visited. I'm wondering if something I said actually got through to her."

"Doubtful," he told her. "Remember, I went to school with Gaby. She's always been a selfish bitch."

"Caleb!"

"Don't bother defending her to me. You're too good for that family of vipers. Always have been."

"Daniel isn't so bad," she said. At least he never asked her for something.

"Yeah? When's the last time you heard from your brother? When's the last time he checked in on you?"

Good points.

She rubbed her forehead.

"Where are you right now?"

"Um, lying on my bed."

"Where is your man? Why isn't he taking care of you?" Caleb demanded.

"Bain takes care of me just fine," she snapped back.

There was a moment of silence. And she opened her mouth to

apologize, horrified by the way she'd just spoken to him when a small chuckle came from Caleb. "There's my fierce girl."

"Sorry, I didn't mean to snap."

"It's all right, Squirt. If anyone has a right to snap, it's you. And I know how fiercely loyal you are to those you care about. I'm lucky enough to be one of those people you'll defend to the death."

She blushed slightly at those words, not knowing that she deserved such praise.

That person in the background spoke again.

"Prince Kassim just told me to offer you a place to stay in Escana. He said that they will keep you safe from this stalker and your awful family. His words, not mine," he said hastily. Probably because in the past she had defended her family from any slurs.

No more.

"It's okay, they are awful. And thank Prince Kassim but I have a place to go. I just have to get there. I need to get rid of this threat first. I can't have this following me around. I don't think I'll ever feel safe."

"I know, Squirt. We're not going to let that happen."

"I hope not. Not sure if I'm more worried about my stalker or my family," she tried to joke.

"I know who I'd be more afraid of."

She let out a scoffing noise. Like he feared anything.

"Call when you get here tomorrow, I'll have Dominic come down and let you guys in through the basement. It will be safer for the princes, right?"

"Learning some tricks from your bodyguard?" he teased. "We will, thanks, Squirt. Are you sure you still want us to come over?"

"Yes, please. Soon you'll be going back to Escana and I won't see you again for ages."

"Well, you could take Prince Kassim up on his offer. Come visit us. Even bring the big guy."

"Not sure I'd manage to visit Escana without him."

The door opened and the man in question walked into the room.

"Squirt, go find that man of yours. He should be looking after you."

"He's here now."

Bain plucked the phone from her hand. He took a quick look at the screen. "Bain here." He grunted. "Yep. I got her." Then he ended the call.

"I might have wanted to say goodbye," she told him

"I did it for you."

She rolled her eyes. He studied her for a long moment. Then he turned away. She thought he was going to leave her alone. That's what she wanted, right? Some peace and quiet on her own?

Then he started rummaging around in one of her drawers. He came back with a bikini and held it out to her. "Let's go for a swim."

"You swim?"

"Yep."

"Huh."

He quirked an eyebrow. "What? You thought I'd sink like a tank? Did you forget I was a Navy SEAL?"

She bit her lip. Whoops. That was maybe a bit rude. "Sorry. I'm not sure I feel like a swim."

"Be good for you. Clear your mind. Stop you from thinking."

She sighed and rubbed her temples. "Not sure that's possible."

"Could give you a spanking. Have the same effect."

She glared and then sat up and snatched up her bathing suit. "I'll go for a swim."

His lips twitched. "Damn. And I was hoping for the spanking."

"Bet you were. Pervert."

He wiggled his eyebrows. "Only when it comes to you, baby."

With the day she'd had, the last thing she'd imagined she'd be doing was smiling. But somehow, this gruff ogre always made her feel better.

They walked out to the swimming pool in silence. It was chilly, and she was thankful she'd put a robe on after getting into her dark blue bikini. Bain didn't seem to notice. He just stripped off and climbed in naked. She glanced around, but it was dark and there was only one building overlooking them. Even if someone was watching, they were still unlikely to see much.

He dove in. Okay, he couldn't just swim.

He could *swim*.

He was so graceful that she just watched him for several minutes as he moved up and down the pool. She untied her robe shivering slightly. It was a bit cool to be swimming. But the pool was heated and as soon as she submerged herself in the warmth, she let out a sigh of satisfaction.

Bliss.

She dove under the water, her hair floating out behind her. She started swimming laps. Going slow and steady. She swam under the water until her lungs were burning. Then she burst up to the surface.

She did lazy lengths until her mind cleared, and her body started to tire then she moved to the side and looked out over the edge to the city. The Manhattan skyline was lit up. She enjoyed the view. But she found herself wishing for the stars. The peace and quiet of the mountains.

A large body pressed itself against her and she leaned her head back against his shoulder. He grasped hold of her hair in his fist, pulling it to the side so he could nibble on her neck.

"Keep your arms against the side of the pool."

Her heart skipped at the command. She'd discovered how much she loved being ordered around in the bedroom. Which was lucky, since Bain grew even bossier during sex.

How that was even possible, she didn't know.

"We can't do anything here, someone might see."

"It's dark. They can't see much. And you're gonna stay under the water." He moved his hands around to her breasts, plucking at her nipples. She gasped as they hardened.

"Changed my mind," he muttered.

Disappointment flooded through her. Even though this was far riskier than anything she'd ever done, she certainly wasn't leading a rock'n roll lifestyle that was for sure, she didn't want to stop.

"Reach back and put your arms behind my neck. Want you completely accessible."

Oh. He didn't want to stop then.

She slid her arms back and grasped hold of his neck. He slid the cups of her bikini up over her breasts, baring them. He rolled her nipples between his fingers and thumbs.

"I'm gonna make you come. Want to hear you scream as you come. Going to wash away all the bad shit that happened today. Replace it with good."

"Oh. Oh," she cried as he moved one hand lower, down her belly.

"So fucking beautiful. And all mine. Tell me."

His finger slid under her bottoms, just resting it on her clit. "Please." She tried to thrust her hips, to make him move but he removed his hand.

"Nooo!"

"Tell me."

"Yours. I'm yours." Did it even need to be said? They both knew she was his. Always. Forever.

"Damn fucking right you are. Hold on tight, baby. Keep looking out. Let me make you feel good."

He always made her feel good. Whether he was giving her pleasure or not.

"My Little. My girl. My angel." He slid his finger back under her bikini bottoms. But this time, he slid his finger straight inside her. She clenched around him.

"That's it. Suck me in. Fuck, baby." He drove his finger back and forth as he played with her nipple with his other hand.

"Damn, want to taste you. Gonna take you to the other side." He moved backward, pulling her along with him, into the darker side of the pool.

"Float on your back, hold onto the railing." He helped her lie back with her arms over her head, grasping hold of the railing. Then he grabbed hold of her bikini bottoms, dragging them off and throwing them to the side of the pool.

She made a mental note to get them later. She didn't need Dominic finding them. Then her brain stopped working, all thoughts leaking away as he moved between her legs, drawing them over his shoulders as he grasped her around the waist and raised her pussy out of the water so he could feast on her.

And feast he did.

Her breath came in harsh pants as he circled her clit with his tongue then flicked at it firmly. He removed one hand from her hip and reached under her to part her cheeks. Her breath hitched.

"When we get back to your bedroom, one of those training plugs is going in this ass."

She groaned at the thought. Christ. That just drove her arousal higher. He pressed a finger against her back hole. She tensed, then relaxed as he just lightly massaged over her puckered entrance. His tongue continued to flick at her clit, driving her more and more insane. She had to use all her control not to move or thrash around, not wanting to send waves of water everywhere.

Her breath came faster, the sensation of him playing with her ass only drove her wilder.

"Please! Please!" she cried out.

"Come, baby. I want your screams."

It seemed those were the words she needed to hear as she gave in, falling over the edge, a scream of pleasure erupting from her lungs. He continued to lightly lap at her clit until she came down from her high. Then he gently helped her out of the pool, wrapping her in a towel, grabbing one to pull around himself before drawing her up into his arms.

Just as well, since she didn't think her legs could hold her. He carried her to her bedroom and through to the bathroom, setting her down next to the shower. He turned the heater on then the shower.

"Take your top off then turn around and grasp hold of the counter, legs spread wide."

Oh fuck. He really was going to plug her. He disappeared before she could say anything. With fingers that shook from a mixture of excitement and trepidation, she undid her bikini top. Then she turned and grasped hold of the counter, pushing her legs out as he walked back in.

He held a plug in one hand, a tube of what she guessed was lube in the other.

"Good girl," he told her in a low voice, filled with approval.

Damn, he was so hot. He'd lost the towel and was walking around naked. All those muscles encased in silky skin.

Scrumptious.

Her body didn't care that she'd just had a spectacular orgasm. She wanted more. She grew more turned on as she watched him lube up the plug. He moved in behind her, his eyes catching hers in the mirror above the sink.

"Want this, baby?"

She nodded.

"Words," he prompted.

"Yes, please."

"Remember, you have a safeword."

She did. But she wouldn't need it. She knew he wouldn't push her past her boundaries. He pressed her ass cheeks apart.

"Just relax," he murmured to her. "Deep breath in."

She felt the tip of the plug against her back entrance. Holy shit. Her clit was throbbing in anticipation.

"Now out. Good girl." He slowly pressed the plug inside her.

Fuck. Yes. It slid slowly inside her. There was a slight burn. The feeling of being stretched. But once it was fully inserted and she clenched around it, waves of need surged inside her.

More. She wanted more.

"Fuck yes. That's gorgeous. Good girl. Such a good fucking girl to take my plug. Let's get you clean, huh."

She stood and held his hand as he led her into the shower. It felt kind of weird to walk around with something in her ass. She clenched her bottom cheeks around the plug. Knowing her luck, the damn thing would fall out. He washed her reverently, covering every inch of her body, even washing her hair for her.

She turned to him when he was finished, squirting some shower gel onto her hand. He'd moved his stuff in here, after rumbling about having to smell like vanilla and citrus. She started with his shoulders and arms. Strong. Hot. Masculine. He watched her with heated eyes as she ran her hands over his chest.

God, yes. She loved the feel of him. So strong yet smooth. Leaning in, she flicked her tongue over his nipple.

"You planning on washing the rest of me?" he asked in amusement.

She made a humming noise of enjoyment. "Soon."

He chuckled. But she squeezed out some more gel and had him turn around so she could wash his back. Not that she was any less obsessed by this side of him.

His whole body was a thing of beauty, but that ass... holy hell. She squeezed the cheeks.

"You have an amazing ass." She had to force herself to move lower, washing his legs then waiting until he turned to grasp hold of his cock. He let out a strangled groan as she ran her hand up and down his shaft.

"Got to make sure all of you is clean."

"Yep," he agreed, his eyes falling to half-mast, his breath coming faster as she played with him, running her thumb over the head of his cock.

"Fuck, baby. Not gonna last, you keep doing that."

"So come," she told him.

He shook his head. "Nope. Not coming like this. Turn around, bend over."

She pouted but he gave her a stern look. She turned and placed her hands on the small seat built into the shower wall. He pressed her ass cheeks apart so he could play with the anal plug he'd inserted.

Fuck. Fuck.

Her bottom clenched around the plug. Oh hell. Felt so good. It stretched. It burned slightly, but her body welcomed the intruder.

Ass play seemed to be her thing. Who knew?

She tried to straighten, but he laid one hand on her back. Her clit was throbbing. Her pussy felt empty. Her arousal was growing.

"Bain, please," she begged.

"Part your legs," he commanded.

She slid them apart as she felt the head of his cock press against her pussy. He pushed inside her, pausing for a moment to let her get used to the feel of his thick head inside her. Then he drove forward.

"Fuck yes, baby," he groaned, seating himself deep. "I can feel the plug in your ass. So tight. Damn."

So could she. She needed him to move. She attempted to drive her hips back, but he smacked her bottom sharply.

She cried out, clenching down on him. *More, please. More.*

He grabbed her hips, holding her steady as he fucked her. His movements were hard, fast.

"Play with your clit, Ari," he commanded.

Oh hell. He didn't have to tell her twice. She reached down to flick her clit. She circled it, tapped it, her need rose and rose.

"Come with me, baby. Come now," he yelled.

She cried out as she came. Only managing to stay upright because of his hold of her hips, her legs buckling beneath her. He let out a roar as he followed her over, leaning one hand against the wall, his breath coming in harsh pants, his free arm wrapping around her waist and holding her to him.

A place she never wanted to leave.

It wasn't until later that she remembered her damn bikini bottoms. Bain went and got them for her.

Ever the gentleman.

23

Dominic walked into the living room the next afternoon just as she finished smashing Bain's butt at Candyland. She was starting to think he just might be letting her win.

"Sorry to interrupt. But Ari's family is downstairs, along with Larry and they're insisting on seeing her. What do you want me to do?"

"Ari?" Bain turned to her, a frown on his face.

She rubbed at her temples. Crap. "We knew this was coming. Their timing could have been better, though." Caleb, Aleki, Wolfe and the princes were due soon.

"I can tell them to fuck off," Dominic suggested with a wolfish grin. "It would be my pleasure."

"No, let's get it over and done with and then at least stop worrying about their reaction." She took in a deep breath. "But if they overstay, I'll let you both kick them out."

"Fine," Dominic grumbled. "I'll put them in your office. But let them wait for a while."

"Another game?" she asked Bain.

He just grinned.

She wished she could have made them wait while they played one more game, but the truth was, she wanted to get this over and done with. So ten minutes later, she walked into her office, her hand in Bain's. She didn't give a rat's ass what her family thought about that. It was well past time that she stopped caring about their opinion of her. Her parents and sister were sitting in the exact same places as last time. They were all dressed impeccably, while she wore a pair of worn jeans and an old T-shirt.

Larry on the other hand, stood directly across the room, leaning against the wall.

"Arianna, we need to talk. Alone. Without the staff listening in." Her mother sneered at Bain.

What? No hello?

Immediately, Arianna straightened her shoulders. She may have put up with barely-veiled insults flung her way, but she wasn't going to let anyone talk or treat Bain badly.

"Bain is not the staff. He's my boyfriend. And Dominic is my friend. They both stay." Although maybe Dominic would like to leave. She sent him an apologetic look. "As long as they both want to."

He just winked at her. She handed him her phone. He took it with a nod, knowing Caleb was going to call her when they left their hotel. Dominic would go down and let them in through the garage.

Bain drew her against him.

Her mother gave her a pitying look. "Arianna, it's so sad how delusional you are. These people are not your friends. They are paid to be here. As soon as you stop paying them, they'll leave."

"I'm not being paid to be here," Bain rumbled. "I'm here because I love Arianna."

Her mother sniffed. "You love her money, more like. Tell me, how much debt did your wife leave you in? Must be a relief to find a rich, vulnerable woman to help pay off all those debts."

Arianna glared at her mother. How dare she!

"Don't know where your information came from," Bain growled. "But you might want to ask for a refund because I don't have any debts. And I'm not with Arianna for her money."

Her mother looked him up and down. "Right. And you just expect us to believe that."

"You can't judge everyone by your standards, mother," Arianna snapped.

Her mother narrowed her gaze. "And what does that mean?"

"It means not everyone wants something from me. Bain is with me because he likes me, he sees me, he doesn't care about what I can do for him, or how much I'm worth."

"And you're saying that's how your mother sees you?" her father barked. "She is your mother. The woman gave birth to you. You shall treat her with respect."

"Like how the three of you treat me?" she asked quietly. "You've never once shown me any respect or care. As a child, you were embarrassed by me. You hid me away. I was a nuisance. Only once I was worth anything to you did you pay me any attention."

Her mother waved her hand in the air. "Oh, for goodness sake, Arianna. Grow up. What did you want from us? To coddle you? To hold you every time you had a nightmare? Whatever we did, it was for your own good. If we'd catered to your issues it would have made them worse. You were always given the very best. And still you complain."

It was pointless, they'd never understand.

"We're getting off track," Larry said impatiently. He moved around restlessly. "Arianna, you cannot be serious about moving to some backwater cabin with your bodyguard. You cannot leave your career. You have obligations. Do you think the royalties will just keep coming in, because believe me, they won't. And when this ape dumps you and you're out on your ass you'll have nothing."

Bain let out a low rumble which had Larry blanching. But she grasped hold of his arm.

"First of all, I know I have obligations, and I'll fulfill those."

Relief filled Larry's face. "Good. I'll get started on—"

"You misunderstand. I haven't changed my mind. You're no longer my agent, Larry. I'll deal with the record label and what they want. I'll find a new agent if necessary. But I no longer wish to work with you." She turned to look at her family. "As for the rest of you, I'm not bankrolling your lifestyles anymore. I'm moving with Bain to Montana. I never wanted this life. I love creating music, but performing in front of huge audiences, all the publicity, the pushing myself to breaking point, it's not something I want. I did it to please all of you. Because I thought I owed you. Because I thought that if I did what you wanted, you might love me. But my only worth to you was wrapped up in how much money I could make and that's not right."

She stared up at Bain. "I now know what it's like to have someone actually love me. Someone who cares about me. Who puts me first. And it's made me realize that I've never had that. You may keep anything I've bought for you, of course. But as of now, you'll need to get jobs or live off what you have left in your accounts."

"This is preposterous." Her father jumped up and pointed at Bain. "This is your fault! We know you're doing this because you want her money. I don't know what you did to her, but I will find out."

"This is all my fault."

She frowned, glancing over at Larry as he shook his head, staring at her sadly. She tensed. Something was happening here. Something she didn't understand. Larry looked far too happy for someone who had just been fired.

"What?" she asked.

"Bernadette, Frederick, I'm so sorry. I failed you both. You and your daughter."

"What are you talking about? Failed how?" Arianna demanded.

"No, Larry," her mother said sweetly. Her mother was only ever sweet when she was about to get her own way. Or stab someone in the back. "It's not your fault. It's ours. You are her agent; we are her family. It was up to us to look after her. Like we have done all our lives. But we thought she was doing better. Arianna, how long have you been off your drugs, dear?"

"What?" she asked, confused.

"Come now, you don't need to pretend not to know what we're talking about." Her mother stood and walked closer. Arianna really wanted to step away, but she made herself stand her ground. She knew better than to show weakness. "Mr. Grady, I'm not sure what Arianna has told you about us, but I'm afraid you can't really believe what she says. Not when she's off her medication. She makes up wild stories about how we treat her. I bet she told you that we used to lock her in her room at night?"

"Preposterous," her father stated. "We would never do that to our own daughter."

She gaped at her father, betrayal hitting her hard. She knew they could lie. She knew they could be heartless. But she didn't expect this.

"You did do that." She turned to her sister. "Gabrielle, you remember that, right?"

Gabrielle kept her gaze on her manicure. "I have no idea what you're talking about."

She sucked in a breath. She would not cry. Maybe her sister didn't remember, she'd been a child.

"Arianna, dear, why did you stop your medication? You know it helps with the delusions."

"What delusions?"

"I'm afraid our daughter isn't very well, Mr. Grady," her mother said to Bain. Her face was filled with fake concern. "She hasn't been well for a long time, but she manages with the help of medication. You see, unlike what she probably told you we never wanted her to enter this career. We thought the pressure of being in the spotlight would be too much for her and our worries have come true."

"What are you talking about? You pushed me into this."

Her phone rang and Dominic stepped out of the room, speaking into it quietly.

Her mother shook her head. "Oh, Arianna, where did we go wrong?" She looked back up at Bain. "She's had issues ever since she was a child. What was she? Six? Seven? When she stopped talking?" She turned to her husband.

"I was four," Arianna gritted out.

Her mother ignored her. "We thought it was just for attention. Ari is our youngest and our neediest. Frederick worked a lot and I had taken on too many obligations. I didn't notice soon enough that something was wrong with her. That's when the nightmares and sleepwalking began. She had the best therapists and tutors. Gradually, she became better. But then she got it into her mind to pursue a career in music. We tried to protect her. But her problems returned. The pills help with those bad thoughts, Arianna. Remember? Doctor Jones said you had to remember to take your pills."

"The only pills I've ever taken are for anxiety, not delusions."

"If only that was true." Her mother shook her head sadly.

No. No, this couldn't be happening. Bain didn't believe them, right? She glanced up into his face but couldn't tell what he was thinking. He was giving nothing away.

"I want you all to leave. I've had enough of the lies. I don't have delusions. I don't take any other medication."

"We can call Doctor Jones, have him explain to everyone," her mother said. "But we're trying not to embarrass you, dear."

Right. Like they cared. They were trying to separate her and Bain so they could keep her under their thumb. What they didn't realize was that she wasn't going to let them bully her any longer.

"We have to tell them everything, Arianna," Larry implored. "We can't keep this up. Not with the police involved. It's against the law and I can't keep lying for you."

"What are you talking about now?" That sick feeling in her stomach was growing. She wanted them gone.

Bain squeezed her hand and she reminded herself that she wasn't alone. He wasn't going to abandon her. He wouldn't believe her parents over her.

She felt the room spin and she leaned her head against Bain's arm. She wouldn't panic. There was nothing they could do to her.

Larry gave her a false look of sympathy. "I wish I didn't have to do this, Arianna. I know you'll feel betrayed by me. But we can't continue on with this lie."

"What lie? There is no lie!"

She heard voices behind her. She recognized Caleb speaking but she couldn't focus on him right now. Larry had something up his sleeve. One last play. And she just knew it wasn't going to go well for her.

"Oh, Arianna. I guess it's up to me to come clean." He turned to Bain, straightening his shoulders. "There is no stalker."

Her mouth dropped open. The silence in the room was suffocating. Her heart raced so hard she felt ill.

"What are you talking about? What do you mean there's no stalker? Those letters. . ."

"Oh, Arianna," Larry said with false sympathy. He turned back to Bain. "You can't blame her. If I'd known she was off her meds, I never would have agreed to this. I shouldn't have agreed to it anyway. But I didn't know it was all a fabrication until she handed me the letter before the concert. I told you that I found it in her dressing room. Truth is that she gave it to me to pretend to find. She told me to go to the press with it." He turned to Dominic. "You saw her give me the letter while we were in the dressing room."

"I saw her give you a piece of paper, but I didn't see what was on it," Dominic said gruffly.

She frowned. "That was a list of things you wanted me to sign off on for the concert organizers."

"Please stop lying, darling," her mother said. "You're only hurting yourself."

"Arianna invented a stalker for publicity purposes," Larry declared. "She sent those letters to herself."

"What the fuck!" Caleb exclaimed.

"I did no such thing."

"You cannot blame her," Larry said to Bain. "She sometimes has delusions when she's off her medication. She may well have convinced herself that this stalker is now real."

She'd never wanted to hurt someone more. "You lying asshole! I don't have fucking delusions and I never made up the stalker."

Larry sighed. "Arianna, we both know you're lying."

The words made her gasp. Her legs wobbled. Even worse, though? Bain let go of her hand. He believed them? He couldn't believe them!

She saw everything slipping through her fingers.

"This time, things have gone too far, Arianna," her mother said. "You involved these nice men. You involved the police. Of course, Larry should never have agreed to help you."

"I was wrong. But I care about Arianna a great deal. I wanted to make her happy."

A slow clapping filled the room. She spun and saw Caleb standing there. His face was granite, but his eyes were blazing with anger. "What a command performance. You know, Lars, you and the wicked witch here should go into acting. You could take that comedy routine on the road."

Relief flooded her. At least someone believed her. But Bain. . .she turned back to him, but he wasn't looking at her. Instead his gaze was on Larry.

"Caleb," her mother spat out with thinly-veiled dislike. "I didn't know you were back in the country. Aren't you living in some third world hellhole?"

"Third world hellhole?" an accented voice drawled.

She turned toward the voice. How had she missed them? Well, she guessed these were special circumstances so she could be excused for being a bit distracted. Wolfe and Aleki flanked Caleb who stood, glaring at her family. But behind and to their right stood four truly gorgeous men with dark hair.

She wasn't sure which one had spoken, but when she looked them over, they all reacted differently. The first one stood tall and straight, his glare directed at Larry. His brother next to him was scowling at her mother. He was slightly shorter, but much thicker with muscle. The next brother grinned and winked as her gaze moved over him. He had longer hair; it lay in a shaggy mess that was really quite adorable. The fourth brother wasn't looking at anyone. He'd half-turned to glance out the window, seemingly oblivious to the tension in the room.

"Did you hear that, Kassim?" the smiling one said.

"I did," the first brother replied. "Funny, I thought we were the second wealthiest country in the world."

"Well, our bank account did dip below fifty billion the other day," the grinning one said. "Perhaps that's why this bitch thinks she can look down on us."

Her mother gasped. Whether over being called a bitch or hearing how much the brothers were worth, she wasn't sure.

"Who are you?" her father demanded. "This is a private conversation."

"Arianna, tell these people to leave," her mother demanded. "I'm sure you don't want an audience for this."

"Arianna, my offer still stands," Prince Kassim offered. "Our private jet can be ready within thirty minutes. You are welcome in Escana for as long as you like."

"A private jet?" Gabrielle asked, smiling at the four brothers. "I wouldn't mind visiting Escana."

"You weren't invited." Surprisingly it was the fourth brother who spoke, the one who hadn't even seemed to be paying attention.

Gaby gasped, unused to being rejected.

"The invitation is for Arianna," Kassim added coldly. "Not anyone else in her family."

"And if anyone is going anywhere, it's the four of you," she told her mother.

She let out a breath, trying to slow her racing heart. She just wanted them to leave. Their lies had cut deep. It showed how little they truly cared about her.

"I have proof," Larry stated.

"What?" Bain barked.

"I have proof. That Arianna made up her stalker."

"That piece of paper she gave you could have had anything on it," Dominic told them. "It's proof of nothing."

"What about proof that she wrote it? I saw her do it. On her laptop. The other letters are probably there too."

"What are you talking about? Why are you lying?" Tears threatened and she fought to keep them at bay. Her entire body shook with reaction.

Did Bain believe this bullshit? Surely not.

Maybe he thinks I lied to him the way his ex-wife did.

Caleb leaned a hand on her shoulder, and she waited for Bain to say something. He was incredibly possessive. But his gaze remained on Larry.

"Show them, Arianna," Larry urged.

"There's nothing to show." This was all so preposterous.

"Then you won't mind proving it," Larry said smoothly. He opened her laptop. The screen came up, asking for her password.

"You don't have to," Caleb murmured to her. "Let me get rid of them."

It was tempting. So tempting.

But she couldn't help but feel like Bain might always doubt her if she didn't prove that she was telling the truth.

"I have nothing to hide. Here." She walked over, unlocked her computer and opened up her documents. She froze. What the fuck was that? Under recent documents there was a new file. Labelled Letters.

Larry came around and put his hand on the small of her back. She thrust his hand away. "Don't touch me."

Bain stepped up, forcing Larry to take a few steps back. Relief flooded her at the move. Maybe she was imagining things. Maybe he had drawn back because he'd gone into bodyguard mode.

"Easy, man. I wasn't going to hurt her. I care deeply about Arianna."

"Sure, you do," Caleb mocked.

"Well, what is that file, Arianna?" Larry pointed at the one labelled Letters. Now she wished she'd never opened her laptop. She didn't know what the file was, had never seen it before but she knew what she was going to find in it.

"I never put that file there," she said hastily, looking over at Bain. "It's not mine."

He gave her a slight nod. Did that mean he believed her?

"Arianna, please, we know it's not your fault, darling. Just let us help you." Her mother walked up next to her and opened the folder. Inside there were three documents. She knew what was going to be on them before her mother even clicked on them.

No. No, no, no.

Her breath sawed in and out of her lungs. Nausea bubbled in her stomach and if it wasn't for Caleb wrapping his big arm around her waist, she thought she might have lost her balance.

"I didn't write those."

"They're on your laptop, darling," her mother pointed out. "How else would they have gotten there?"

"Someone planted them."

"And who would do that? How would they do that?" her mother asked.

She had no idea. She just knew that somehow, someone had. She glanced over at Bain, desperate for some sign he believed her. He frowned at the letters, going through each one. Then he turned to look at Dominic. They held some sort of silent communication.

"So who delivered them?" Bain asked. "Because that sure wasn't Arianna."

"She told me she paid someone to deliver them," Larry said. "And that she gave him a card to gain access to this level."

She felt so hurt at their betrayal she couldn't even speak.

"You need to leave now," Dominic stated firmly.

"Excuse me?" her mother exclaimed. "We are Arianna's family. She is obviously ill. She needs our help. We are not leaving here."

"You have no right to be here," Dominic told them. "You'll leave now, or we will call the police. I'm sure you don't want that."

Her father stood and took hold of her mother's arm, quietening her. He said something in her ear that no one else could hear.

"Fine. We will go for now. But we will be back. Of course, you will be paid in full for your time here. I'm just so sorry my daughter wasted your time."

"Don't come back," she told them.

"Excuse me?" Her mother stood straight. "Arianna, you don't know what you say. You're ill—"

"I'm not ill," she spat out. "And I'm not the liar here. All of you are. Do you really think this will get me to change my mind? To continue to support you all? It won't. All it's done is really shown me your true colors. I knew you were all selfish. I knew that you didn't care about me. But deep down, there was always hope that you loved me. That's gone now. Now I know that you don't love anyone but yourselves. Larry, you're still fired and from now on, I no longer have a family."

Her mother gasped. "Oh, the hurtful things you say."

"You cannot do this, Arianna. You need me!" Larry's face was red, his hands were clenched into fists. "I made you who you are!"

"No. I did," she said quietly. "I've had enough of you trying to manipulate and control me. All of you. Now go. Before I have you thrown out."

"Come along, Bernadette." Her father glared at her. "Just ignore her. You know she'll change her tune once her boyfriend dumps her and runs."

Was that what was going to happen? Bain was going to believe them over her?

Her family left, with Larry in tow. Suddenly, Bain appeared in front of her.

"Bain. . .I. . .you can't—"

He took hold of her shoulders and gave her a quick kiss on the forehead. "Stay with Caleb and Dominic. Do not leave the apartment. I'll be back soon."

Then he was gone.

"Easy, Squirt." Caleb wrapped an arm around her, walking her over to the same sofa where her family had just sat and eviscerated her.

Holy hell. Had that really happened?

"Wolfe, get her a drink," Caleb ordered. "Aleki, get on her laptop. See how the hell they managed to get those files onto there."

"I'll be back, stay here with Caleb," Dominic ordered her.

She nodded, feeling numb with shock as Caleb sat with her on the sofa, his arm around her shoulders.

But it should be Bain holding her. Bain who was looking after her.

Why had he just left? Where was he going? Would he be back?

"Why would they lie like that?" She was dimly aware of three princes taking up seats around them. The fourth one, the one who hadn't seemed that interested in what was going on, remained by the window.

Maybe he just liked the view.

"Why would they do that? I don't understand any of this. How did those letters get on my laptop? I never wrote them. I swear I didn't."

Wolfe returned with a glass of Scotch. She didn't drink it. She only kept it here for her father and Larry. She wrinkled her nose. Caleb took it from her and held the glass to her lips. "Just have a sip, Squirt."

"It won't help."

Nothing was going to help. Her family were treacherous liars. And Bain. . .where had he gone? Why had he barely looked at her? Did he believe them?

A sob broke from her lips.

"Karisma, drink the Scotch," a cultured voice said gently. She looked up through blurry eyes. It was the brother who hadn't spoken at all yet. "It will help settle your nerves."

"I. . .I. . ."

He took the glass from Caleb and crouching, held it to her lips. "Drink." His voice held a firmer note of command and she took a sip, grimacing at the burn. "Good girl."

She blinked at him.

He smiled. Holy hell, he was gorgeous. Was it wrong to notice things like that when she had a man? When she loved Bain?

"He believed them," she said.

His smile dropped from his face. "If he did then he is a complete fool. Anyone with a brain could see that they were lying."

She sniffed. "You didn't believe them?"

"Not a word, Karisma. And if your man has any sense, he will know they lied."

"He's smart, but his ex-wife lied to him all the time. Maybe he thinks I'm like her."

"If he knows you at all, he'll know you're not a liar," Wolfe growled.

"Shall we introduce ourselves?" the kind prince asked. She suddenly realized who she was talking too. Eek! Where were her manners?

"Oh, excuse my manners, your-your majesty. I. . .uh. . .umm. . .can I get you. . .umm. . .Scotch?" she squeaked. She tried to rise but the prince put his hand out and shook his head.

"Please, do not treat us any differently than you would Caleb, Aleki and Wolfe."

"She's never once offered me Scotch," Aleki moaned.

"That's because you don't drink it. You're a beer only man," she countered. She turned back to the prince in front of her. "Sorry, please, I'd love it if you told me your names."

"Of course, Karisma. The one standing, looking so stern by the door is my oldest brother, Kassim. The fool behind me who is trying to steal Scotch without being caught is Aric. The moody one looking out the window, is Matek. And I am your greatest fan. Tavi."

"You wanted the concert."

"I still do. Maybe you should come to Escana and give it?"

Her eyes widened. "I would love that Prince Tavi, but. . ."

"But your heart lies elsewhere."

"What does Karisma mean?"

"It is equivalent to beauty."

They thought she was beautiful? She blushed.

The door to the room opened and Dominic stepped inside.

"Where's Bain?" she asked, trying to look around Dominic. "I need to talk to him."

She stood and Tavi stood with her. When she wobbled slightly, Tavi clasped hold of her arm to steady her. She gave him a small smile.

"Ari, who had access to your laptop?" Aleki asked before Dominic could speak.

She didn't want to talk about her damn laptop. She wanted to know where Bain was. Why wasn't he here? Did he really believe her family?

"Don't worry, Ari," Dominic said to her. "He'll be back soon."

"But where did he go? Did he believe them? I didn't lie!" Tears dripped down her face. Everything was crashing down on her. What if he left her? Panic seized hold of her lungs. She couldn't breathe. She flashed hot then cold, her entire body trembling.

"She's having a panic attack," a deep, accented voice said. "Sit her down. Breathe, Arianna. Calm down and breathe. In. Then out. You can do this. Just breathe."

She tried to follow the voice. *Breathe, Arianna.*

"That's it. Calm down. All will be well. Good girl."

The black dots swimming in her vision faded away as she took in a deep breath then let it out. As she became more aware, she was shocked to find that it was Matek crouched in front of her. Who had been guiding her through the panic attack.

She met his gaze, noted the deep concern and something else. Something dark and tortured.

"In. Out. Good girl. In. Out. All will be well."

"If he d-doesn't believe me?" she whispered.

"Then he is a fool and I shall chop off his head."

She gaped at the stern-looking man. Then he grinned. A

couple of people gasped, and she wasn't sure why. "Or just beat him up for you?"

She shook her head. "You never told me they were all crazy," she said to Caleb without thinking.

Tavi and Aric laughed. Kassim smiled but Matek kept his stern gaze on hers.

"Oh, sorry, I didn't mean any disrespect." She ran her hand over her face. What was she doing? These guys were princes and they were Caleb, Aleki and Wolfe's employers.

"None taken, little one," Kassim told her.

Dominic looked over at her. "Bain didn't believe them, sweetheart. Not even for a second. He just wanted to speak with them."

"What's taking so long?" she whispered. She needed him. Needed him to reassure her that he knew they spouted bullshit. That he loved her. "Are you sure he doesn't think I'm like his ex and lied to him?"

Dominic snorted. "No way would he ever think you were like that bitch. Bain knows exactly who you are. But he wanted to have a chat with your family. In private."

Caleb made a rumbling noise of agreement. "Good."

"Arianna," Aleki said, getting her attention. "I need you to focus. Who had access to your laptop yesterday? Was there someone else in the apartment besides you, Dominic and Bain?"

She frowned. "No one else had access. Why?"

"Your sister was here," Dominic said.

"Oh yes, I forgot she was here."

"Was she left alone in here? At around quarter to three?"

"Yeah, it would have been that time," Dominic said. "

"Bingo. Got you bitch," Aleki said smugly.

"What are you saying? That my sister planted those letters on my laptop?" She shook her head. "How would she access it? Its password protected."

"What's your password, sweetheart?" Caleb asked dryly.

"Oh, umm, *Soul and Heart*, all one word."

Tavi shook his head. "You used the name of your first album as your password?"

She blushed. "Okay, maybe not the smartest idea. But how did Gaby guess it? She wasn't in here that long."

"Larry ever see you unlock your computer with your password? Any chance he knew it?" Aleki asked.

She rubbed her pounding head. "Yeah. It's likely he knew it. Oh God, you really think she planted those letters?"

"The file was put on your computer at 2:48pm yesterday. Gaby didn't even try to hide her tracks. Any idiot could figure that out."

"It's only the first three letters," Dominic said, looking over Aleki's shoulder. "Because they didn't know about the fourth. Their story was so weak it was ridiculous. She's off her meds? Seriously? She hired someone to deliver the letters? She got Larry to go along with it all? They must think us all idiots."

"They're blinded by greed," Caleb rumbled. "Always have been the most self-centered, morally corrupt people. Don't know how my girl was even born to the same family." He turned to her "I'm proud of you for standing up to them, Squirt."

"For so long I just wanted them to notice me, to love me, now I'm thinking I might have been better off if I'd always stayed in the shadows."

"Arianna Silvers never belonged to the shadows," Caleb told her. "You shouldn't have been relegated to the background and you never will be again. Some things are sent to make us stronger. And you are the strongest person I know."

She leaned into Caleb and he wrapped her up in his arms. "Don't know what I would have done without you all these years. You were my only real friend for so long. Then you brought me two more friends." She looked over at Wolfe and Aleki. Wolfe just smiled.

Aleki leaned back in his seat. "Brothers, babe. He brought you brothers."

"Family doesn't have to be blood," Wolfe added. "You might think you lost something today when really you gained something. Freedom. They held you back. They kept you down. They wanted you under their command, doing their bidding. That's not what family is. Family supports you. They make you better just by being there, by loving you. And you've had that for years."

Tears blurred her eyes. She nodded. "You're so right."

She stood and gave Wolfe a hug then Aleki.

"Someone take a photo," Aleki said jokily. "Might as well torture that man of yours. He seems the possessive type."

To her shock, someone did take a photo. She turned around to glare at Aric who just grinned at her. "Shall I put it on Instagram? *Singing sensation's secret love.* Has a nice ring to it, yes?"

"Don't you dare," she growled. She strode over to the prince. "Give that back."

He just whistled and put the phone in his pocket. She put her hands on her hips, giving him a stern look. "Do you think I won't grab that out of your pocket?"

"Ahh, please do, I think the headline would read, *The princess of pop meets her very own prince.*"

Tavi groaned. "That was a terrible one, brother."

"No good? Hmm. I shall think on a better one."

She gave up on Aric. She wasn't worried about photos going on Instagram. She knew he wouldn't really do that and right now, it was the least of her concerns.

"How did they get the letters though?" Kassim asked. "Do you think they just re-typed them?"

She rubbed her forehead. "I took photos of them to send to Caleb. Soon after Bain and Dominic arrived, Larry demanded I send copies to him as well. I didn't even think about it. . . he claimed he wanted copies so that he was kept up-to-date on what was going on. In case the police wanted to talk to him or something. I just gave them to him to shut him up. I guess he typed them out into a word document."

"Not your fault, Squirt," Caleb told her.

She just couldn't believe any of this was happening. And she really wanted Bain.

"Shouldn't Bain be back by now? How long a chat is he having with them?" she asked Dominic.

Dominic frowned. "I'll try calling him."

She needed him. Needed to have him reassure her that he believed her. That he loved her.

THOSE MOTHERFUCKING BASTARDS. He stepped out of the stairway, having run the whole way down ten flights of stairs rather than wait for the elevator and risk losing them. He walked into the foyer just in time to see them walking past.

"I want a word with all of you," he said, storming up to them. How dare they make up lies like that?

They turned. Arianna's mother gave him a haughty look. Her father appeared furious. But Larry blanched, looking worried.

"Mr. Grady, I can assure you that every word we said up there is the truth," her mother said coldly. "If you would like to consult with Doctor Jones, we can arrange that."

Bain folded his arms over his chest. "Is that so?"

"Yes, of course. I'm sure he'll see us straight away."

Oh, so not only would he willingly break patient-doctor confidentiality, but he could fit them in immediately? He wondered how much of Arianna's cash was being used to grease the doctor's palms.

He turned to Larry, watching the other man until he started

fidgeting. "You know making false reports to the police is an offense, right?"

The other man swallowed. "Yes, but I was trying to help Arianna. And if I get into trouble so will she. Surely you won't be taking that further."

Bain raised his eyebrows. "But according to you all, Arianna has delusions. I'm sure the police wouldn't hold her accountable."

Larry started sweating. So he should.

"Didn't come down here for proof or because I believe any of you. You're all miserable excuses for human beings. Arianna would never make up such a hoax like that. She isn't a liar. She doesn't have delusions. She's honest and kind. Nothing you jerks would know anything about."

"Well, really," her mother huffed.

"Yeah, really." And he realized he believed every word. He hadn't believed them. Not for a minute. She was nothing like Jillian. "Ari is worth a million of you. She's finally doing what she wants. Not your bidding."

"And what she wants is to move to the backwoods with you?" her mother sneered.

"Yes," he said firmly. "If you're all wise, you'll leave without making a fuss. But from now on, you stay away from Arianna. You don't call her. You don't message her. You don't do anything to hurt her. Or I will come after you. And it won't be pretty. Any secrets, anything you've been hiding, I will hunt them down and expose them. Hurt Arianna and I will destroy you."

Her mother just sniffed, looking undaunted. But the other three all appeared worried. Good. Maybe now they would behave themselves. If not, he would be watching. He'd have Corbin start looking into their backgrounds now in preparation.

"You can leave now. Might want to go home and start on your resumes."

"Well, I never—" her mother began to say, but Arianna's father grabbed hold of her arm, tugging her away.

Fuckers.

He waited until they left, before turning around. He needed to get back to Arianna. He hated having to leave her immediately, but he needed to make sure her parents knew exactly how he felt. He hadn't wanted to threaten them in front of her.

"Hey, um, Mr. Grady."

He looked over as Rob, the head of security approached him. He sighed. "What?"

"Can you come into my office? Found something on the camera feed you might find interesting."

Bain eyed him. He'd never been useful before. But then, it wasn't going to hurt to look.

"Sure. I only have a minute, though."

He followed Rob into his office, moving towards his desk.

"What is it?"

Too late, he sensed the attack coming in from behind him as something landed on his head.

Then he knew nothing.

BAIN WOKE up with a splitting headache.

Instead of immediately opening his eyes, he took a moment to figure out his surroundings. His instincts screamed at him that something was wrong.

Wherever he was, it was cold. Damp. He could smell diesel.

Was he in some sort of basement? His hands were behind him, secured together. He tried to move his legs. Tied as well. All right. What was his last memory?

Ari. Her family. Listening to their plans. The superintendent. Rob. Then pain. Had that bastard hit him with something? No.

Not Rob. He'd been in front of him. Someone else. Someone else had been hiding behind the door and had hit him on the head. Then they'd somehow dragged him to where? Down to the basement? Made sense.

There wasn't much street noise. Was he in a boiler room?

He couldn't hear anyone near him, but they could be silent, waiting. Finally, he heard a door creak open.

"This wasn't the plan, Jerome," someone whined. It sounded like Rob. "He can't be here, what if someone finds him? I'll lose my job."

"Shut up, Rob. Who cares about your job? As soon as Arianna is mine, I'll give you enough money to move to some island and live out your days drinking Mai Tais and sunning your white ass. My girl is loaded."

"You better," Rob said in his nasally voice. "So what are we going to do about him? Why did you hit him over the head?"

"You overheard what her sister said to the doorman yesterday, she's moving to Montana with this prick. If you'd put listening devices in her apartment like I told you to we would have known about this earlier and come up with a better plan. I had to move on the fly."

"They've upped security. I couldn't get into her apartment without one of them finding out. What makes you think it's this guy she's moving away with?"

"Because her sister said it was the big hunk. That sister always was a slut. Might have to take care of her. And the rest of her family. They never treated her right."

"What makes you think she'll want to be with you if she's planning to go away with him?"

There was the noise of a scuffle and it took all of his control to stay still. He tugged carefully at the ropes around his wrists. There was some give there. Perfect.

"I told you, we have a connection. She kept my secret for all these years. She could have told. Could have gotten me in trouble. But she didn't. She even shared her cookies with me when my bitch mother wouldn't give me any."

Fuck. Who was this guy? How long had he known Ari? And why the fuck was he going on about damn cookies?

"Fine. Fuck. She's yours. Whatever. Let me go." Rob sounded winded. Like this mystery guy was holding him by the neck.

"Then that bitch got fired and we were separated. It wasn't until I heard her message that I knew she needed me. I came to rescue her. But this asshole is in my way."

He kicked Bain's boot. He forced himself to stay relaxed. Slumped.

"But what if she hires other bodyguards?" Rob asked. "Then you won't be able to swoop in as the hero to save her from her stalker."

So this guy was the stalker and Rob was his partner. Made sense.

"The plan has changed. It wasn't working, anyway with these bodyguards around. They kept her from me. I couldn't make a move with all the new security measures."

"Should we be talking about this in front of him?" Rob whispered.

"He's unconscious. Besides, even if he is listening in, he's not going to get a chance to talk."

"What does that mean? I never agreed to kill anyone," Rob's voice squeaked.

"What are you going to do with him? Let him go? Don't be a wimp, Rob."

"Don't call me a wimp, Jerry."

"Don't call me Jerry. It's Jerome. Everyone fucking calls me Jerry. And it's not my name."

"Fine. Fine, chill out. So now what? What do we do? How are you going to get to her now?"

"I just need to get her alone. To tell her I understand her secret message to me." He started to sing off-key,

"Won't anyone save me
From the depths of my despair
Please won't someone save me
Before I disappear."

Jesus. That was the secret message? Those could have been lyrics from any song from any artist. This guy was completely cuckoo. Which didn't bode well for Bain.

"So what do we do?" Rob asked nervously. "There's still that other bodyguard up there with her."

They didn't know about Caleb and the others? That was good. It meant Arianna had plenty of protection.

"How we going to get to her? They're going to notice he's gone soon."

"Okay...okay...just let me think."

He opened his eyes a slit. His head was slumped forward so he couldn't look up. He could see two pairs of shoes in front of him, so he continued to tug carefully at the ropes around his wrists.

"We need to get her out of the apartment and away from her bodyguard but what would draw her out?" There was a moment of silence. "I have it. This guy. We'll use him."

"Use him how?" Rob asked.

"We'll pretend we've kidnapped him."

"Ah, we have kidnapped him."

"Yes, but we'll pretend we'll release him if she goes to a certain place alone. Then I'll go grab her. You stay here with him. Once I have her, you can kill him and join me."

That was the worst plan ever. Like Dominic would ever let her out of the apartment alone.

"How will we send a message to her without giving ourselves away? We need to give proof that we have him."

"We'll send a photo and a message asking her to go to the park where she'll receive further instructions. I'll snatch her and then you can kill him."

"What if she doesn't go to the park? What if she resists?"

"She'll do it if she cares about him. Obviously, he's not her soulmate like I am, but my girl has a big heart and she had no idea I was coming for her. But if she puts up a fuss, I'll inject her with a sedative. I'll meet her at dusk when there won't be as many people around."

"Fine. Fine. How do we send the message? We can't send it on our phones."

"Where's his phone?"

"I turned it off. I didn't want them tracking us."

Dumb asses. It would still ping his last location. Corbin would be able to figure out he was still in the building. Not that he was planning on waiting around to be rescued.

"Go buy a prepaid phone," Jerry ordered. "This plan is going to work. I can feel it. I'm going to get my girl."

"WHERE IS HE? He shouldn't be gone this long, right?" Ari paced back and forth across her office, feeling ill and jittery. Everyone else was sitting or standing around the room. They all pretended to be relaxed but she could see the tension in Caleb's shoulders, in Dominic's jaw.

Wolfe had gone downstairs to see if he could find Bain. What if he hadn't believed her? What if he'd taken off?

No. He wouldn't leave you, Ari. Have some faith.

The door opened and Wolfe stepped in. He looked over at her and shook his head. Her shoulders slumped. "Couldn't find the head of security either. His office was empty."

"His phone is still going to voicemail. I don't like it," Dominic said. "I'm gonna have our tech guy ping his last location before his phone was turned off."

He moved out into the passage. She continued to pace.

"It will be all right, Squirt," Caleb reassured her.

Would it? She had this horrible feeling in her gut that it wouldn't be.

"Is there something you would like to help soothe your nerves?" Prince Kassim asked her.

She shook her head, rubbing at her tummy. The ball of stress there made her feel ill.

Dominic walked back in, frowning. "His last known location is this building."

Which meant nothing. Just that he'd turned his phone off before leaving. Or before someone made him leave.

Suddenly, her phone went off with a text message.

She scrambled over to grab her phone off her desk. Matek had luckily moved out of the way or she might have bowled him over in her haste. Disappointment filled her as she saw the strange number.

She opened the message, her stomach knotting further as she read what it said.

"Oh God." She looked over at Dominic.

"What is it?" Dominic rushed towards her. "What's wrong?"

"It. . .it's Bain! Someone has him!"

24

"I'm going," she said firmly.

"You're not going."

"I am going, Caleb, and you can't stop me."

"It's a fucking trap, Arianna. For all we know, Bain is already dead and all you'd be doing is sacrificing yourself as well."

She gasped, swaying as black dots danced in front of her vision. He couldn't be dead. That wasn't possible.

"Jesus Christ, Caleb, watch what you say," Aleki snapped, wrapping an arm around her.

"I can't just wait here and do nothing. Do you know how helpless I feel right now? Everyone has always made the decisions for me. This is my decision and I'm going to do it."

Dominic shook his head. "I can't let you do that. I'm your bodyguard, Arianna. I can't let you do something dangerous."

"Then you're fired," she said quickly. "The rest of you, figure out a way for me to do this safely but do it quick because we've got fifteen minutes left."

Fifteen minutes to meet this asshole at the west corner of the park. It was nearing on dusk. There wouldn't be many people out now. She knew it was a trap. But if she didn't go and something happened to Bain. . .

"I'd never forgive myself if something happened to him."

She didn't know who had him or how they'd captured him. But she did know she had to help him.

Dominic crossed his arms over his chest. "Not happening."

She turned to her best friend. "Caleb. Please."

Caleb sighed.

"There are ways to manage this," Kassim said quietly, surprising her. "We have time to set up if we go now."

"You guys can't get involved," Caleb protested.

"No, no of course not," she said. "Kassim, you and your brothers need to stay here. I'm sorry, I wasn't thinking. Of course, Caleb, Aleki and Wolfe need to stay with you."

Caleb gave her a look while Aleki rolled his eyes. But it was Wolfe who spoke. "We're going with you."

"You seem to all think we are helpless children," Matek said coldly. "You forget our skills."

"You don't have your sniper rifle here, Matek," Caleb reminded him.

Sniper rifle?

"If you have a spare gun, I will try to get close enough to provide cover," Matek said to Dominic.

Dominic tensed then looked around at them all. "Fuck. Shit. I'm not going to be able to stop you all, am I?"

"I have to do this, Dominic. Please understand."

He groaned. "For the record, I don't agree with any of this."

"Noted," she said grimly. "But the only way you're stopping me is to tie me down."

Dominic looked thoughtful.

"No," she told him. "Come near me and I'll run. I will fight you."

"Fuck. When Bain kills me, I expect a nice funeral," he muttered.

She shook her head. She didn't care about facing Bain's anger. Because that meant he would be alive and back here. With her.

Caleb grabbed hold of her shoulders. "We're going to position ourselves along the route you'll take to the park. Matek and Wolfe will be in the park, hidden. You'll never be alone."

She nodded.

"We're going to get this guy," he added. "We'll get him to tell us where Bain is."

As long as he hadn't killed him already. She took a deep breath, panic threatening to flood her again. She pushed it deep. She could do this. She had to do this.

Bain was counting on her.

25

He managed to get his hand free just as Jerry left. Shit. It would have been far quicker if he hadn't tried to do it quietly. He released his other hand, then grabbed the rope so it wouldn't fall to the floor.

His ankles were still tied to the chair.

Rob was pacing back and forth. The scent of his body odor wafted out. Bain opened his eyes, watching him walk by before he flew forward, slamming into Rob. The chair came with him, slamming into his back, but he ignored the pain. The other man fell backwards, hitting his head on a shelf and crumpling to the ground in a heap.

Bain stared at him for a moment, but he lay still. Fuck. Had he killed him? Shit, he hadn't meant for that to happen. But he wasn't going to feel guilty. Or waste time checking on him. Asshole had been going to kill him after all.

Christ, he hoped they hadn't let Arianna leave the apartment. He'd fucking kill them all if they had. He managed to get himself turned so he could work on the ropes around his ankles. It took longer than he would have liked.

He stood and moved towards the stairs. Now he had to make a choice. Go upstairs to the apartment or to the park.

Fuck.

SHE WAS SO nervous that she thought she might vomit.

She took a calming breath as she walked close to the corner of the park. She couldn't see anyone around. But she knew the guys were out there somewhere, watching. They'd made certain of the route she would walk before they'd all headed out to hide. Their one hope was that this guy didn't know how many people she had with her.

She prayed this guy didn't spot any of her guys. The message had told her to come alone or that Bain would die.

She swallowed. She couldn't live without Bain. He was everything. If anything happened to him, she didn't know what she would do.

She came to a stop a few feet away from the west corner gates. Where was this guy? She glanced around. Nerves tightened her stomach. Shit. Shit.

"Hello, songbird."

She nearly gasped at the words, jumping into the air and glancing around frantically for the source of that voice.

Songbird? That's what her stalker called her.

"Hello? Who's there?" she called out loudly when she didn't see anyone straight away. She didn't know how far away the guys were. This corner of the park was quiet. It wouldn't take much for someone to grab her and wrestle her into a car.

Someone stepped out of the shadows of a tree and she frowned. He was pale. Tall and kind of thin. His dark hair was shaggy, as though it hadn't been cut in a while. But it wasn't stylishly done like Aric's was.

There was something oddly familiar about him, but she couldn't place it. Had she seen him before?

"Hello, Arianna. Miss me?"

"Miss you?" she asked cautiously. Last thing she wanted was to set him off. That had been Caleb's advice. Don't get close to him. Keep calm. Don't rile him.

He stepped forward, closer to her and she resisted the urge to step back.

"Of course, don't you remember me, darling? I heard your message to me. I'm so sorry that I didn't realize you'd been trapped all these years, songbird. It was your awful family. They've always held you prisoner. Treated you like you were less. Especially when you retreated into yourself. When you stopped talking. I know why you did that, though, don't I, songbird? It was to protect me."

What the fuck was he talking about? To protect him? Did she know him from her childhood? She tried to think back. Then she studied him again. The dark hair fit. And he was probably about the right age.

"Jerome?" she whispered.

He smiled wide. "You remember me. I knew you would. I'm here for you, songbird. To set you free."

"You sent me those letters? You're my stalker?" She glanced down at his hands, spotting what looked to be the same tattoo as the man they'd caught on camera delivering the last letter.

He frowned. *Shit, Ari. Don't make him mad.*

"I'm no stalker. I made those letters to get your attention. I was going to be your hero, your protector. But you hired those stupid bodyguards. I'm glad to see you came without the other one. I couldn't let you leave me, songbird. We belong together."

"Is Bain all right?" she asked worriedly.

Jerome's eyes narrowed, anger filling his face. "Why do you care about him? I'm your soulmate!"

"Of course you are," she soothed, remembering Caleb's words about not angering him. "I just don't want anyone to get hurt."

"You always had a soft heart. That's why you need me to protect you. You always have since you were four. We were only together a short time, but I took care of you. Until my slut of a mother got fired and we were forced apart."

She licked her lips. "You said I went silent to protect you?"

Did he know why she stopped talking? What her nightmares were about? The sleepwalking? Was he the reason for all of that?

"Yes, songbird. You never told anyone. I knew you wouldn't. Because you were loyal to me. Don't you remember?"

"Of course. But I guess I never fully understood it all."

"You were young. You must have followed me out of the house one evening. I didn't see you. But I know you just wanted to be with me, so I'm not angry."

Okay. She guessed that was good.

"Mr. Longley deserved what happened. He yelled at me the day before. Just for walking on his lawn on my way home. He didn't yell at your brother for doing the same. Because he thought I was nobody."

Mr. Longley. Wait, didn't she remember Mr. Longley? He'd lived next door to them for a while. Until his house. . .

"Wait. . .you. . .you set his house on fire." Horror filled her. She vaguely remembered the flames. The screaming. "You were only what? Eight? Nine?"

"That was the biggest fire I'd ever set. I started small. Then I went on to bigger and bigger things. That fire was beautiful. Glorious." His face filled with happiness. Was he a pyromaniac?

She tried to think. To remember. "Was he hurt?"

"Some third-degree burns. Nothing he didn't deserve. He didn't die."

How could he be so callous? And how could he have done that

270   LAYLAH ROBERTS

at such a young age? And she'd seen it? Why hadn't she told anyone?

"You saw me there."

"Yes, of course I saw you." He frowned. "I had to drag you back to the house. You started crying and screaming. So I put my hand over your mouth and told you that if you told anyone what you'd seen that I was going to hurt Squiggles."

Squiggles. Her toy cat. She gulped. Oh God.

"I had to threaten him. I couldn't let you tell anyone."

She just stared at him.

"It was just a toy, Arianna. And I only chopped his tail off as a warning."

She was going to be sick. She remembered now. Waking up to find Squiggles on the floor. His tail cut off and lying a few feet away.

A warning to a four-year-old to keep quiet.

That's why she'd stopped talking. She'd been too scared to. In case she blurted out what she'd seen and then he would hurt her favorite toy.

"I had plans to have you be my little helper. Then that bitch mother of mine got caught stealing from your parents and we were out on our asses."

She held back a sob. Poor Mr. Longley. All this time, she'd suppressed that memory out of fear. Until she'd forgotten it. How many more people had he hurt? Because she hadn't said anything?

"Did you set the fire off at the concert?" Had he set someone else up to take the fall?

"Ahh, no, that actually wasn't me. I wouldn't risk you, songbird. You're mine to protect."

She shook her head. No. "Where's Bain? Where is he?"

She didn't care about Caleb's warning any longer. What if this psycho had done something to him?

Jerome reached for her and she stepped back, stumbling and falling onto her ass. For once her clumsiness came in handy.

Her name was roared across the park and she froze. That sounded like Bain. Jerome bent over towards her, and she noticed something in his hand. A syringe? She scrambled backward just as someone slammed into him from the side. She was grabbed from behind, pulled onto her feet. She fought back. She wouldn't be taken. She wouldn't!

"Easy, Karisma! It's me. Tavi."

She stopped fighting. Tremors continued to rock her body, though as she stared down at Wolfe who had Jerome pinned to the ground, his hands were being twisted behind him. He was screaming.

"Fuck, quiet him before someone calls the cops," Caleb said, racing forward.

But all her attention turned to the man running towards her, his face filled with thunder.

"Bain!" she screamed, wrenching herself out of Tavi's arms. She ran forward and flung herself against him with a happy cry. "Bain! Oh God. You're all right. You're all right."

She burst into tears. Bain picked her up, hugging her tight. She wrapped her legs around his waist as she sobbed into his neck.

"I was so scared. I thought he was going to kill you. Oh God."

"Shh, angel. Calm down. I'm fine. I'm fine. Take more than that idiot to do me in. Hush, now. You're going to make yourself ill."

"Bain, you're alive then," Caleb said.

"Looks like it," Bain replied.

"Bain. Fuck. Where were you?" Dominic demanded. Where had he come from? Oh, who cared. She didn't care about anything except that Bain was all right.

"I was fucking tied up in the basement of the apartment building," Bain snapped. "Where the fuck were you and why weren't you guarding Arianna? Who the hell let her leave the apartment?"

There was silence except for muffled screaming coming from Jerome. She guessed someone had gagged him. She wasn't moving from her perch in Bain's arms to check.

"Well? She should never have been out here. She should never have been in reach of this fuckwit. He was going to drug her and fucking kidnap her so does someone want to explain whose stupid idea it was to let her come out here to meet up with this fucked-up asshole?"

"T-that would be mine," she sobbed out, trying to lean away from him. He held her tight. "D-don't be angry with Dominic and the others. It was all me."

Bain just growled.

She rubbed his back then leaned up to whisper in his ear. "And I'd do it all over again to save you. I love you."

"I love you too. But you're going to pay for this stunt. Remember my warning about what would happen if you ever placed yourself in danger? You aren't going to sit properly for a week."

She tightened her hold on him. She would take whatever he'd dish out, if it meant that he was here and hers.

BAIN DIDN'T WANT to let her go. Not even when the cops arrived. Someone must have seen or heard something and called them. The princes had quietly left with Aleki when they heard sirens. It was best if they weren't involved in this, being visitors to the states and royalty. He still didn't know what Dominic, Caleb and the others had been thinking, letting Arianna do this.

That asshole could have hurt her.

Arianna had put a call into her lawyer when the cops threatened to take them all downtown for questioning. Finally, the detective they'd dealt with over the letters was called. They were all escorted back to her apartment while the cops took Jerome to the police station. Bain had remembered to send someone down to the basement to get Rob. Surprisingly, he'd still been alive.

Now it was hours later, and he just wanted them all gone so he could take care of his girl. She was pale and shaky and completely exhausted.

Any scolding or punishment would have to wait.

Nobody had mentioned the princes or Aleki being there. If there were any cameras around that might be a bit trickier to explain away. Although only Tavi had gotten close to Jerome.

Finally, with warnings not to go anywhere in case they had more questions, the cops left. As soon as they were escorted out by Dominic, Bain pulled Arianna onto his lap on the sofa. He ran his hand up and down her back.

"Can't believe it was that asshole, Jerry, stalking you," Caleb said in shock, running his hand over his shaved head. Only he and Wolfe were left. "And he set Mr. Longley's house on fire. Wonder if his mother had any idea?"

She shook her head. "I can't believe I never told anyone. That I totally suppressed that memory."

"Baby, you were four. You were terrified. He threatened you. Of course you didn't say anything," Bain told her soothingly. He wasn't having her blame herself. "You weren't to blame, angel."

She snuggled in closer and he held her tight. He knew she was feeling guilty and he hated it. Dominic returned to the room, giving him a nod. Cops were gone at least.

"That bastard wasn't right in the head. Everything he did was his fault, not yours. He and Rob were in on it together. They sent you those letters to scare you. They had some stupid plan where Jerome would swoop in to rescue you from your stalker. Rob was just in it for the money."

"They. . .they were going to kill you."

"Don't think they would have gone through with it. Rob was too nervous. I wasn't worried about me. Was worried about you."

"Must have been Jerome delivering the letters, which is why there was no prints from Rob on the letters," Dominic said. "I checked and he has the same tattoo on his hand that the person on the camera had. But Rob must have given him access. Don't know how he got into your dressing room at the concert without being caught on camera."

"He was likely getting on and off via the basement, not the main entrance so no one saw him, and Rob likely wiped the cameras," Caleb added.

"He heard Ari's sister telling the doorman that she was moving to Montana," Bain said. "Then he kidnapped me when the opportunity presented itself. But he didn't have much of a plan."

"You should get your head looked at," Arianna told him worriedly.

"I took some painkillers. I'm fine, angel."

"Pretty sure his head is made of rocks," Dominic joked.

Bain narrowed his gaze at the other man. He hadn't forgotten that he'd let his girl walk into a dangerous situation. It was going to take a long time for him to get off Bain's shit list.

"Thought you would have enough fucking sense to keep Arianna in the apartment where she would have been safe."

"I have a feeling I'm going to be hearing about this for a long time to come," Dominic said dryly.

"Too fucking right."

"Dominic's getting a scolding," she said.

He nearly smiled at the note of teasing in her voice. He was still worried about her but if she could tease right now, she'd be okay.

"I'm so glad you're all right," Arianna told him. "I was worried that you thought I had lied to you and that's why you left."

"Why? Why would you think that?" He pulled her back,

gaping down at her in amazement. "Didn't Dominic tell you that I was going after your parents to chat with them?"

Dominic held up his hands as Bain scowled at him. "I did, man. I promise. But when you didn't return, Arianna got really worried. And then when we received those messages, there was no stopping her. She was frantic."

"She's five foot nothing and weighs a hundred pounds soaking wet, you're telling me that you couldn't keep one tiny little girl from throwing herself into a dangerous situation," he growled.

"Bain, please," Arianna begged. "Everything's okay now. Can we just forget about it?"

Forget about it? Hell, no. But he could stop talking about it for now. Especially when there were more pressing issues.

He cupped her face between his hands. Then he lightly kissed her. "Angel, not for one second did I think you were lying to me. I stayed mostly silent because I wanted to hear what they had to say, wanted to wait for them to hang themselves. But I never believed a word that came out of their mouths. They could have come up with all the fucking bullshit evidence in the world and I still would have believed you. I trust you, angel. Totally and fully."

Tears dripped down her cheeks.

"Hey, now. No more crying."

She nodded. Caleb handed him a tissue and he dried her face, wiping her nose.

"There's something fishy about the doctor who gave you that medication, though." He looked over at Dominic. "Think we need to look into him."

She glanced up at him. "What did you talk to my parents about?"

He grimaced. "May have threatened them a bit. Followed them down to foyer to do it away from you. Didn't want you to get upset."

She wrapped her arms around him. "How can I be upset when you were taking care of me? Like always."

"And I always will."

"I'm sorry my stalker knocked you out and kidnapped you."

He shook his head. "Life always going to be this exciting with you?"

"God, I hope not. All I want is some peace and quiet and you."

He kissed her gently. "Then that's what you'll have."

AFTER THEY'D SAID goodbye to Caleb and Wolfe, Bain carried her into her bathroom, stripped her off and washed her in the shower. He didn't linger, setting her down on the small built-in seat as he quickly cleaned himself.

She swayed where she sat. If she'd been alone, she'd probably have fallen into bed, fully dressed. But she was glad he insisted on a shower. She felt decidedly gross and dirty.

She could picture Jerome's face as he stared at her. That insane glint in his eyes. She shuddered.

"Angel, don't go to sleep yet," Bain told her.

She opened her eyes. She hadn't even realized she'd closed them. He turned off the shower and climbed out, grabbing a towel and wrapping it around his waist before picking up another one. He held out a hand to her and she took it, letting him help her up. She climbed out of the shower and amazingly, managed to stand all on her own as he dried her off.

Go her.

He picked her up, setting her on the counter. Obviously, he didn't have as much faith in her ability to stand without falling over as she did. He dried himself off and she watched the towel move over his gorgeous body.

"Yum."

He snorted. "Yum? Are you eating me with your eyes?"

"Are you objecting?" she asked.

He threw the towel away then picked her up in his arms, holding her against his chest. She didn't even have the energy to wrap her legs around his waist. She just let him take all her weight. He didn't seem to mind, though.

"You can eye-fuck me any time you like." His voice was a low rumble that sent a wave of pleasure through her. "But tonight, you're not up to anything more than a cuddle and sleep."

"I don't wanna sleep."

"Angel, you're dead on your feet." He carried her into the bedroom and set her down on the armchair. Then he pulled back the covers on the bed. "I'm worried you'll keel over."

"It's a legitimate worry." She watched as he set out her sleep sack. A happy sigh erupted from her. Maybe with her sack and Bain holding her tight, she might be able to keep the nightmares at bay.

"Still don't wanna sleep."

He turned back, his hands on her hips. "Why not?"

"I'm gonna dream about it."

"About nearly being taken by Jerome or about your parents?"

"About you being kidnapped," she whispered. "I nearly lost you."

He knelt on the floor in front of her, pressing her legs apart and moving in close to her, his hands resting on her hips. "Angel, trust me. I was fine. Those two idiots had no idea what they were doing or who they were up against. I have no intention of ever leaving you."

Tears dripped down her cheeks. God, you'd have thought she was out of them by now. "I can't lose you, Daddy. I can't."

"You won't. I promise."

She leaned forward and wrapped her arms around his neck. He ran his hands up and down her back. "But you got to know, I'm gonna have nightmares too. And all of mine are gonna be about you risking your life like you did."

He drew back, cupping her face between his hands. "It is totally unacceptable to me that you put yourself in danger."

"I didn't want them to hurt you."

"I can take care of myself. And no matter what, no matter the situation, you always come first. Dominic should have fucking realized this and made you stay safe. You. Come. First. I'm tough. Can handle myself. But you, my angel, are infinitely precious."

She knew she couldn't promise not to risk herself for him again. She loved him. That's what you did for the people you loved, right? You put them first. And he came first with her.

Still, she wanted to be allowed to leave her bedroom before she was old and gray, so maybe she shouldn't tell him that she'd do it all over again.

"When all this is done with and you're feeling more like yourself, you're going over my lap every night for a week. Got to pay for the gray hairs you've given me."

"What about the gray hairs you gave me? Do I get to spank you every night for a week?"

He huffed out a laugh. "Not the way things work, angel. Besides, I was knocked out and kidnapped. You went willingly into a dangerous situation to meet with your stalker."

Ugh. Her stalker.

"I can't believe it was Jerome. He never crossed my mind. I feel like I barely knew him. I can scarcely recall anything about him."

"You were young. Plus, something traumatic happened to you that made you retreat inside yourself."

"I can't remember the details. . ."

"Which might be for the best." He grimaced. "I'm no head doc though."

"I don't. . .I don't think I want to remember it all."

"Whatever happened between the two of you created some

bond in his head. He thought you were destined to be together. And those lyrics in your latest song convinced him that you were asking for his help."

"Stupid thing is those weren't even my lyrics. I didn't write those."

"He wasn't right in the head, angel. Nothing you did made him this way. It was all him. He's behind bars now. He can't hurt you. Nobody will hurt you again. Not while I'm here."

"Don't ever leave me."

"I won't. I promise."

Bain pulled her back into his arms and she rested her head against his neck. Her head was thumping, her stomach still churning. Too much stress and not enough food or water.

"Maybe we should have called a doctor," he muttered. "Gotten you something to help you sleep."

"No. No, I don't want to take anything. I'll be okay. Unless you want to get a doctor for your head. Do you think I should wake you up every hour and check on you?"

"No, baby. I'm fine. You are definitely not staying awake to watch over me," he said firmly. He studied her for a moment. "You got a headache?"

"A small one," she replied.

"When's the last time you ate?"

"I can't eat. I'll throw it up."

"All right. You okay with letting me take over? Giving me control? Might be what you need to clear your mind."

She shuddered. "Yes. Please."

"Okay, little bit. Daddy is going to get you settled in bed then I'll go heat up a bottle for you."

She made a murmur of protest. A bottle? She wasn't sure about that. But he placed a finger on her lips. "Daddy is in charge. You're exhausted, probably dehydrated. You need something in your belly. You need to go potty?"

"No," she whispered.

He frowned. "Let's get you into bed." He stood and held out his hand to her. Then he helped her slide into her sleep sack. It settled around her, hugging her tight. Although nothing felt as good as his arms around her.

"Good, angel?"

"Yes, Daddy."

"I'll go get some painkillers and a bottle."

"No! Don't leave!" She couldn't have him leaving her. Couldn't be alone. Her breath started to come fast despite the comfort of being swaddled.

He sat next to her, running his fingers through her long hair soothingly. "Shh. It's all right. I won't go anywhere. Just let me find my phone. Think it's in the bathroom. Won't go any further than that. Shh."

He returned quickly with his phone and a bottle of pills which he set on the table by the bed. He tapped out something on his phone then sat facing her on the bed, running his fingers through her hair soothingly rubbing at her scalp.

"Does your cabin have a porch, Daddy?" she asked, needing him to talk to her. And she was curious about his home.

"Does *our* cabin have a porch? And yes, it does. It has a small one out the front and a wider one out the back."

"Has it got a porch swing or rocking chairs?"

"It doesn't. But I think we need to remedy that. Wouldn't mind a rocking chair for inside, either. I think I'd quite like rocking on a chair with my baby in my lap."

Yeah, that sounded pretty perfect to her as well.

There was a quiet knock on the door, and he stood, walking over. A light shone in from the passage and she heard Dominic speak quietly.

The door shut and Bain walked back. Only her night light was on, sending stars across the ceiling.

"I can't wait to sleep under real stars."

Bain set a bottle of water and another bottle with white liquid in it on the bedside table.

"Isn't that a baby's bottle?"

"It's a special one. From the same shop I bought the other things from."

"Before we leave, I might have to visit that shop."

"That can be arranged. As can the sleeping under the stars. Here, baby." He grabbed the bottle of painkillers and tapped out a couple, placing them in her mouth before picking up the water and holding it to her mouth. She drank several sips. He took a couple of painkillers himself before settling in against the headboard.

He pulled her onto his lap and then grabbed the other bottle. The rubber teat was placed against her mouth and she opened her lips, taking it into her mouth and sucking on it experimentally.

"I had Dominic put some warm almond milk in it," he told her as the sweet, warm liquid hit her tongue. "Thought it would be easier on your tummy than normal milk."

That was really thoughtful. Maybe tomorrow, she'd be embarrassed about Dominic preparing her a bottle. But right now, she didn't have the energy to care.

She closed her eyes and suckled. Reveling in the feeling of Bain holding her tight and secure in his arms. He sang her some lullabies in a surprisingly good voice. She'd have to ask him to sing with her some time.

She drifted off to sleep, barely aware of him tucking Patches in against her and the rubber teat of the bottle being replaced by her pacifier.

And held in his arms, safe and secure, she didn't dream at all.

26

S he managed one breath. Then another.

In. Out. Slow. Steady. Just breathe.

Bain's face appeared through her tears. She clasped hold of his hands, feeling his steady presence soothe her. When the shaking subsided and she could breathe more easily, she managed to give him a small smile.

His frown deepened. Yeah, he wasn't buying her act for a second.

"Hey, it's better than yesterday right? This is only my first one today."

It had been a few days since Bain had been kidnapped and she'd been suffering from regular panic attacks. She'd also been having nightmares.

This morning, Caleb and the others had left to go back to Escana. She already missed them like crazy. She'd spent yesterday watching movies and playing board games with Tavi and Aric. Kassim and Matek had holed up in her office with the others, discussing guy stuff. Aric and Tavi had told her some interesting things about life in Escana. How most relationships there were a single woman with many husbands. How women were cherished, worshipped and closely guarded.

She'd made plans to visit them later in the year. With Bain, of course. She still needed to give Tavi that concert.

Bain sat beside her on the bed then drew her onto his lap. He rocked her back and forth. "Wish I could help with these, angel."

"You do help," she told him fiercely. "They'll stop eventually. It's just. . .I keep imagining you getting hurt. Killed."

"I'm fine. You're fine. Nothing is going to happen to either of us."

She nodded her head. Logically, she knew they were both all right. But that didn't mean that her body still didn't go into panic mode. That her brain didn't go over everything that could have gone wrong.

"At least they both confessed."

Rob had been taken to the hospital but had woken several hours later. He had immediately confessed. That had enabled the detectives to put pressure on Jerome. He'd caved. He still refused to talk about any crimes in the past. But he had admitted to sending her those letters and kidnapping Bain.

"Don't forget about Larry," Bain rumbled. "He's finally getting what he deserves."

Turns out, Jerome hadn't left the letter in her dressing room. The police had done some digging into Larry and they'd found he'd made a series of large withdrawals in the days leading up to the charity concert. It hadn't taken him long to confess to writing the letter he'd 'found' in her dressing room and paying someone to set the fire and take the fall. He'd done it for publicity, to raise her profile and increase sales. He'd also thought it would make Bain and Dominic look incompetent, that she'd get rid of them and turn back to him. Someone could have been hurt and all he'd cared about was himself. Asshole.

There were also some questions around his financials and

whether he'd been embezzling money from her. She felt so stupid for trusting him so much.

She hadn't heard from her family. That was one positive. It still hurt, their betrayal, their lies. But she knew she was better off without them.

"I still think you should talk to someone about all of this."

She shuddered. Apparently, the doctor who lived at Sanctuary had a brother who was a psychiatrist. And she had to admit, she was thinking it wouldn't be a bad idea.

"I'll think about it. After our RV trip."

"Still can't believe I agreed to that."

Dominic was due to fly back to Montana tomorrow. After she got her apartment on the market, and packed up what she wanted, she and Bain were going to drive back. In an RV.

She was so excited. It wasn't quite camping, but it was still exciting.

Bain ran his fingers through her hair. "What you want to do now, angel? How would you like to play a board game? We might be able to rope Dominic in."

"Candyland! Candyland!"

Bain shook his head. "All right, Candyland."

"Yay!" She climbed off his lap and did a victory dance as Bain grinned at her. They walked out of her bedroom and down towards the living room.

Dominic stepped out of the kitchen, a sandwich in his hand. Like normal. How did the man eat so much and not gain weight?

"Dom-Dom, we're playing Candyland. And I'm going to whip your ass."

Dominic groaned. "Dom-Dom, really?"

"Yep."

He looked over at Bain. "I think I preferred it when she was closed off and overly polite."

"No, you don't," Bain commented.

Dominic winked at her to let her know he'd just been joking.

"Candyland again?" Dominic asked.

She nodded excitedly.

"I'll go get it ready," Dominic moaned.

Bain grabbed hold of her hand as she went to follow him. He tugged her in against him. "I know these past few days, hell, weeks have been hard on you. Your family's betrayal. The stalker. Just want you to know. I'll always take care of you. Always protect you. Always believe in you."

"My family didn't suddenly change. I was just blind to their faults. Or maybe it was more that I was in denial. Now that they're gone. That the threat of the stalker is gone, I feel free. Sure, I'm still having panic attacks and nightmares, but they'll go eventually. Now, I have everything. I have you."

"You do. Always."

EPILOGUE

"Arianna? Arianna! Where are you? You better not be hiding from me!"

Well, she hadn't been. But now that she'd heard the scolding note in his voice, she thought it might not be a bad idea.

There was just one problem...

She kind of needed him to rescue her. Seemed that while she might be a champion tree climber, she was not a champion at getting down from said tree. And it also seemed that she might have developed a slight problem with heights since she was a child.

This had been so much easier when she was eight.

"Arianna!" The worry in his voice decided things for her.

"Up here, Daddy!" she called out.

"Where?"

"Here! In the tree." Okay, she realized how silly that sounded once she said it. They were surrounded by trees. "The really big one."

"This really big one?"

His voice sounded closer and she glanced down to find him staring up at her, his hands on his hips, a scowl on his face.

"Yep."

"What did I tell you about climbing trees, Arianna?" he rumbled at her.

She bit her lip. "Not to do it without you."

He folded his arms across his chest.

"I'm in trouble, aren't I?"

"Oh yes," he drawled. "Big trouble."

Yeah. Damn it. That's what she'd thought. She'd been dying to climb this tree ever since she'd seen it, but every time she'd asked, he'd refused to let her, claiming it was too high.

Turns out, he was right.

But she wouldn't tell him that.

She knew she'd be in trouble if she got caught trying to climb it, but she'd figured she could get up and down before he got home.

Turns out, she was wrong.

She also wouldn't tell him that.

She'd lived here at Sanctuary Ranch for three weeks now and she loved it. The press was still hounding her for her story, but it was much easier to ignore them from here. Before they'd left Manhattan, her parents had turned up at her apartment. A last-ditch effort to get at her. But after Bain had a word with them, they'd left. Bain had refused to tell her what he'd said. Which might be for the best.

Before embarking on their RV adventure, she'd called Estelle. Just because Joe hurt her, didn't mean she had to cut herself off completely from the older woman. Estelle told her that she believed Larry had discovered Joe's gambling issue and had played him. Apparently, Larry would often give Joe inside tips he'd heard about different horses and races. In the beginning the tips had paid off, then things had started to go downhill.

Just another way Larry had been trying to control her life. By pulling Joe's loyalty away from her.

Larry's lawyer had contacted her, asking her to meet with him, since her ex-agent wasn't legally allowed to be in contact with her. She'd refused. Bain had wanted to call the lawyer and tell him where he could shove his request, but she'd managed to calm him down.

The lawyer had then sent her an email from Larry. He'd tried to explain his actions. He'd pleaded with her to forgive him. Told her he had nothing to do with Jerry or Rob. He'd just been blinded by opportunity and greed. He'd even tried to convince her that he'd done it all for her.

He was a fucking asshole.

Although, both Jerry and Rob had told the police that they hadn't been working with Larry.

His career was over. He would now have a record. He would be blackballed from the industry; she'd heard from her record label that no one wanted anything to do with him.

He deserved it all. He'd known those letters were real, yet he'd been willing to risk her safety by trying to convince Bain and Dominic that she'd made them up. He'd paid someone to set a fire. People could have gotten hurt, including her. He'd put pressure on Joe to gamble then used him to keep tabs on her. He hadn't cared about her safety that night at the concert. Hell, he'd made Joe drive him home rather than wait for her.

Scum.

Bain had also paid Doctor Jones a visit and he'd admitted to taking money from her parents to give her medication she didn't really need. Both he and her parents were under investigation. She could have tried to protect her parents. But she was done with them. They'd made their bed. They could lie in it.

Once they'd gotten out of the city and on the road, she'd been able to put most of it behind her. The worry. The stress. When they'd arrived here, she'd immediately felt a sense of home. This place was so beautiful. The mountains. The trees. And the people here had been so kind and accepting.

Most mornings, she got up, had breakfast and went off into her music room for a few hours. She didn't know how Bain had managed to have the soundproof room built onto the cabin before they'd gotten here. But it was amazing. Not only did she have her own music room, but he'd had the second bedroom turned into a playroom for her.

The record label had been really supportive of her creating her own music. She'd have to go back to New York at some time to record it. And there would be some publicity events she'd have to attend, but Bain had promised he would do what he had to in order to be there with her. She hadn't yet convinced him to sing with her, but she knew he would eventually cave.

After a few hours of feeding her soul with music, she'd emerge feeling refreshed and amazing. Then she'd spend time with Bain, if he was home. He'd been working from the ranch while she settled in. He didn't want to go away until he was certain her panic attacks and nightmares were under control. And that she wouldn't sleepwalk.

A lot of her time spent with Bain was as Little Ari. Honestly, that had done more to help her with her nightmares and panic attacks than anything else could have. But she'd still started Skype sessions with Doc's brother, who thankfully had a much nicer manner than his brother

She'd been worried that her presence here might be disruptive or not welcome. The last thing she wanted was to cause any problems. But everyone here had been so welcoming. Especially the other Littles. They'd planned a board game night this weekend.

She was going to kick all their asses at Candyland.

She'd never felt more secure or happy in her life.

Bain had even arranged for a porch swing to be installed on

the back porch. She loved spending most of her time out there. Even if she got into trouble for letting herself get too cold or not wearing enough clothes.

For someone who had always tried her best to please people, she seemed to manage to get in an awful lot of trouble.

"Get down from there, Arianna."

"I would if I could."

"You can't get back down?"

She shook her head, squeaking as she felt the branch beneath her shift. "No! Help me, Daddy. Please!"

"It's all right," he reassured her. "Daddy's coming. Hope this tree can hold my weight."

She did too.

She clung on for dear life as he made his way up the tree. When he reached her, he stood on the branch below and wrapped his arm around her. His heat surrounded her.

"It's okay, baby. I got you. Gonna guide you down. That's it. Let go now. Move your foot here. Good girl. I won't let you fall."

She followed his calm instructions, feeling much braver with him there. She knew he'd never let her fall. Bain could do anything. Even rescue a naughty Little from up a tree.

When they were both on the ground, she threw herself at him. "Thank you, Daddy! I was scared!"

He picked her up and she wrapped her legs around his waist. He carried her as he walked through their cabin and into the living room. He sat on the sofa with her straddling him and held her close until they both stopped shaking.

"You're okay," he muttered to her. "You're okay."

She wasn't sure if he was trying to reassure her or himself. Finally, she pulled back to look at him. She knew that as soon as he got over his fright, she was going to be in big trouble.

"I sorry, Daddy. I thought I could get back down on my own."

He narrowed her gaze at her. "You're not supposed to climb trees without me."

"I know." She hunched her shoulders miserably.

"And especially not that tree. What did I say about that tree?"

"That it was too tall, and I'd get stuck."

"And that's just what happened, isn't it? What were you going to do if Daddy hadn't come home?"

"Wait until you did."

"It's growing cold and you didn't have a jacket on. What if you'd slipped and fallen? Little girl, don't you know how much you mean to me? What if you'd been hurt?"

She sniffled, feeling miserable. "I'm so sorry, Daddy. Is you gonna punish me now?"

"I sure am."

She wiggled off his lap and stood with her head lowered. "Do I gots to get my naughty girl paddle?"

Bain had bought the naughty girl paddle after she'd gone to the park to meet with Jerome. During their trip here, she'd thought about throwing it out the window several times. But he'd warned her that he'd just buy another one and use it every night on her ass for a week if she did that.

"Yes. Off you go."

Her naughty girl paddle wasn't that big. It was black leather with heart shapes cut out on one side. The inside of the hearts was red. It hung from a hook in her playroom. Next to it sat her time-out chair. Something else she wasn't fond of.

Her feet dragged as she walked back towards him and held the paddle out. "Here it is, Daddy."

"What do you say?"

"Please, Daddy, will you paddle me?"

"I will." He stood. "All right, angel. Take off your pants and panties. Pull them right off. Then bend over, hands on the seat cushions."

She pulled her clothes off her bottom half then leaned over.

"Spread your legs wide."

Already, she could feel tears welling. She knew she'd frightened him and that he really was serious about her safety.

"I'm sorry, Daddy."

"Me too, baby. It's a count of ten."

Without any further warning, the paddle landed on her ass several times. She rolled up onto her toes. Holy fuck! That hurt!

There was a pause and he struck again. She shuffled from foot to foot. "Ow. Owie."

"I know, baby. Gonna need you to stay still."

She took in a shuddering breath. The next two were no less painful. The heat built. Her poor ass throbbed. She wasn't going to be sitting comfortably for a while.

Another two. Ouch. Ouch.

"Two more." The next one landed and she started to cry. Sobs racked her body. She hated that she'd scared him. She'd been frightened too. She'd been worried he wouldn't be home for hours and that she'd be stuck there, cold and afraid.

The last one landed and she collapsed against the sofa. He immediately pulled her up into his arms, carrying her to their bedroom where he lay on his back with her sprawled on his chest. He ran his hand up and down her back, talking to her in a low, soothing voice.

"Love you, baby. I don't handle it well when you scare me. Not when you go to meet your crazy stalker. Not when you climb high trees. Need you to stop giving me gray hairs."

"I'm sorry, Daddy. I try not to scare you again."

"Appreciate that. Love you, angel."

"Love you too."

"DADDY! WHERE ARE WE GOING?" she squealed.

After having her butt paddled, Bain had put her down for a nap. When he'd come to get her, because she wasn't allowed to get up on her own, he'd told her he had a surprise. Then he'd slipped a bandana over her eyes to blindfold her. Now he was leading her through their cabin. Towards the back door? Were they going out? But no, he would have told her to get dressed warm if they were doing that.

He was nothing if not ultra-careful with her health and protection.

"Gonna sit you down so I can put some thick socks on your feet, all right?"

So they were going outside?

"Okay, Daddy."

"Good girl."

He helped her sit then put some socks on her, as well as a hat, gloves and a scarf. She thought it would have been easier to do this before she'd been blindfolded. But, oh well. . .

"Right, come here, little bit." He picked her up in his arms.

"Good thing you're so strong, Daddy. Since you like carrying me around."

"Seems like I was made just for you, doesn't it, angel?"

Oh yes. It certainly did.

He had to shuffle her weight around to open the door then a rush of cold air hit her. She didn't care. Montana was magical. Even the chill in the air as it grew closer to winter. She just wanted to hole up in her little cabin with the fire going and snuggle into her big, cuddly ogre.

"What was that thought that put a smile on your face?" he asked as he walked. Where was he taking her?

"Just thinking about what a snuggle bunny you are."

He made a dark, rumbling noise and her smile grew wider. "Snuggle bunny? I ought to spank you for that."

Such an ogre.

"All right. Gonna set you down now."

He put her on her feet, holding her shoulders until she was steady. Then she felt him move behind her.

"Gonna take the bandana off. But keep your eyes closed for a second."

"Okay, Daddy."

The bandana was untied, and she kept her eyes close.

"Open," he commanded.

She opened her eyes, blinking a few times to clear her vision. Then she gasped in delight, clapping her hands. "Daddy! A swing! For me?"

He grinned. "All for you."

It had a large wooden seat, almost long enough for two people and was hanging from a large tree in their backyard.

"You like?"

"It's amazing! I love it!" She couldn't believe he'd remembered that she said swings were her favorite.

Then again, it was Bain. He didn't miss much.

"Can you push me in it, Daddy?"

"Of course. But got something else to show you too."

Something else? He turned her and she gasped. In the clearing there was a big pile of huge, outdoor cushions set up, partially covered in a number of thick blankets. With more cushions at one end. Behind the nest was a projector set on a table. And at the other end there was a portable screen.

"For movies. And to lay under the stars once it's dark. But no sleeping out here. Too cold for that," he warned sternly.

She turned then threw herself at him. He caught her, barely moving at her impact.

"Thank you, Daddy! Thank you! Thank you!"

"You're welcome. Anything for my angel."

"How did you do this?"

"Had a bit of help while you slept," he admitted.

"Push me? Please!"

She climbed onto the swing, wincing slightly as she sat on her hot ass. But she soon forgot about that as he drew her back, letting her go.

"Higher! Higher!" she squealed.

"Not too high," he warned.

Party pooper.

But he pushed her for ages. Until he claimed his arms were tired. She didn't believe that for a second. But she wasn't too disappointed since she got to watch a movie outside.

He carried her over to the big pile of cushions, since she had no shoes on and set her down on the cushions.

"It's so comfy! What are we watching?"

"Here, get settled under the blankets." He held some blankets up and she snuggled in. He stood and walked back to the projector. The screen lit up and she let out an excited cry.

"Shrek!"

"Thought you might like it."

"Quick, Daddy, get in, it's gonna start!"

He climbed in under the blankets with her, pulling her into him so her head was resting on his chest.

When the movie was finished, the screen went dark.

"Look up at the sky," Bain murmured.

Oh. She hadn't even noticed that it had grown dark. She let out a contented sigh as she stared up. "There they are. The stars."

"Yep. It's just you, me, the quiet and the stars."

This was her happy place. And it had nothing to do with the stars and mountains. The trees and quiet.

No, her happy place was him.

LET'S KEEP IN TOUCH!

Don't miss a new release, sign up to my newsletter for sneak peeks, deleted scenes and giveaways: https://landing.mailerlite.com/web-forms/landing/p7l6g0

You can also join my Facebook readers group here: https://www.facebook.com/groups/386830425069911/

HEAL ME, DADDY

Montana Daddies, book 8
Coming July 8th

Can two brothers work together to heal the pain of a woman who swore she'd never love again?

Headed to an isolated cabin to try to work on their fractured relationship, Doc and his brother run into a spot of trouble. Their savior is an unlikely one, a Little with a shield so thick it will take both of them working together to penetrate it.

Caley isn't interested in the real world. She much prefers to live through the stories in her head. At least then, she's guaranteed a Happy-Ever-After.

She's lost everyone she ever loved. She's not interested in risking her heart again. Not even to two men whose sweet promises fill her heart and whose hot looks stir her body.

And whose loving, protective, possessive Daddy sides call to her Little.